THE
CABIN

By

Donna Mabry

To Judy & Bill
Thanks for your
help.

Donna Mabry

Acknowledgements

Thanks are due to the many people whose contributions made this work possible, starting with my Creative Writing teacher in high school, Mr. Paul Garbe.

Shelby MacFarlane, whose home was a shelter for me when I was growing up, whose friendship has supported me throughout my life, and whose willingness to read and repair my sketchy first drafts somehow survives.

Sandy Novarro, who keeps asking for the next manuscript and telling me when she likes it.

My cadre of advisors who do their best to mend my mistakes:

Mary Millard
Barbara Winters
Elaine Stubbs

Especially, I owe great thanks to Joyce Mochrie, who did wonderful the final proofreading and edit. If you see any mistakes in here, I made them after her work was finished.

And, most of all, my Melanie, who inspired Alexandra, and who performs the technical demands of publishing a book.

The Cabin

A Manhattan Story

Copyright by Donna Mabry

This is a work of fiction. All of the characters, names, incidents, and dialogue in this novel are either the products of the author's wild imagination or are used fictitiously.

Smithtown, Nevada
Sierra Nevada Mountains
1929

Chapter 1

Nancy ran until she couldn't run any more. Gasping for air, she leaned against a tree to catch her breath. A cramp in her side felt as if it would cut her in half. Stretching her right arm high above her head, she bent sideways to stretch out the muscle. Her long braid of dark blonde hair fell over her shoulder and snagged on the bark of the tree. Tugging it loose, she straightened up, looked ahead at the trail, and started out again, walking this time, instead of running.

The further she went from town, the thicker the forest became, until the pine trees were so close together she couldn't see more than a few yards ahead. It was October and the needles on the top layer of the forest floor were fresh, covering decades of accumulated fall. They crunched under her feet, sending up a sweet aroma. The sunlight was fading, and there was a chill in the air. *How far have I run?* The only thing more frightening than the darkening forest ahead of her was what had been left behind.

She was doing her morning chores at their home on the edge of town when her younger brother, Matthew, came to fetch her, and she hurried to the house. Nancy had been spared the kind of discipline most of the other children in the town were raised on. They learned to be obedient by a beating with a flexible tree branch the size of a man's thumb, but she still dreaded making her father angry. Hurrying, she emptied out the bucket of corn in the yard of the chicken coop and trotted to answer the summons.

When she reached the house, her older cousin, Abner, was sitting in one of the rockers at the end of the porch. Married to her younger sister, he watched her with a wolfish smile as she trotted up the steps and into the house. He had three wives, her sister Linda, a year younger than Nancy, and two other women. The village blacksmith, he operated a livery stable and had a good amount of business coming in from renting and trading horses. He was a huge man in his late forties, with a rotund stomach pressing against the front of his bib overalls and fingers so short and stubby he couldn't close them together. His protruding lower lip hung down over the top of his beard and he had to make a conscious effort to close his mouth.

Nancy ignored his leer and the smell of man-sweat that always followed him, and rushed past. Her father was sitting at the kitchen table and waiting for her. Lucas Smith, in his late sixties, had a body stout from lifting bulky merchandise that he sold at his general store, a bushy gray beard, and a ruddy face. Except for Sundays, it was unusual for him to be off his feet in the daytime. Always up long before dawn, he took his breakfast early and worked in the store until sunset. His workday lunch came from a basket one of his wives would bring to him and was eaten in bites taken between waiting on customers.

He looked at Nancy with a furrowed brow. "Sit down, girl."

Nancy pulled out one of the wooden chairs and sat cater-corner to him. He reached out and patted the back of her hand. "You're going to be eighteen in a few days. It's time you were married. Your cousin Abner is willing to take you."

Nancy felt as if someone had jerked a leather strap tight around her chest. She jumped up so quickly she overturned the chair. "No! I don't want to marry Abner. I don't want to marry anyone."

He pointed a thick finger at her. "This isn't up to you. Abner and I have come to an agreement, and the wedding will be Saturday."

"I'm not going to do it. You can't make me."

His face turned red and he barked out, "I *can* make you, and I will if I have to." His tone immediately softened and he coaxed her. "Now, Nancy, Abner is one of the wealthiest men in these parts. His wives each have their own homes and anything a woman could want. It won't be so bad."

"No! Linda told me what he does to her. It's nasty and disgusting. I'll never let any man do that to me."

"It isn't that bad. If a husband is considerate, some girls even come to like it."

"He isn't considerate at all. Linda says she feels like she's being crushed, and every time she gets her--her--monthlies, he beats her because she hasn't conceived."

Lucas's face paled. He pressed his lips together and closed his eyes. "As you know, I'm not one to use that method, but as long as he follows Biblical guidelines, a man is allowed to discipline his wife as he sees fit."

"Discipline? It isn't her fault if she can't have a baby, and Abner torturing her certainly won't make her conceive. She said that when he's beating her, he looks like he enjoys it."

"Let's pray that the Lord will bless her with a child one day, but, in the meanwhile, Abner is complaining that he has to support a woman who's

4

barren and not even the one he wanted. He asked for you in the first place. He only settled on her because you refused him. I've promised to give you to him now to make up for it."

Nancy pleaded, "How can you do that to me? I don't want to get married. I don't want to let him, or anyone else, touch me the way he does her."

"Be reasonable, Nancy. You have the misfortune to take your looks after me instead of your mother. You're big boned, and aren't the prettiest girl in town."

It was true. There was nothing delicate about her, but the words cut deeply. Lucas patted her hand again. "No one else has asked for you. Every man around has heard your sharp tongue and knows how willful you are. You're lucky Abner is willing to take you. You're well past the age where you should have had babies and a home of your own. Don't you want to be a mother?"

Nancy fought back her tears. "I don't want to do those things you have to do to get a baby. Not ever."

Her father's voice grew sterner. "You have to marry and have a family. A woman without children cannot enter the kingdom of heaven."

"I don't care. If God would keep me out of heaven because I refused to get married then I'll spend eternity with Linda in whatever hell she goes to."

Lucas's jaw dropped open and his face turned red. He raised his hand as if to slap her, but quickly lowered it. "Don't blaspheme, girl." He ran his hand over his face and slowly shook his head. "What will happen to you if you don't marry? I'm getting older. Who will take care of you when I die?"

"If you hadn't left the real church so you could keep marrying young girls and having children, you wouldn't have to worry about that."

He jumped up from his chair. This time, his hand lashed out and struck her cheek so hard she fell backward out of her chair and landed on the floor. He loomed over her and shook a finger in her face. "I won't have you sassing me like that. *This* is the real church, the one Joseph Smith founded, and the one the Lord intended. Those people in Salt Lake City are the heretics. You'd do well to mind your tongue. The Lord could strike you dead for talking to me in such a manner. Remember the fifth commandment, 'Honor your father and your mother, that your days may be long upon the land which the Lord your God has given you.'"

Nancy's eyes rimmed over with the tears she could no longer hold back. She sniffled and wiped her cheeks with the back of her hand. "I don't care.

I'd rather be dead than married, especially to Abner."

Lucas shook his head and sighed. His face softened again, and he held out a hand to help her to her feet. He wrapped his arms around her and patted her on the back. "I know it's my fault you're the way you are. You've always been my favorite. I've spoiled you just like I spoiled your mother over my other wives, giving you store-bought dresses and bringing home licorice sticks from the candy jar at the store. I never did that for the others."

He kissed her forehead. "I know you don't want to be married, but it's already arranged. You can have a new dress and a nice party, and the other women will give you gifts for your new home."

She nestled her head on his shoulder and sniffled. "I don't care about a party and presents, or any home I had to live in if I have to let Abner do those terrible things to me."

Smith pushed her away from him and held her at arm's length. "You don't have the luxury of saying no. If you don't do as I say, I'll turn you away from home and no one in town will take you in. It's settled. You'll marry Abner this Saturday."

"No! I won't do it!" She spun around and ran out of the house, past a leering Abner, down the steps, and into the woods. She kept going until the stitch in her side forced her to stop.

As she walked further, she was terrified. It was getting dark. She heard unfamiliar animal cries. *Are those coyotes? There's bears in these woods, too, and wolves, and snakes.*

The boughs of the trees closed in over her head, filtering out what was left of the sunlight and casting gloomy shadows. The musty smell of night began rising from the forest floor and overpowering the sweet pine needles. She jumped at every strange sound, but kept walking, even though she had to peer at the ground to make out the trail.

As the last of daylight faded into night, and she could barely see where she was going, it grew colder. Her breath became visible in the air. She shivered and ran her hands up and down her arms to warm them and hugged herself. She had a nice, warm coat at home, and she ached to go get it and slip into it. *Abner would be waiting for me there.* She shivered again and kept walking.

Pushing through two young pines so close together she had to turn her body to get through, she came to a clearing and walked out of the pine canopy and into the moonlight.

Chapter 2

A cabin stood in the middle of the clearing, and in the pale light Nancy could make out a large shed to one side. A water trough and pump stood next to it. There were no lights showing inside. A gust of cold wind cut into her and she fought the impulse to run up the steps and fling open the door. *I have to find shelter somewhere or I may not make it through the night. Maybe it's been abandoned.*

She walked up the steps onto the porch and knocked on the door. "Hello?" she called. There was no answer. She knocked harder, scraping her knuckles against the rough wood. "Hello-o-o?"

Another blast of frigid air blew her cotton dress around her legs. The thin fabric provided no warmth, and her teeth were beginning to chatter. After waiting a moment, she walked back to the yard and found a stone the size of her fist. She used it to pound on the door. *I don't want to go into someone's home uninvited, but if I don't find a place to get warm, I'm going to freeze to death.*

There was no doorknob, only a latch. She pushed it up and shoved on the door. It slowly gave way, opening into blackness. She stepped inside, closed the door behind her, and heard the latch fall back into place. For a moment, she panicked at the thought of being closed in and not able to get out, but when she ran her hand over the door, she felt a handle. She held her breath and lifted it. The latch went up and she was able to open the door. Relieved, she huffed out a visible stream of air into the cold night and closed the door again.

Another shiver ran through her, and she rubbed her arms harder to encourage circulation. The inside of the cabin wasn't much warmer than the forest, but at least the wind was shut out. She took a deep breath. The cabin smelled of wood, ashes, and humans, but it wasn't musty smelling, the way it would be if it had been abandoned and the doors and windows closed up for a long time. *Someone lives here. I wonder how long they'll be gone.*

Her body ached with fatigue. *How long have I been walking? It seems like forever. It gets dark around five o'clock now, so I left home over six hours ago.* She began to feel dizzy. *Maybe there's some sort of bed in here or a cot where I can lie down and rest.*

She felt along the wall to her right. There was a table with a bucket on it, and one chair. The bucket had a cloth on it and when she took it off and felt inside, there was water. She hadn't had a drink since morning. Leaning over it and sniffing, it seemed all right. She cupped her hand and brought some to her mouth, dipping the tip of her tongue into her palm. It tasted good. She slurped up several handfuls, replaced the cloth, and kept going along the wall, walking inches at a time and feeling her way.

She turned the corner, and on the next wall was a window with closed shutters held in place by a crossbar, and seamed so tightly no moonlight penetrated. A few steps further, she felt a large wooden box the size of a steamer trunk. She turned the next corner and made out a stone fireplace. There was a wide mantle, and as she felt along the items sitting on it, she made out a lantern, three cast iron pots in different sizes, a box of matches, and a big frying pan. The stones were cold to her touch. The fire must have been out for some time.

On the third wall was a cot with thick wool blankets on it. What strength she had left drained out of her in a rush and she didn't care what might be beyond the cot. She had to lie down or she'd fall into a heap on the floor. She sat on the cot, pulled off her shoes, and got under the blankets, pulling them up around her chin and drawing her knees to her chest, making herself into a ball. After a few minutes, the wool of the blankets captured the heat from her body and wrapped her in a warm pocket of air. She stopped shivering and drifted off to sleep.

A horse's whinny woke her. She jumped up from the cot and strained to hear. She could make out the sound of horse's hooves clopping on the hard ground--no, two horses--and she could hear a man's voice, but couldn't understand what he was saying. She felt her way to the window, slid the crossbar to one side, and pushed the shutter open far enough that she could see the shed. There was the dim light of a lantern glowing through the door. She could see his shadow as he moved back and forth, but she couldn't see inside. He came out carrying a bucket, filled it with water at the pump, and went back to the shed. A moment later, he came out again carrying the lantern in one hand and a bundle in the other. He headed for the cabin.

Terrified, she closed the shutter and felt her way back to the cot, where she took one of the blankets and wrapped it around herself. She made her way along the wall to the far corner and slid into a sitting position on the floor, hugging her knees and pulling the blanket over her head. The broad wood planks of the floor were cold under her thin dress, and in only a matter of seconds, she was shivering again, partly from cold, partly from fear. *If I can stay hidden until he goes to sleep, maybe I can sneak out of here without him finding me.*

She heard the man open the door latch and she pushed the blanket aside far enough to see him.

As he walked in, his head came to the top of the doorframe. In the light of the lantern he carried, she could see that had a short, dark red beard and mustache, but under the broad brim of his western style hat she couldn't make out much of his facial features. He used his foot to shove the door closed, put the package on the table, and took off the rifle slung across his back. He hung it on a wall rack before unbuckling the gun belt he wore fastened around the outside of his coat. That went on one of the pegs that made a row under the rifle rack.

She could see a long-barreled handgun in his holster, like the Colts her father sold at the store. Next, he took off a second belt that held a hunting knife on one side, a smaller hand gun on the other, and oddly enough, a tin cup. The second belt went on the hook next to the Colt. He took off his coat and hung it on the last peg. When he removed his hat, it revealed a wild thicket of auburn curls that covered the collar of his shirt.

The eerie shadows made by the lantern as he walked back and forth made Nancy's skin crawl. He went back to the table and pulled the string to unwrap the bundle, pushing aside the paper around it to reveal a loaf of bread, which he set aside before taking some of the papers to the fireplace where he spread them out. Adding a handful of kindling from a bucket standing there, he stacked some logs on top and lit the paper with a match

13

from the mantle. A blaze jumped out. He watched it for a moment before he went back to the table.

Picking up the loaf of bread, he pulled the knife from the holster to slice off two pieces, then unwrapped a wedge of cheese and made himself a crude sandwich. Nancy's breakfast was long since digested and at the sight of the food, her mouth watered, and her stomach growled so loudly she was sure he must hear it. She tried to make herself smaller.

After taking a large bite of his sandwich, he chewed while he pulled the cloth from the bucket sitting on the table and dipped the tin cup into it. He ate quickly without sitting, washing down the meal with water.

He stretched and yawned. Nancy was startled when he spoke. "If I don't get some sleep, I'll be no good tomorrow." *Does he know I'm here?*

He stripped off his jeans and shirt and draped them on the back of the chair. Still wearing his one-piece, long winter underwear, he turned down the wick on the lantern and the light faded out. In the flickering of the flames from the fireplace, she could see him walking toward the cot. *Will he notice the missing blanket?* She heard another yawn, and then a clunk. "What the hell?" he said. He reached down and picked up one of Nancy's shoes.

My shoes! I forgot about my shoes.

She ducked her head and pulled the blanket tight over it. She heard him walking again, then the sound of a match being struck. She made herself as small as possible. Her heart was beating so hard she thought he might find her just by listening to the racket it was making.

He was going around the cabin slowly and his footsteps were coming nearer. The blanket was jerked away and her hiding place exposed. She cowered against the wall as he stood over her. The lantern gave an eerie light, and it made him look like a giant. "Who are you?" he growled. "And what are you doing here?"

Chapter 3

Nancy was so afraid she could barely speak. "I'm Nancy Smith. I was out taking a walk and got lost."

"Don't start out with a lie. You didn't just go for a walk and get lost, you ran away from home, and you left in a hurry."

"How would you know that?"

He pointed at her. "Who would go for a walk out in the middle of the forest this time of year dressed like that? Look at you. You aren't even wearing a sweater."

"Oh." Nancy's heart pounded. She looked up at him. "I'm sorry. I didn't mean to break in or anything. I knocked and called hello, really I did. It was freezing out there. I had to take shelter somewhere or I would have died from the cold. I didn't have anywhere else to go."

"Well, you can't stay here."

"You mean you'd put me out there to freeze and die?"

He pressed his lips so tightly together they disappeared between his beard and mustache. He considered her for a moment before he waved a dismissive hand. His voice wasn't so harsh when he said, "It's not freezing yet. This is only an early cold snap. It'll pass, but if that cotton dress you're wearing is all you have to keep you warm, you could die from the cold tonight. I don't reckon there's any harm in you spending the night, but you'll have to get out of here in the morning."

The tone of his voice made Nancy feel somehow safer, and she relaxed a little. "I will."

"How long you been out there gallivantin' round the woods?"

"Since noon, I think. I hadn't had lunch yet."

"You hungry?"

"I'm starving."

He waved at the table. "Sit."

She got to her feet and sat watching while he made her the same sort of sandwich he'd eaten. When he handed it to her, she thought a prayer of thanks and took a bite. It was nothing but bread and cheese, but it was divine.

He filled his tin cup with water and put it on the table in front of her. "You can wash it down with this."

"Thank you."

While she ate, he strode over to the big wooden box against the far wall, took out another blanket, and tossed it at her. "Make yourself a pallet out of this. If you get closer to the fireplace, you'll stay warm enough. I'm too tired to argue with you. My pack horse came up lame and I had to put his load on my saddle horse and walk the last mile or so home. I'm beat, and I'm not about to give up my bed for someone I don't even know."

"Thank you." She swallowed the last of her meal, stood, and folded the blanket into three's in front of the fireplace, then lay down with her back to him, and spread the other blanket over her. Her whole body was tense as she waited to learn what he would do next.

She listened for his movements and heard him return to his cot. In a matter of minutes, she heard deep, regular breathing that told her he was sleeping. She let herself relax and drifted off.

Chapter 4

When Nancy woke, she could smell oatmeal cooking. She opened her eyes to see sunlight streaming in the open front door and windows. Standing only a foot away from her pallet, the man faced the fireplace and stirred a pot that hung from a cooking bar. She stood and said, "Good morning."

He twisted his body to look at her. "Morning. Looks like that cold spell is over. The sun is warming things up right well. Breakfast'll be ready in a minute. The outhouse is in the back."

Nancy could feel herself blushing. "Thank you." It didn't feel all that warm to her. She wrapped one of the blankets around her shoulders and went out of the cabin. She walked down the steps and around the house. From the shed, she heard the horses nickering.

Relieved to find that the outhouse was clean, free of spiders, and smelled decent, partially because of one wall being lined with cedar, she relieved herself and then stopped at the pump to wash her hands in the clear, cold water, drying them on her skirt.

When she went back in the cabin, he stood at the table with the pot in his hand. He appeared puzzled. One bowl and two cups sat on the table.

He looked up at her. "I don't get much company out here. As a matter of fact, I never had any company at all. I don't have any extra dishes or anything much besides what I use myself and one extra cup."

She thought it over and said, "One of us can eat out of the bowl and the other one out of the pot. Do you have two spoons?"

"No, but if you use the regular spoon, I can use the stirring spoon." He scooped out some of the oatmeal into her bowl and set the pot on the table before he sat on the chair. She stood there awkwardly. He frowned. "Oh. I forgot there was only one chair." He got up, dragged a small barrel over to the table, and said, "You can sit on the flour barrel. It's 'bout the right height."

In the daylight, she could see his hair and beard were a coppery auburn, and what she could see of his face seemed nice enough. His eyes were deep green, and the crinkles in the corners made them look kind. She found comfort in that. *He's fairly good looking. I wonder how old he is.* She sat down and again thought her prayer of thanks instead of saying it out loud. She picked up her spoon. "Is there any milk and sugar?"

He shook his head. "No cow, no milk. I do have some sugar." He reached behind him, took a brown cloth sack from a shelf, and handed it to her. Aware that sugar was expensive this far west, she sprinkled only a little of it on her oatmeal.

She had to keep herself from laughing at him when he started eating with the big spoon he used to stir the oatmeal. He had to lip the food from the tip. He ate silently, keeping his eyes on his food, and it seemed to Nancy that he was tense. She finally blurted out, "I'm Nancy Smith. What's your name?"

"Jacob Belk. My friends call me Jake."

Nancy waited for him to say something else, but he didn't. She said, "You don't sound like a person from around these parts. Where's your home?"

This brought a small smile from him, the first she'd seen. It made him seem nicer. "This cabin."

"I mean, before that. Where did you come from?"

"Kansas."

His scant answers began to irk her. "Where in Kansas?"

"The northeast corner."

"What town?"

He laid down his big spoon and rested his forearms on the table. He had the expression of someone trying to be patient with an irritation. "Manhattan."

"Manhattan? I thought that was in New York."

"There is one in New York. This was the other one." He scooped the last of his share of breakfast from the pot.

"Why did you leave?"

"One reason or 'nother. I have to be going. Wash the dishes before you leave. Do you know your way home?"

"No. I don't have any idea."

"I take it you live in town?"

She nodded her head. "I did, but I can't go back there."

"Why not?"

"Saturday is my eighteenth birthday. If I go home, my father is going to make me marry my cousin Abner or he's going to disown me. I'd rather die."

"He can't make you marry someone you don't want."

"Yes he can."

"Is this Abner such a bad man?"

"He's horrible. He's already married to two other women and my sister. He beats her, and she told me that from the look on his face, he likes doing it. She's watched him slaughter the hogs and chickens and says he acts like it's the most fun he's ever had, --and at night, he does disgusting things to her. She told me all about it."

22

He nodded. "Renegade Mormons."

Nancy stuck out her chin. "Yes. My family is Mormon, but I'm not going to be any more. Not if I have to marry a man I hate and let him--let him--you know."

"I can't say as I blame you. I've seen men like you describe this Abner before. I wouldn't want anyone I cared for to be married to someone like that. What do you plan to do if you don't go home? Is there someone else who will take you in?"

Nancy pouted. "No," she whispered. "I don't have anyone but my family in Smithville."

He took his coat from the hook and pulled it on. "I don't have time to talk about it now. I have to go check my traps. While I'm gone, you decide where you want to go, and I'll see to it that you get there."

"Can't I just stay here with you? I'll clean and cook for you to earn my keep. I'm a good cook."

Without answering, he strapped on his gun belt and picked up the knife holster.

She asked, "Well?"

He sighed and looked down at the floor. "You're going to be a grown woman in a few days, so I'll talk to you like one. You know those disgusting things your cousin wants to do to you?

I'm a man like any other man, and I want to do them, too."

Nancy shrank back from him and crossed her arms over her breasts. He waved a hand at her. "I didn't mean I would force you, but it's a hardship for me just to have you in the cabin. Last night, soon's I saw you were a girl, those feelings jumped up inside a' me. It's one thing for me to be here all alone for over two years, but it's different when there's a beautiful young woman standing right in front of me. I have to fight my nature every minute."

Nancy blinked in surprise. "Beautiful? No one ever called me beautiful in my life. My father was always telling me how plain I was, and that I was pudgy."

His eyes roamed over her body, from her head to her feet and back up. They settled on her face. "He's wrong."

"Really?"

"Really." He grinned at her. "But then again, like I said, I been here by myself for a long time."

His smile eased her fears. She asked, "If I can't stay here, what else can I do?"

"You think about it while I'm working the line. There's enough logs for you to keep the fire burning all day. When I get back, you can tell me where to take you."

Before she could answer him, he turned around and strode out of the cabin. Nancy watched him disappear into the woods.

There was nothing to think about. She had nowhere else to go. She either had to go home and marry Abner, or find some way to convince this man to let her stay in the cabin with him, without ever letting him touch her. She thought about it all day, but no solution came to mind, none at all.

Chapter 5

Maybe I can do enough work that he'll see I won't be a burden to him. She started by cleaning up after breakfast, drawing water from the well, heating it over the fireplace in the pot used to cook the oatmeal, and washing the few cups and bowl.

Three shelves lined the wall over the table. On the top one, a stack of soft white cloths she took to be flour sacks was on the end, and a row of filled burlap bags came next. She stood on the chair to see what was in them. One held apples, three had potatoes, and in the last, onions. On the next shelf, another stack of flour sacks sat next to a cast iron skillet and a cooking pot, larger than the one he used for the oatmeal. *We could use the skillet for a plate.* She took it down and set it on the table.

The last shelf had two boxes of ammunition, one for the rifle, and one for his revolvers, several empty Mason jars, a small wood box filled with lye soap formed into irregular bars, sugar, a bag of salt, a fork, the loaf of bread, now wrapped in a white cloth, and a few other small items. A broom that looked handmade stood upside down in one corner and she used that to sweep out the plank floor.

When there was nothing else she could find to clean or straighten, she decided to investigate, starting with the big wooden box. Like the broom, the furniture, and most things around the cabin, it looked handmade. The lid was heavy, and she had to use two hands to lift it high enough to let it rest against the wall. The box itself was made of pine, but the inside was lined with cedar and the fragrant aroma rose up to meet her.

On the top, lay a big King James Bible. She took it out and put it aside. Under that was another wool blanket, an assortment of men's clothing, a pair of jeans, two work shirts, a navy blue suit, white shirt, necktie, and an assortment of underwear. One at a time, she laid them on the floor beside her.

Something made of light blue calico was next. She held it up and it unfolded to reveal a woman's dress. *What is he doing with this?* When she stood up and held it in front of her, it was pretty much out of style, but looked as if it would fit. There was another dress next to it, this one fancier, yellow lace with a wide satin sash, the kind the wealthier women in town wore to church. A few more dresses made of ordinary cotton were in the bottom of the trunk. *Too bad there isn't any women's underwear. I could use a change of clothes.*

Nothing else held any interest, and, except for the Bible, she put the items back in the same order she found them. *When I finish looking this place over, maybe I'll read the Bible for a while. There could be an answer to my problem in there.*

She closed the box and went out to the porch. It was much warmer than a few hours before, and she held her face up to the sun and closed her eyes for a few moments before she continued her inspection.

At one end of the porch were a rocker and a small table. *Does he sit out here in the evenings?* She walked down the steps and looked around. The clearing was much larger than she'd realized the night before. The big shed was on one side of the cabin and a garden on the other. A long, narrow work table sat in back of the shed. Next to it was a stack of wooden boards standing on end and leaning against the wall. They looked like thin tabletops.

She walked to the garden on the other side of the cabin. Except for a row of turnips and a few carrots, it was almost bare of vegetables. There were still neat rows of dirt where things had grown. A rooster and a few chickens scratched between the rows. *I never even heard the rooster crow this morning. How deep was I sleeping?* She wanted to see the shed and the horses first. When

Jake left, he was walking, so the horses would still be in there.

She noticed a small building several yards behind the shed and looked inside. It was the smokehouse. Pieces of meat wrapped in cloth hung from the ceiling, and the room smelled of apple wood and oak. She closed the door and turned her attention to the shed.

She found two horses inside, a tall sorrel she assumed was his saddle horse because of his height and build, and another, a chestnut that must be the pack horse, shorter and broader across the back, with sturdier legs. They both turned to look at her and nickered, as if asking her in. The shed was roomy enough for the horses to move around.

On one side was a waist-high wall where the saddle and tack hung. When she looked behind the wall, she saw a bale of hay and several large, closely-woven sacks. Two of them were stamped *Salt*. Next to them was a bag of lime. *He must use that to keep the outhouse fresh.* On the wall, the lantern now hung next to a row of tools, a hammer, screwdrivers, and three kinds of saws among them.

One of the horses snorted and drew her attention. *I wonder if it will be safe to pet them. You never know about a strange horse.* Approaching cautiously, she stepped in front of the saddle horse first, not getting too close, and held out her hand. "Hello. I'm Nancy. Can I give you a scratch?"

He tossed his head a little, as if he were saying, "Sure." Without getting closer, Nancy reached out and pushed aside his forelock to scratch under it. He closed his eyes and nickered again. She stepped a little closer and scratched his neck.

The pack horse whinnied loudly and startled her. She jumped back but he stuck out his neck and put his head in front of her, bobbing his chin up and down, as if saying, "It's my turn." She laughed and gave him a good scratch, too.

Next, she went to examine the garden. The chickens scurried away from her and disappeared in the woods. The ground that had been cleared for planting was about forty feet square, with built-up rows of dirt about a foot apart. Between each row were lines of marigolds, still blooming. *How strange, that he would plant flowers.* In the woods beyond the garden, she saw the purple heads of asters nodding in the breeze. *If he wanted flowers in the cabin, why not just cut some of those?*

At the end of the garden were poles that supported what was once tomato and bean plants, their skeletons browning in the autumn air. Most of the garden had been harvested, but there was the row of turnips that looked ready to pick, and a few carrots still grew in one mound. Along the back side of the plot was a row of five feet tall apple trees, barely old enough to bear a few pieces of fruit.

The trees surrounding the clearing were mostly pines, but the others, mostly oaks and ash, were dressed in autumn colors. She hadn't noticed them the night before, but in daylight, Nancy marveled at the beautiful gold, orange, and red leaves.

She looked up at the sun. It was almost directly overhead. *It's barely past noon. What can I do now? I wonder when he'll be back.* She went back inside, added some logs to the fire, and brought the Bible out to the porch with her. She sat down in the rocker to read for a while.

Having studied it since she first learned to read, she knew the book well, and knew whole passages of it by memory. On the first page, it said, *Presented to,* and the handwriting said, *Jacob Belk, by his mother and father, Matthew and Emily Belk, on October 1, 1915.* The next page was the *Family Registry.* On the line for *Husband,* it said, *"Jacob Belk,"* and on the line for *Wife, "Lucy Irene Miller Belk."*

The next page was the *Births.* On the first line was written, *"Timothy James Belk, September 23, 1916."*

So he's married, or was married, and has a son. I wonder where they are. Did he run off and leave them? She turned another page and under *Deaths,* in a trembling script, it said, *"Lucy Belk and Timothy James Belk, September 23, 1916."* His wife and son died on the same day. *Oh, Lord! What happened?*

She closed the Bible with her finger holding the page and thought about what she read. *How did he come to live here?* After a while she opened the book, turned to a random page, and began reading in the *Song of Solomon.*

The first few chapters got her to wondering about the whole mystery of physical relations and why men were so obsessed with it. *I wonder if Daddy is right about some women liking it, too. The Bible is full of stories of people getting into trouble because of it.*

She turned to a less erotic section of Bible, the New Testament. Even there was the story of Salome. She read all the Gospels before her eyes began to droop. She nodded off and woke with a start when the chickens, who had wandered back into the yard, began squabbling.

I wonder what time it is. The sun was sinking to the level of the tree tops and she estimated that it was around two in the afternoon. *I could cook dinner. It ought to please him to come home and find a meal waiting for him.*

She returned the Bible to the big box. Before she closed the lid, she checked to see if everything was in the same place where she found it. She didn't want him to think she'd been snooping.

Dinner would be difficult without a proper stove, but she had seen how he cooked the oatmeal and thought she could manage. In the fireplace, the logs were still smoldering. There was only one stick of wood on the rack that stood by the fireplace, so she fetched some from the pile stacked on the side of the shed, added them to the embers, and poked at them until she was satisfied the new logs were burning.

She brought a bucket of water and filled the big pot halfway, and it was hung on the fireplace rod so the water could come to a boil. *Potatoes or turnips?* She thought she should use the turnips first. Potatoes would last longer without spoiling.

She pulled up two large turnips, washed them at the pump, and then brought them inside. *A knife, I don't have a knife. How will I peel and cut up the turnips? How can I cut a piece of meat from one of the hanging bundles in the smokehouse?*

She remembered the row of saws in the shed and ran to get the smallest, a hacksaw with a thin blade and washed it at the pump. In the smokehouse, she un-wrapped the cloth from the lowest bundle without taking it off the hook. *I wonder what kind of meat this is.* She smelled it, but could make out only the oak and apple wood aromas. She cut off a chunk of meat that looked the right size for two dinners.

After re-wrapping the meat, she carried the piece into the cabin, dropped it into the pot, added some salt from the sack on the shelf, and wished there were pepper to give it a little kick.

When she put the turnips on the table to cut, they wouldn't hold still for her to slice them, but kept rolling around. The best she could do with them was to stick the fork in to hold them down and try to hack off pieces. She tossed them into the pot along with the greens, and then chopped up an onion as best she could before dropping it into the now boiling concoction. *I wonder when he'll be back. This needs to cook for at least two hours.*

Nancy took a flour sack from the stack on the shelf and shook it out. It had been cut open to make a rectangle. *Good, this'll do for a tablecloth.* She spread it out over the table before she put the skillet down on one side and the tin bowl on the other. The only spoon went next to the bowl and the one fork next to the skillet. Remembering the Mason jars, she filled one with water and then went back to the yard to pinch off a half-dozen of the asters to add a pretty splash of color to the table. She was arranging them when, out of the corner of her eye, she caught sight of Jake emerging from the woods. His rifle was slung over his shoulder, and he was carrying animal pelts in both hands.

She was surprised at the shock of pleasure that ran through her when she saw him and ran out the door and down the steps to greet him. "I was wondering when you would be home. I have dinner cooking, but it won't be ready for a while."

Jake blinked several times. His eyes narrowed and he looked at her as if she were a rattlesnake. He almost seemed afraid of her. He turned his head and strode toward the shed. "I have work to do."

She followed him. "What is it?"

He plopped the animal skins on the table and nodded at them. "I have to season these." He took off his jacket, hung it on a nail sticking out from the side of the shed, and rolled up his sleeves. A Mackinized apron from another nail was hung over his neck and tied in the back.

He spread out one skin with the fur down, drew his knife from the scabbard, and began scraping the remnants of flesh from the inside.

Nancy crinkled up her nose and told her stomach to settle down. "What are you doing now?"

"I clean them off and salt the inside of the skin down before I stretch them out on a board and hang 'em to cure. After a while, I take 'em to town to sell. It's what I live on."

"What happened to the rest of them, their bodies?"

"Left them behind today. The critters will have an easy meal tonight."

"That's nice of you to think of them."

He snorted. "Nothing nice about it. Too much weight to carry. I only bring the bodies home when I need meat."

She looked at the pelts. There were raccoons and rabbits. He was working on a beaver skin.

"It's very pretty." She reached out and ran her fingertips along the fur. "It's soft, too."

He nodded. "Brings extra money in town. Back-East ladies like to make coats and such out of them. Keep your fingers back if you don't want 'em cut."

She jerked her hand away. It was growing cold again. She shivered and hugged herself to keep warm. He looked up at her. "You best be going inside. Close the door and windows. I'll be in later and get the fire built up."

"I already did that, so I could cook."

He stopped scraping the pelt and looked up at her. "Did you now?"

She nodded. She saw the corners of his mouth curve up and he almost smiled. "That's a good thing to know, how to keep a fire going--and how to cook. Now get on in the cabin 'fore you freeze to death. I got to get this finished 'fore dark."

Nancy stopped by the woodpile, picked up an armload of logs to take with her, and once inside, stacked them on the fireplace rack. She placed the lantern in the center of the table, closed the door, and pulled the window shutters together. *I could go get the lantern and light it so I can see, but he might think it's a waste of oil.* The cabin was too dark with the windows and door shut, so she opened the door a crack, stirred the stew, re-folded the blankets, and moved the dish and frying pan around on the table, fussing around the cabin to keep busy.

For the next hour, she kept going to the window and peeking out to see if he was finished with his work, but he was always bent over the table, his arm moving back and forth as he scraped the skins and rubbed the salt into them.

She wrapped a blanket around her shoulders and sat on the front porch rocker to watch him. It was almost dark before he carried the last board to the smokehouse and walked toward the cabin. He stopped at the pump and washed his apron, knife, hands and forearms, then went back to the shed to hang up the apron and get his jacket.

She thought he was coming inside and was disappointed when he went back in the shed. She saw the light of the lantern that hung there being lit and shadows of him moving around. He came out once, carrying the horse's water bucket, filled it, and went back. It was another half-hour before he came out again and walked to the cabin carrying the lantern.

When he saw her sitting in the rocker, he stopped at the bottom step. "You'll get sick sitting out here in the dark."

"I'm fine. I wanted to watch what you were doing."

This time he did smile, but only with one side of his mouth. "Doing? I was doing my work, and taking care a' the horses."

"I know."

"Then why you sittin' out here?"

"It's dark inside. Out here I can see the moon and the stars."

"Oh. Well, we best be getting inside or the bears will be after us."

He stood back to let her go in first and went toward the table to set down the lantern. When he saw the flour-sack tablecloth and the flowers, he stopped and stared. She waited to see what he would say, but he didn't speak. He placed the lantern at the back of the table and sat down in the one chair. He looked at her. "Somethin' smells good."

"I hope it tastes good, too. I don't know what kind of meat is in it."

Using a flour sack for a potholder, she brought the pot to the table and put it in front of him. He scooped out some of the stew into his skillet with the ladle and then some into her bowl. Instead of sitting down, she un-wrapped the cloth from the bread and began slicing it with the hacksaw.

He threw back his head and guffawed loudly, leaned back in his chair, and ran his hands through his hair. "Lord Almighty, girl. I heard say 'Where there's a will, there's a way,' but you sure do put that into practice. Is that how you cut the meat?"

"You took the only knife with you. It was all I could find."

Still chuckling, he said, "I reckon I been getting by with the least I needed for so long, I forget what civilized folk live like." He took a taste of the stew and nodded. "This is right good, but it needs a bit of pepper."

"I couldn't find any."

"That's 'cause I don't have any."

She sat down on her flour barrel, dropped her head, closed her eyes, and thought her prayer. If he noticed that she gave thanks for her food, he didn't comment. She started eating. It *was* good. *I wonder what it is I cooked.* "What kind of meat is this?"

He took another bite and chewed on it for a minute before answering. "I don't rightly know. It could be raccoon or rabbit. The smoking makes 'em all taste pretty much the same."

They ate in silence for a while and he said, "Don't you have some questions to ask me?"

"Questions?"

"You been here alone all day with everything I own right in front of you. I figured you'd be full of questions."

She felt herself blush. "You think I went through your things?"

He smiled his half-smile again. "You're a woman. It's only natural that you'd snoop, and there's things here that you would wonder about. It's all right. I been 'specting it. Go ahead and ask. Then I got some questions for you."

"Tell me about Lucy."

His face fell and he nodded. "Stands to reason that'd be the first thing you wanted to know." He put his head down for a moment before looking up to show her a face etched in sorrow.

"Lucy was my wife. We grew up together back there in Manhattan, Kansas. Both our places were a ways out of town and, outside of church and school, we didn't see much of the other kids. She lived a short piece down the road from us. I don't know how to make it sound sensible, but we always knew we'd marry and raise a family. I thought we'd be together our whole lives."

He stopped and smiled wistfully before he went on. "Our wedding was the first weekend after we graduated from high school. My mother had a fit. Both my mom and dad had their hearts set on me going to the University in New York where my dad went, but the only thing I could think about was that if I went away, Lucy couldn't go with me, and I would never leave her behind." He put a forkful of food in his mouth and started chewing.

Nancy wanted to know more. "What happened to her?"

He swallowed, sighed, put down his fork, and laid his hands in his lap. She could see his shoulders sag and he dropped his head again. "Bout a year and a half after we married, she gave birth to our baby boy. He never drew a breath. She named him Timothy, and she died a few hours after he was born. The doctor said it was one of those things that sometimes happen, and that she could have had any one of a bunch of things go wrong--but I always thought she died of a broken heart."

"Is that her wedding dress in the box?"

"No, we buried her in her wedding dress. I kept the blue calico because that was her favorite, and she looked so pretty in it. The blue matched the color of her eyes. I kept the yellow one 'cause I had saved up for it the whole time she carried the baby and was complaining about being fat. I was going to give it to her as a surprise when she got slimmed-down again. She never got to wear it."

Nancy saw tears in his eyes and found that she had some of her own. She didn't say anything, and after a pause, he went on. "We put our baby in her arms and buried them together. That day I wished I could lie down in there with them and die, too, but the Lord didn't take me. Maybe He has something else planned for me in this life."

"Do you have any pictures of her?"

"Not here. I have a whole book full of 'em at my mom and dad's place."

Nancy wiped her cheeks with the back of her hand. "That was a long time ago. What have you been doing since then?"

"This and that. Maybe someday I'll tell you about it."

Someday? Is he going to let me stay here? Will he leave me be at night, or will he turn out to be just like Abner? Her question was answered when he said, "You been thinkin' 'bout where you're goin' to go?"

"I don't have anywhere I can go. I thought maybe you'd let me stay here and take care of the cabin and cook for you."

His eyes met hers and flickered down over her bust. His face turned red and he looked away and stared down at the table. "I already told you, you can't stay here, and I told you the reason why."

Nancy's heart fell. "Oh."

Without looking back at her, he said, "I'll take you into town in the morning and you can see if someone will give you work. There's one or two wealthier families that might need a maid."

"No! I can't. Every person in that town knows me and knows my father, and probably knows why I ran away. If I go back there, my father will make me marry Abner. I can't ever go back."

"Well then, what do you want to do?"

Nancy's shoulders slumped and she pouted. "I don't know."

He stood up and put his coat back on before he picked up one of the blankets. "You think about it tonight. I'll be expecting you to get on out of here in the morning."

"Where are you going?"

"I'll sleep in the shed with the horses."

"You don't have to do that."

He looked her over from top to toe and then met her eyes. "Yes, I do. It'll be the only way for me to get any rest. Don't worry about me. I've slept there before."

"Why?"

"When I first found this clearing, I knew right off I wanted to live here. I slept in a tent until I built the shed, then I spent my nights in there with Charlie and Pete until I got the cabin put together."

"You slept with the horses? How long did it take to build the cabin?"

"All summer. We had one at home that I kept in mind as a guide, so I already knew how big I wanted it to be. I put the fireplace up first. I was able to do that and cut the logs by myself. I had a friend who lives a short piece from here to help me cut the planks for the floor and the outhouse. I got it built far enough along to sleep inside before the snow started. I'll be all right in the shed. You go ahead and sleep on the cot--for one night. In the morning, you'll have to go."

Before she could answer, he left and closed the door behind him.

Chapter 6

The sound of the rooster crowing woke Nancy. *He might like it if I do a share of the work.* The sun wasn't up yet, but she jumped from the cot, slid her feet into her shoes, and tied them in a hurry. She took care of her morning needs and then picked up a few logs from the stack by the shed. She could hear him inside, talking to the horses. Back in the cabin, she poked at the embers in the fireplace with one of the logs, and when the flames shot up a little, lay more logs on top. She heard the sound of him working the pump, grabbed one of the buckets, and hurried out. "Good morning."

"Morning."

"Did you sleep all right? I felt bad about taking your bed away from you."

"I slept sound enough."

When he finished filling his bucket for the horses, Nancy placed hers under the pump and he kept working the handle until the bucket was almost full. He pointed to the cabin with his chin. "I'll take that inside. It's a might heavy for a girl."

She picked up the bucket and walked quickly toward the cabin. Over her shoulder, she said, "It's not heavy. I'm used to hard work."

By the time he came back from the shed, she had the oatmeal ready, and they sat down. Jake started eating as if he were in a hurry. Before she picked up her spoon, Nancy bowed her head and said a silent prayer. Jake stopped with his spoon in mid-air. "I guess I got uncivilized living out here by myself. You can say that prayer out loud if you want."

"I can't do that when there's a man in the house. I was taught that women have to let the men take the lead."

He chuckled. "My mom would have smacked me for eating without praying. You want me to say it?"

"It would be nice, but I'll understand if you don't want to."

At home, her family held hands while the blessing was given, so when he bowed his head and closed his eyes, Nancy reached out, took his hand, and bowed her head. She could feel his hand under hers jump a little and then relax. He said, "Lord, thank You for this day and for the food You have provided. In Jesus's name, amen."

"Amen," Nancy added.

He pulled his hand away and started eating. With his head bowed over his breakfast, he asked, "You been thinking 'bout what you want to do to get on out of here?"

Panic surged up in Nancy, and her chest tightened. "I've thought about it, but I don't have any ideas."

"Then I'll take you on in to town."

She made no effort to hold back her tears. "Please! Please don't take me back there. My father would make me marry Abner, and I think I would kill myself before I'd marry him."

"You said you grew up there. Isn't there anyone, maybe some lady, who would give you work and a place to stay?"

"Everyone in town is Mormon. None of the women would be allowed to help me if I went against my father."

He pursed his lips and peered at her from under his eyebrows. "Then what are you going to do?"

Nancy sobbed. "I don't know!"

He lay down his spoon, put his elbows on the table, and pressed his palms together, patting his hands as he thought. "There's a bunch of young women who work for the railroad called Harvey Girls. They serve food at the station restaurants. They get a place to live and wages. I hear it's all respectable and on the up and up. Maybe if I could get you to one of the depots where they work, they would see fit to give you a chance."

Nancy's heart leapt. "How far would I have to go?"

"I think there's a station in 'most any railroad town of good size. You'd have to go to the depot in Reno and ask. They could tell you."

"Can you take me to Reno?"

He shook his head. "I can take you to town, and you could take the bus and connect to get a train to take you there."

"I can't go into town at all. As soon as I did, someone would tell my father I was there. Besides, I don't have any money to pay for a ticket, not even for the bus, much less a train." She started sobbing in earnest, her body convulsing.

He jumped up from his chair. "Lord A'mighty. Stop that wailing. It tears me up to hear it." He paced the floor a few times. "Tell you what, I'll think on it today. Up to now, I never used all my traps at one time. I only put out enough to bring in as much money as I needed to get along. Maybe I can put out extra traps and get enough pelts to make cash for a ticket."

Nancy sniffled. "You would do that for me?"

He shrugged and half smiled. "I got to find some way to get shed 'a you."

"Thank you so much."

"The money's only part of it. Once't I get that, I have to come up with a way to get you to the next station down the tracks."

"Sometimes, at home, when I was in bed at night, I've heard the horn from the late bus that must go out around ten o'clock. I could wait out of sight and you could go in the station and buy my ticket for me. If it were dark, and I stayed out of sight until the last minute, maybe I could get on that bus and be gone before anyone saw me."

"That would work."

Nancy was beginning to get excited about her possibilities when one thought made her heart plummet. "What if I get to that Harvey place and they won't hire me? What would I do?"

He ran his hands through his hair. "I didn't think 'bout that." He paced some more and stopped by the fireplace. "There's only one thing a girl without money can do to get along, and I'm not about to let you do that."

"What?"

"Think on it."

Nancy realized what he meant. "Oh. You're talking about being a harlot, like Rahab." *It's hopeless. If he doesn't let me stay here, there's nothing else for me.*

She inhaled deeply, huffed out her breath, and said, "There is something else I could do."

"What's that?"

"I could wait until the bus got up some speed and then step out in front of it. I'd rather die than earn my living letting men touch me."

He held out his arms in the air and let them flop down. "I don't know what to tell you. I'll go ahead and set the traps. Maybe as the day goes on, one of us will come up with some sort of plan."

He strapped on his knife and guns and almost charged out the door. She watched him as he went to the shed and came out carrying a load of his unused traps. He disappeared into the woods.

Nancy busied herself with what little cleaning there was to be done and then went out to explore the area a little further. Walking around the clearing, she gathered juniper berries to use as a substitute for pepper, filled one pocket with them, and her other pocket with pine nuts. She found a patch of dandelions and gathered the greens for a salad.

Still using the hacksaw, she hacked off a piece of meat and tossed it into the pot, peeled two of the potatoes and an onion and added them. *A little salt and a few juniper berries will give it flavor. He'll like having something with a new taste.* She brought in some purple coneflowers to dress up the table.

It was almost dark by the time he came back. He went to the work table behind the shed, lit the lantern, and scraped and salted the pelts he'd brought home before he came in the cabin.

She had dinner ready. He stopped in the doorway and smiled his crooked smile at her. "Something sure smells good. Makes my stomach growl."

She felt herself blush. "I made us a stew with some of the meat, a few potatoes, and a carrot from the garden. I seasoned it with juniper berries I found at the edge of the trees."

He chuckled. "I'm ready to get to it. I left here without taking something for lunch. All I had was a few strawberries I found."

"Strawberries? I love strawberries. Will you show me where they grow? I'd love to have some for tomorrow."

"There's no one partic'lar place. They grow here and there. If I run across more, I'll bring 'em home with me."

They sat down and Nancy bowed her head and reached out for Jake's hand. This time, his hand didn't flinch at her touch. He gave his same brief prayer, and they ate. He seemed more relaxed and in better spirits than he had been since the first moment they met.

She started the conversation with the weather. "It was such a beautiful day. I sat on the porch to read in the sunlight and fell asleep."

"There won't be many more like it. Charlie and Pete are growing extra winter hair. Out in the woods, the caterpillars are all fuzzed up thick. It'll be a hard winter, prob'ly lots of snow."

"What do you do if you can't get to town for supplies?"

"I normally go in 'bout once't a month, but the first winter I spent here, I was snowed in for four months."

"How did you survive?"

"I was 'specting it, so I'd already laid in flour and such, chopped enough firewood, and had a stack of feed for the horses. There was plenty of meat in the smokehouse. I ran out of potatoes and apples and such early on and had to make do with what I could find around the clearing to take their place."

"What was that?"

"Some of it was the pine nuts like you put in with the dandelion greens here. They're easy to find, 'cause the pine cones don't all fall off the trees in autumn and a good hit on the trunk will shake them loose. The fruit stays on the kinnikinnick bushes all winter. That's not bad. I knew where there was a stand of sulphur flower in the summer and dug up some of the roots to boil."

"How did you learn all this?"

"Some of it I learned in Kansas, growing up near Deep Creek. Grandma Mimi is a Kansa Indian, and she taught me a lot of it. Some, I learned from Henry, a pal of mine, a Paiute, who grew up in these parts. He and his wife used to live in a cabin 'bout a mile from here. We met in town at the general store one day and struck up a friendship."

At the mention of the general store, Nancy's pulse sped up. *He's done business with my father, but I'm not going to tell him about the relation.* "Do you still see him, Henry, I mean?"

Jake shook his head. "Not for over a year. I asked 'bout him in town, and they hadn't seen him either. I went looking for him at his cabin, but it looked like he was gone for good. The bed and table were still there, but all his gear was gone. It was a disappointment to me. We got along pretty well. I helped him when he needed a hand, and he helped me when I needed one. We dug the well together, and he's the man who held the other end of the saw when I cut the planks for the floors here."

"When will you be going into town again?"

"Depends on how many pelts I have. I've had some pretty good luck in the last few weeks. I'll load up Pete and make the trip Monday. I need to start bringing in extra supplies for the winter. Can't carry it all in one load."

"When you go, if you could get some baking powder and powdered milk I could make flapjacks, and if we had cornmeal, I could make cornbread. Oh, and would you get an extra fork and bowl, and a kitchen knife so I can use something better than a hacksaw?"

He looked at her for a long moment and gave his head one quick nod.

After they ate, he put on his coat and picked up his lantern. "I'm going to go ahead and bed down the horses and get some sleep. I'll see you in the morning." He stopped at the door and gave her a small smile before he left.

On this third day since she first arrived, he hadn't mentioned her leaving, and she'd made no attempt to bring it up. She cleaned up after the meal and lay down on the cot.

It was hard for her to get comfortable. With no nightgown, she'd been sleeping in her dress. Clean by nature, wearing the same thing for so many days without it being washed was irritating. She had rinsed out her undies in the stream while he was gone, but had nothing else to wear except the one dress. As sleep came to her, she thought about what was in the trunk. *I wonder if he would let me wear Lucy's blue dress. It looked about the right size. Then I would have one dress to wear and one to wash.*

In the morning, Jake lined up the logs in the fireplace to make an evenly topped fire and brought in a side of bacon from the smokehouse. He unwrapped it and sliced off a half-dozen thick pieces. "Today's Sunday. I mostly let the chickens keep their eggs to make chicks, but if you look around where they roost, you can bring us in some of the fresh ones. Look for a nest with only one egg in it. I eat oatmeal or mush six days a week, but on Sunday I have bacon or ham and eggs."

She got the big frying pan from the mantle and rinsed it under the pump. While he cooked the bacon, she gathered the eggs.

When breakfast was on the table, she bowed her head for the prayer and he reached for her hand first and held it tenderly in his. She held her breath, shocked by the racing of her heart. *I can't be feeling things like this. There's only one place it could lead, and I'm not about to go there.*

After the prayer, she drew her hand away from his and he seemed reluctant to give it up, but let her slide it away from him. Not wanting to meet his eyes, she looked out the window to see the horses grazing at the edge of the clearing and told him, "Charlie and Pete have gotten out of the shed. You better go get them before they get away."

He kept on eating. "They been in there all week. I let them out so they could move around a little. They won't go anywhere."

"They won't? I thought it was in a horse's nature to roam around. Daddy would never let his horse graze outside the fence."

"These two are smart enough to know when they have it pretty good. They'll stay put."

"Aren't you afraid the wild horses will call them and they'll go join up?"

"The wild herds don't gen'rally come this deep into the forest. A horse likes to be where he can run away if something gets after him."

She waited a while and when he didn't say anything else, she took a deep breath and blurted out, "I need a bath and some clean clothes. Would it be all right if I wore Lucy's things?"

He stared at her as he chewed. When he swallowed, he looked down at his plate and said, "I reckon it'd be all right. They been folded up in that box for an awful long time, not being any use to anyone."

He ate a few more mouthfuls, and added, "I guess I could use a bath myself. Bein' up here alone, gettin' a bath isn't the first thing on my list, especially once't it starts gettin' cold. I'm used to going down to the creek and washin' up out of a bucket this time of year. Unless there's ice on top, sometimes I jump in to rinse off just for the fun of it. Grandma Mimi used to think it was healthy."

"Healthy? I would think it would give you a death of cold."

"She was full-blood Kansa. They're tougher than white folk, had to be. I don't know if you can stand that water, though, even washin' out of a bucket. It's always cold, even in the summer."

He looked around the cabin and scratched the back of his neck. "I think I know of a way to fix you up a bathtub. You can heat up some water and get your bath inside the cabin while I go get mine at the creek." He smiled his crooked smile. "I reckon I'll be a lot easier to be around when I get the man-sweat and the smell of horse manure off me."

Nancy ducked her head and mumbled, "You're not all that hard to be around--at least, now that you aren't so cranky."

"I'm sorry 'bout that. I don't take well to surprises, and you sure pulled a big one on me, showin' up here like you did. I'll try to do better. I'm startin' to get used to you now."

"Does that mean you'll let me stay?"

He stared at her until she felt his gaze would cut right through her, and he drew in a long breath before he said, "The only thing worse for me than you bein' here and not being able to—to have you, is the thought that you might leave, and I'd be alone again. It wasn't too bad until my dog died a while back. I used to talk to him and, sometimes, I was pretty sure he understood everything I said."

He hesitated and then said, "I didn't know 'til you showed up how lonely I been. I mean, I go into town once't a week and say hello to the folks I trade with, but it isn't the same as havin' someone waiting at home at the end of the day. I been livin' out here like I wasn't much more than one of the animals myself for over two years."

He choked up, dropped his eyes, and cleared his throat. It was the longest speech he had made thus far. "If you left now, I'd have to pack up and leave, too. I don't think I could live here another winter by myself. I want you to stay. I won't hurry anything. I'll wait for you. You're eighteen, a grown woman, and sooner or later, nature will draw you to me, and you'll stop being afraid."

Nancy felt as if a weight had been lifted from her chest. She wanted to stay as long as he wouldn't force her into a physical relationship. She was happy to be there, but she didn't want him to think she'd come to his bed. "I'm sorry. I don't think my nature will make me want to do those things."

"It will, I promise you. That's God's plan for us, to be drawn to one another." He grinned at her. "Besides, I'm the best looking man here, ain't I?"

She chuckled, "I suppose if I'm the most beautiful woman, you're the handsomest man." Relief flooded over her. *He's going to let me stay, and he as much as said he won't try to have relations with me if I don't want to, and I never will.*

When the meal was over and the dishes cleared, he emptied out the trunk, setting the contents on the bed. He went to the shed and came back carrying a big tarpaulin and a hammer. "This here's my old tent. It's been Macadamized to keep the rain out. It stands to reason it'd be just as good at keeping water in."

He spread the canvas out inside the trunk and folded and then nailed the corners to the sides of the box. "Let's fill up the buckets and we'll let the water get hot over the fire."

They filled several pots with water, set some next to the burning logs, and hung a few on the cooking rod in the fireplace. He gathered a bucket, his clean set of clothes, a chunk of soap, and a towel. "I'll go get myself cleaned up in the creek. I'll stay outside until you open the door to let me know you're finished."

"All right."

When he was gone, she took the blue calico dress and shook out some of the wrinkles. There wasn't anything to iron it with. It would have to do. *Most of the wrinkles will come out with wearing it. I'll wash my own dress so it'll be fresh for a change after my next bath.*

She went to the fireplace and stuck her finger in one of the buckets. The water had been icy cold when it was drawn, and now it had hardly lost the chill. It would be a while before it was hot enough. *Maybe I shouldn't be so fussy about cold water. He's out there washing in that freezing cold water right from the creek, and he probably won't complain a bit about it.*

59

The picture of him without his clothes came into her mind and made her curious. Except for changing the babies and her wizened, dying grandfather, she had never seen a naked man. Her curiosity began to get control of her. Almost against her will, she went out of the cabin, down the steps, and walked softly to the woods. She could hear him singing loudly. He didn't have much of a singing voice, and it made her laugh. She clapped her hands over her mouth so he wouldn't hear her and kept going, a few steps at a time. When she reached the pines, she crept forward until she could see him.

His clothes were in a pile on the ground. He had his back to her. He had lathered his whole body with the soap and was scrubbing himself with a handful of pine needles. She couldn't take her eyes off him. When he finished cleaning himself, he filled the bucket with water, held it up over his head, and let it slosh down over him, rinsing away the suds. His body was lean, and his skin stretched tightly over muscle and sinew.

Almost in a trance, she stepped closer one foot at a time until she was only a few yards away. *So many scars!* His body was peppered with them, large and small. The worst was a thick, jagged line that began at the top of his shoulder and ran diagonally down his back, stopping an inch or so above his waistline near the spine. There were others, less dramatic, but still, so many. She was compelled to come closer. He picked up the towel and began drying off.

She took several more steps. When she was close enough, she reached out and ran her finger down the diagonal scar. He stepped away from her. Without turning around, he said, "Don't touch me. It's more than I can bear."

She turned and ran at full speed back to the cabin and up the steps, slamming the door behind her. She pressed her back against the door and panted until she caught her breath. *What a fool thing to do. Now there's no telling what he'll do to me.*

She peeked out the window, but there was no sign of him. She decided after a few minutes that he wasn't going to follow her. Steam was beginning to rise from the water heating in the fireplace. She looked out the window again and still didn't see him. *It'll be all right. He'll keep his promise and stay outside until I open the door.*

One pot at a time, she poured the water into the make-shift bathtub, pulled her dress and chemise over her head, and stepped out of her step-ins and into the water. It was still only a few inches deep, but it would do. She slid down in the water to cover as much of herself as possible, turned to get wet all over, and sat up. She lathered the washcloth with the lye soap and ran it over herself before she splashed off the suds.

At home, they had a proper bathtub, and she could fill it high enough that the water reached her chin, but it had never felt as wonderful as this. She lay on her back and held her chin up to get her hair wet, then lathered it up and rinsed it. She was reaching for the towel when he opened the door and walked in. She gasped, pulled her knees up to cover herself, and held the towel in front of her. "You were supposed to wait outside!"

He grinned at her. "You were supposed to wait in here."

"I'm sorry. I don't know what came over me."

"I do--woman's curiosity. It's a terrible condition, but one I seen before. It's all right with me."

"Get on out of here so I can get dressed."

"No. I want to see you."

Her stomach turned over. "What? No! Get out of here."

"It's only fair. You saw me."

The heat of a blush ran over her face and neck before she felt it spread down her whole body. "I didn't see all of you."

He chuckled, and in a teasing tone, asked, "Do you want to see the rest of me?"

"No-o-o!" For some reason, his laugh was comforting, and hearing it, Nancy wasn't afraid of him. She stuck out her chin. "Get out," she ordered, pointing at the door.

"Nope." He sat down at the table. "I'm staying right here. You might as well dry off 'fore you catch cold. I won't touch you. I just want to look at you, like you did me. Fair's fair."

There was nothing else for her to do. She couldn't sit in the makeshift tub forever. The water was already cooling, and it was true that she was the one who broke the rule first. She became unexpectedly bold. She stood up, dried off quickly and reached for the blue dress.

He stood up. "Wait a minute." He walked toward her and put out his hand.

She clutched the towel and shrank back. "You promised you wouldn't touch me!"

"I keep my promises. I'm not going to touch you until you say you want me to, but what harm would it do to let me imagine I'm touching you?"

"I don't understand."

"Just be still for a minute. I won't lay a finger on you."

In spite of the blazing fire, Nancy clutched the towel and shivered as he came closer. She made herself believe his promise. *Oh, Lord! Daddy would beat me something awful if he knew this, but I don't have anywhere else to go if he puts me out. Jake has to let me stay here. What else can I do?*

He gently pulled the towel away from her and held up both hands next to her forearms. His palms were so close she could feel the heat of them, but he didn't make contact with her skin. She closed her eyes and held her breath. She could feel the warmth radiating from his hands as he ran them down near her arms, breasts, stomach, and legs. He walked around her and she felt them next to her shoulders, back, and bottom. She heard him gasp and walk away from her.

She opened her eyes and he was standing by the table staring at her. He said, "Don't ever let anyone tell you that you aren't beautiful."

She grabbed the blue dress and he watched as she quickly pulled it over her head. When her body was covered, she tossed her chin defiantly. "There. Are you satisfied?"

He went to the cabin door, where he turned to look at her one last time. "Not by a long shot, Nancy."

She had no doubt what he meant.

Chapter 7

Over the next four weeks, they settled into a pattern of compromise for both of them. Nancy cooked and cleaned while Jake tended his traps and cured the hides. On Sundays, she had her bath, and he watched, but kept his promise and never touched her. After a few times, any fear of him was completely gone. Even though she could see him struggling to keep control over himself, she trusted him to keep his word.

Every time he saw her without her clothes on, the longing on his face was clear. She was beginning to have similar feelings. Sometimes, they frightened her, and sometimes, they excited her. In her heart, she felt a victory of some sort. Growing up as a female, she had never had power over anything, but she had a power over him. The fourth week, when Nancy reached over her shoulder to wash as far down her back as she could reach, he said, "Lucy liked me to wash her back for her."

She didn't flinch, but met his eyes, and found them to be without danger. She handed him the washcloth and leaned forward. "Just the top, above my waist. I can reach the rest by myself."

He slowly ran the cloth over her shoulders and back and forth across her back until he reached her waistline. Sometimes his hand made contact with her skin and an electric thrill ran through her. She had to fight the shiver it produced. She had to keep him from knowing what she felt.

On Mondays, he saddled up Charlie and Pete and took the animal skins he had cured into town to trade at the store. She gave him a list of things she wanted, and every week the cabin was more like a home, with enough dishes, utensils, and even a proper vase for flowers.

Whenever he made the trip, he was always home before dark. Pete would be loaded down with as many supplies for the approaching winter as he could comfortably carry. Knowing how hard it was for him to earn money, she asked for only a few things for herself or for the cabin, cooking staples like baking powder, or scissors, needles, and thread, so she could make herself undergarments and nightgowns out of the flour sacks folded on the top shelf. She longed for a piece of the soft fabric her father sold at the store but was reluctant to ask for such a luxury. He brought home everything she asked of him without complaint.

One morning, she called him several times for breakfast and he hadn't answered. She went to the shed to see what was holding him up, and when she walked in, he was pulling his shirt off over his head. The sight of his bare chest didn't embarrass her. He'd seen her naked often enough that the sight of his torso seemed natural now. She hadn't thought of the scars on his back since that first day she saw them, but now her curiosity sprang up.

"It's a little cold to be taking your shirt off," she said.

"Pete there just sneezed all over me."

"Yuck! I came to tell you that your breakfast is getting cold."

"I'll be right there."

While they were eating, she said, "Tell me about your scars."

The pain that washed over his face startled her. When he didn't say anything, she asked, "Were you in the war?"

He sighed. "I was. I'd like to forget about it, if you'd let me."

"Oh. I'm sorry. It's just that you have so many scars. I never saw one like the big one that runs down your back. Just tell me about that."

"I reckon you won't stop asking 'til I tell you. That one's from a bayonet."

"A bayonet! How did it happen?"

"You're going to make me tell the whole story, aren't you?"

"You'd tell me sooner or later, and you're so stingy with words, you'd probably tell it in dribs and drabs. You may as well get it over with."

He took a drink of coffee and wiped his mouth with the back of his hand. "Well, here it is. I'll tell you this all at one time so's you'll not ask again." He drew in a long breath and began. "I told you how, after Lucy died, I wanted to die myself. I left my home town and took off for Kansas City, the big one on the other side of the Mississippi River. I'm ashamed to tell it on myself, but I lived a life I'm not proud of, one my momma would have whipped me over, if she'd known it."

He went on, "I had a job at a stable takin' care of the horses and so forth, and a sleepin' room in a boardin' house but, after work, I'd go out drinkin' and listenin' to the music in the saloons. I'd been there 'bout a year when I met this woman named Vanessa. She was pretty, and she made me laugh. We got married and--"

Nancy couldn't stop herself from interrupting him. "Married? Where is she? What happened to her?"

"If you'll be still, I'll tell you. It seemed like as soon as we married, she got tired of me. We were only together a few months when America got into the war. I grew up around horses, so I signed up to join the Cavalry. Vanessa acted like she was glad to see me go. When they shipped me off to France, she didn't even go with me to the railroad station."

"Were you one of those soldiers I see pictures of, riding your horse into battle?"

"As it turned out, only officers got to ride. I took care 'a the Army mules that pulled the cannons around. It was pretty much the same job I'd been doing in Kansas City, and it was all right with me. Mules got a reputation they don't always deserve. Some of 'em are right easy to get along with if you know what they want."

"How would you get a scar like that taking care of mules?"

He held up a palm. "Be patient, I'm gettin' to that part. When you're a soldier, you're a soldier first. When the fightin' gets thick, and the supply of able-bodied men gets thin, you take your rifle and go to it. For the time I was over there, I got sent in five times. On the day this happened, it was toward the end of the war and they had been fightin' this battle for three days. I was sent down to reinforce the front and wound up in a trench."

He closed his eyes and Nancy thought she saw him shudder. She covered his hand with hers. "Were you afraid?"

"Afraid's not the half of it. I was scared out of my wits. I never did get over that. Some of the men told me that after a while, I wouldn't worry about it anymore, that I'd take livin' or dyin' as somethin' out of my control, and then I wouldn't be afraid after that, but I never got to that place."

She bit back another question and waited for him to continue. He swallowed hard, leaned back in his chair, and ran both hands through his hair. Looking at the corner of the ceiling as if he were watching something there, he said, "I don't normally talk much, and I never talked about this to anyone 'cept the other soldiers, the ones who lived through it with me and even then, there wasn't much to be said. We all knew how one another felt."

He paused and looked deep into her eyes. "I'll describe it to you as best I can if you'll promise to never ask me about the war after this one time."

"I promise." She leaned forward and rested her chin on her hand.

"All right then. It was around the end of the battle of Argonne. We were fightin' at one end of the line, and the French troops were next to us, holdin' out on the other end. It was only November, but it was freezing cold, and we kind of tried to stay up the side of the trench, a little out of the stream of water that ran down the bottom."

"Water? Why was there water?"

"There always is. Sometimes it comes up out of the ground when you dig down, and sometimes it's the noise from the cannons that makes it rain."

"Oh."

"What you usually do when you make a trench, if you have the time, is dig it and then nail or tie together a lattice out of planks or maybe only strong branches to lie along the bottom so the water will run under it and you won't be walking in mud. There wasn't any time for that when they dug this one. They told us in basic trainin' to always do what we could to stay dry, but it seems like when the cannons get to firin', it always brings on the rain."

She nodded. "That sounds kind of like the rainmakers in the prairies. I read about how they set off dynamite to bring on a storm."

"Are you going to keep interrupting me?"

Nancy snapped her mouth shut. "No."

"I'd been there for a day and a half with this fella I knew from the time I first got off the boat. The Germans made a charge at us. There were cannons and grenades and rifles shootin' all at the same time. It was like being thrown into the worst hell you can imagine. I peeked up over the top of the trench and a German came runnin' at me out of the smoke with his bayonet pointed right at my heart. Funny thing was, he looked just as scared as I felt. I ducked down and the blade stuck into my back up at my shoulder. It skidded down along the top of my shoulder blade until he tore it out where you saw the scar end down by my waistline.

"I rolled back into the water at the bottom of the trench. He jumped down and was fixing to finish me off when my buddy shot him in the back. He fell on top of me and his eyes looked right into mine. He said something that sounded like, 'Study more, lad.' Didn't make any sense to me. The awful thing of it was, he was only a boy, couldn't 'a been more than fifteen, sixteen years old. He kind of gurgled and died right there."

She asked, "Did you ever find out what the boy said to you"

He nodded. "One of my buddies who made it through the battle and spoke a little German told me what he said meant, 'I'm sorry.' It hurt my heart knowing that boy died like he did, and his last words were an apology."

"How awful!"

"Awful doesn't start to say it. I pushed him off 'a me and tried to get up, but I couldn't make it. I reached out my hand to my buddy and he was fixing to help me up when a grenade landed right behind him. I saw it and kind of rolled away from it, but it tore him to bits. I got a load of shrapnel myself. That's what caused a lot of the other scars you see on my back and legs."

"They're all over you, at least, what part of you I saw." She felt herself blushing again.

"Yep."

"It's a wonder you didn't bleed to death before they could help you."

"There wasn't any help to be had for a long time. I was there all night. I fell back down into the water again and they said that's what saved me. It was freezing cold, even had some ice on the top. That's what stopped the bleedin'. They came and got me the next mornin', but I don't remember any of that. When I woke up, I was in the medical tent. They did the best they could to sew me up. The doc even apologized for the scar, but it had been so long since it happened, and the wound was so uneven, it was the best he could do."

"And you came home right after that?"

"No such luck. They found me fit for duty and sent me back to the front. It was the last time I was in battle, though. I was glad for that. I tended my mules and prayed it would all be over, and after a while, it was."

"You made it through the worst part. You're a hero. You must be proud of that."

"I'm not proud of anything," Jake said firmly, "and I'm no hero. I was scared to death and prayin' every minute just to get out of there. I came home with other scars, the kind you can't see on my skin."

"What do you mean?"

"I saw too many things that I wish I could wipe out 'a my mind. There were men getting blown to bits all around me, one of them that fella who was like my best friend. Even that wasn't the worst of it. In the medical tent, they brought in a bunch of our guys that had got hit with mustard gas. They had blisters the size of silver dollars all over them, and I mean all over. It was so bad they had to have their hands tied down to keep 'em from scratchin' and makin' 'em worse. A lot of 'em, their eyes were swole shut, and some couldn't see at all. The docs said their eyesight would maybe come back after a while.

"A lot of 'em were coughin' up blood 'cause they breathed the gas in and their lungs were bleedin' inside. Their bodies were burned so bad the doctors couldn't put bandages or bed covers or anything on 'em. The nurses made a rack like a tent frame on their beds and draped the sheets over the top to keep out the cold air as best they could."

Nancy fought back her tears at the images he painted. She said, "I wasn't old enough that I remember much about the war, especially living where we did. What was that war started about anyway?"

He shrugged. "None of us knew. I still don't know. You think your country needs you, so you don't ask those kinda questions, you just go."

He fell silent and after a while, she asked. "What else? Tell me the rest of it."

"It's been a long time since I said this many words at one time. It would take too much talkin' to tell it all, and you know talkin' isn't what I do best. Besides, it pains me to remember it."

"Was it very long after that before you came home?"

"You're determined to hear it all, aren't you?"

"I guess I am, but don't tell me more about the fighting. I want to know what happened after that."

"After my stitches came out, and I was declared fit for duty, I went back to tending my mules. In a few more months, the fighting was 'bout over." Jake shook his head. "Whew! It was even awful when the shootin' stopped and quiet finally came over the place. There wasn't even the sound of a bird singin'. The whole countryside was burnt up, trees blown away, grass gone, houses smashed to bits. Nothin' left but the mud and the trenches and the barb' wire. I wondered if anything would ever grow there again."

"So you were finally out of danger. It must have been wonderful."

He snorted. "That's what we thought, but we weren't out of danger–not even close. When we got on the ship and it left port, we thought we were safe for the first time in I don't know how long. We were on the trip comin' home when the

Spanish Influenza broke out. It hit the youngest men the worst. Seemed like the older ones didn't get it so bad, or didn't get it at all. It was strange how it would go. Some of us got awful sick and then got well, and sometimes a man wouldn't look sick at all, and the next thing you know, he'd cough and have bloody foam running out of his mouth, and he would keel over dead right in front of you."

Jake shivered at the memory. "I came down with it on the boat, and for 'bout three days, I thought I was going to die. Try as they might, they couldn't keep you clean, what with vomitin' and…" He looked away from her and went on, "bloody diarrhea. Most of the time, you just lay there in your mess. It was awful. There was times I wished I would go ahead and die so it would be over. I lived, but it was a month 'fore I felt like myself. I was weak as a kitten for a long while, and I slept most of the time. When the boat finally landed, they shipped me and a bunch of the others to Fort Riley, right close to where I grew up. They said they would keep us there 'til they were sure we wouldn't give it to anyone else, but it still got out. The nurses and doctors carried it home with them, and their families got it. I heard that the Spanish Influenza went around the world twice and altogether 'bout a hundred million people died from it."

Nancy squeezed his hand and said, "I'm glad you made it through."

He picked up her hand and turned it palm up, held it to his lips, and kissed it. The chills that ran through her whole body took her by surprise. She jerked her hand away from him and put it in her lap. With her head down, she asked, "What was worst, the fighting in the trenches or the flu?"

"Oh, there was things worse than either one of those, but I'm not wanting to talk 'bout them."

"You don't want to talk about much of anything, do you?"

"I'm a talker when I like the subject."

"What subjects do you like?"

He brightened a little. "Horses. I like to talk about them, or dogs. When Skipper, the dog I grew up with, died, I cried for a week, like a little kid, and I was almost eighteen when it happened. We always had two or three dogs growing up, and I had a blue tick hound named Dutch with me here until just a few months ago. He went right with me ever' step I took, even ran behind Charlie all the way into town and back when he coulda slept on the porch. At night, he lay right there at the foot of the cot 'til the rooster crowed."

"What happened to him?"

"He got into it with a bear and it killed him. I know I'll get another dog someday, but right now my heart's still broke over losing him." Nancy thought she saw a glimmer of a tear in his eye. He looked away, swallowed, and said, "I like horses. I could talk 'bout horses all day. Get that from my mom."

Nancy said, "I never had a dog of my own. They were always around, but they were my father's dogs and never paid much attention to anyone else. They followed him all the time, like you said Dutch did you."

"I believe that means your dad has a good heart, for a dog to love him like that."

She grinned at him. "Are you saying since Dutch loved you, it means you have a good heart?"

He took her hand again and she didn't pull it away from him. "I believe I do. I don't think anyone who ever met me could say I ever did something to harm them. Even when I was over there in France, I didn't have to do a lot of shooting,' but when I did, I didn't aim to kill anyone if I could help it. Do your folks have a horse?"

"We did, but the horse belongs to Daddy, and we weren't allowed to touch it unless he said so. He used to let me ride once in a while until I got too old for it to be proper. I'm not much interested in horses."

"Then you won't get along with my mom. She's crazy 'bout 'em."

"Tell me more about the war."

He sighed. "You said I didn't have to talk any more about that."

"Then tell me more about what you did when it was over. It's you I want to know more about. You've hardly told me anything at all."

"I told you about my childhood and my pets and my two wives, and even the war. There isn't much more than that. Why don't you talk about yourself?"

"You already know it all. I haven't lived much of a life. You don't have to talk about fighting any more. Tell me what you thought about the war, you know, the politics of it, and things like that."

He shook his head slowly. "The more I say, the easier it gets to say it. I didn't know 'til you showed up here how I been wantin' someone to talk to, but you're 'bout to wear me out. I'll tell you all 'bout war in a few words. It's ugly. War is evil and low and ugly. Why on earth does a girl like you want to know 'bout things like that?"

"I've lived my whole life up here in these mountains, in that little town, with the same people every day. I've never even been to Reno. The war happened in a different world with different people, and I want to learn about things outside of here, get to know people who're different from my family and the folks in town. I don't know anything, and I've never been anywhere."

His face turned red and his voice grew tense. He jumped to his feet and almost shouted, "Then someday you ought to travel to other worlds, but pick peaceful places, places where men ain't blowin' one another to pieces. Try to meet people who don't want to kill anyone."

Shocked, Nancy shrank back in her chair. He took a long breath and shrugged. "I'm sorry. I didn't mean to yell. I'll tell you one thing, don't think that you don't already know different sorts of people. Kind people are kind wherever they are, and killers are the same all over the world. They aren't all that much different inside, whether they're fightin' in the trenches or killing hogs in Smithville."

He stared into her eyes. "Back when you first told me about your cousin Abner, I recognized him, his kind, I mean. I met plenty of men just like him when I was in the cavalry, men who didn't sign up to fight for their country, they signed up so they could have a chance to kill other men and not get punished for it. Soon's you told me 'bout him, I swore to myself I'd never make you go back there. I didn't know what I was going to do for you, but I wouldn't make you go home and marry a man like that."

She reached out and took his hand again. "So, here we are."

He sat back down, leaned forward, and stared into her eyes. "Yep, here we are, you sleeping in the cabin, and me sleeping in the shed, and winter coming on soon."

She blushed and looked away. "What happened after you got over the influenza?"

"They declared the official armistice, and I was mustered out. I went back to Kansas City, where I thought Vanessa was waitin' for me. She was there all right, livin' in the same place, but I doubt she gave me a thought the whole time I was gone. We spent one night together. When we woke up in the mornin' she looked at me and said, 'I don't even like you,' so I packed up my gear and went to see my folks for a few days. My mom had been takin' care of Charlie for me while I was gone. Even after all that time, he was happier to see me than Vanessa was."

"So you were home again. It must have been wonderful to feel safe after all you went through."

"You'd 'spect so, but I was restless, couldn't seem to get settled down to workin' the farm again. After we visited a few weeks, I knew I wanted to try something different. I got on a train with Charlie and came out here. I used my mustering out pay to buy Pete and some supplies, and then rode around the woods 'til I came to this spot one day and knew it was where I wanted to stay."

"How did you know?"

"It was perfect. There was a stream wasn't too far off to one side, the clearin' was already here, and it was uphill from the water, so it wouldn't flood if it got to raining hard."

"If there was a stream so nearby, why did you go to the trouble of digging a well?"

"It's always good to have water nearby. Buckets of water can get right heavy when you carry them any distance, and it's handier if there's ever a fire. Henry helped me with it."

"Henry?"

"The Paiute friend I told you about."

"Oh."

"There was lots of young pine to use for the cabin and shed and whatever else I needed. I set right in cuttin' trees for the shed and that made the clearing bigger than it was to start with. I been here ever' since."

"Are you cold, sleeping in the shed?"

"It's not too bad. When I built it, I pitched the logs with clay from the stream so it keeps out the wind, just like the cabin. The heat comin' from the horses warms up the space." He grinned at her. "I'd rather be sleepin' in here, but that would be harder on me than sleepin' out there."

She very well understood his meaning. She sat back in her chair a little and nodded her head. *What would it be like to lie next to him, to feel his*

82

body against mine? Would those other things be so terrible if he were gentle about it? He isn't like Abner at all. He isn't mean, and he doesn't weigh a ton. Daddy said I may even grow to enjoy it. I never heard a single one of the women in town say they liked it, but outside of Linda, I haven't really talked with that many of them.

He gazed at her for a moment, as if waiting for her to say something, but when she didn't, he stood up and walked to the door. "I'll get on about my work."

Chapter 8

At the end of each day, Nancy had dinner sitting on the table when Jake came home. One afternoon, he was holding one hand behind his back and grinned at her. "I got a surprise for you." He held out his hand and there was a cloth bundle in it. She took it and unfolded the cloth to reveal a mound of strawberries, each the size of a dime.

"Strawberries!" She popped one between her teeth and pressed it against the roof of her mouth with her tongue. The juice ran over her taste buds. "I never had one that tasted like this. It's wonderful, but they're so small. Do they ever get any bigger?"

"In the summer they do better. These are the last of 'em for this year."

"I love them. We'll share them and have a grand dessert."

He looked at her with a smile that crinkled his eyes. "I'm glad they're still good. I was afraid they'd be sour."

"Didn't you taste them?"

"No. I couldn't find very many. I wanted to save them for you."

She took one of the berries and held it in front of his mouth. "Try it."

He blinked, opened his mouth, and she put the berry on his tongue. A thrill ran over her when her fingers touched his lips. He nodded. "You're right. They are sweet."

After dinner, he said, "I'm goin' into town tomorrow. Is there anything you want me to bring back?"

"Well, if we can afford it, I'd like some ladies' soap. They have some at the store that smells like lavender. One bar is enough. I'll make it last for a long time."

"Is there anything else?"

She felt herself blush. "I know this sounds like a little kid, but would you bring me a few licorice sticks?"

Jake left early the next morning, and as she worked, Nancy thought about her requests. *I hope he doesn't think I'm being foolish asking for things we could get by without, but it isn't very much, a bar of soap and a few pieces of candy. The homemade lye soap is good enough for cleaning, and there's enough to last through the winter, but the smell would never be described as pleasant. Mother always smelled like lavender, and I miss that. Daddy says I'm just like her, and it must be true. She loved the licorice as much as I did. Daddy always said I took after him in looks and took after her in loving licorice and being hard-headed, but he was only joking with us. Thinking of it makes me a little homesick. I wonder if she misses me.*

The day wore on and Nancy kept busy until the sun was touching the tops of the trees. *Why isn't Jake home yet? He doesn't like working in the shed when he has to use the lantern because he's afraid of starting a fire. He always comes home with enough daylight left to unpack the supplies and see to bedding down the horses.*

Every few minutes, Nancy would look out the front door and listen to see if she could hear him or the horses coming home. She grew more anxious with every minute that passed.

Oh, God! What would I do if something happened to him? I could never survive out here by myself. I'd have to go home then. Should I go out and try to look for him? The light was fading away when she heard the sound of a horse's whinny. She hurried to the door, flung it open, ran outside--and collided with her father, Lucas Smith.

He wrapped his arms around her and lifted her off her feet. "Thank the Lord. Everyone said you probably died in the woods, and half the men in town went out searching for you. They all said you were dead, but I knew you weren't. I would feel it in my heart if you were. I never gave up hope."

A panicked Nancy rasped, "What are you doing here?"

He set her down. "We came to rescue you."

"We?" Nancy looked over her father's shoulder to see Abner sitting on his horse. "How did you know I was here?"

"When that mountain man bought that lavender soap and then asked for some licorice sticks, it didn't take me long to figure it out. He's been coming into the store for some time now. I remember him talking about where he lived, and I didn't figure it would take me very long to find this place. While he was going in and out of the store to load up what he bought, I had one of your brothers go out and loosen the cinch on the pack horse a little so the load would fall off the first time he went up a hill. That gave me enough time to get Abner and make it out here."

"But how---?"

"We don't have time now. We have to get out of here before he gets back. We can send the sheriff to arrest him for kidnapping later."

Nancy's heart thudded. She grasped his jacket. "I wasn't kidnapped, and I don't want to go with you."

"You weren't kidnapped?"

"No. I got lost and he took me in. He saved my life."

"How did he save your life?"

"I would have died of the cold."

"Well--"

The sound of a rifle cocking made both of them look in Abner's direction. He held his weapon up to his shoulder, and when Nancy turned her head to see where he was aiming, Jake was sitting on his horse at the edge of the path. He threw his leg over the saddle horn and slid to the ground. "What's going on here?"

Abner shouted, "Stop, or I'll shoot you dead!"

"No!" Nancy screamed. She ran down the porch steps and raced toward Jake. She placed herself in front of him and held out her arms to make herself as large as she could to protect him. "You can't shoot him."

Abner growled. "Why not?"

"He's my husband."

Her father clambered down the steps. "Husband? He can't be. Not one of the bishops in town would marry you to him without my permission."

Nancy stuck out her chin. "It's like you always say. There's man's law and there's God's law. I've been sleeping in his bed almost from the night I came here." Nancy felt a twinge of conscience, but it wasn't an outright lie.

Abner's face contorted and turned crimson with rage. He bellowed so loudly his horse reared, "You can't have her. She was promised to me."

Nancy's father held up his hand. "You wouldn't want her for a wife now, Abner. She's already been with him."

"I'll have her all right. I'll marry her because she belongs to me, but she'll not share my bed. She's been contaminated. She'll be a servant in my house until the day she dies. No one takes what's mine. I'll kill both of them before I'll let him have her." He got his horse under control and raised his rifle.

Smith caught hold of Abner's horse's rein. He drew his Colt from his belt and pointed it at Abner's face. "You'll do no such thing. I'll shoot you myself if you even try."

Abner's mouth fell open. He stared at Lucas and slowly lowered his rifle.

Smith said, "Put that thing away. You won't be using it today."

The corners of Abner's mouth pulled down so far his whole face took on the grimace of a demon. He slid the rifle into its holster.

Smith put his gun back in his belt, turned, and walked to where Nancy was still standing in front of Jake. He held out his right hand. "Mr. Belk, I take it from the way she acts that Nancy is satisfied to be here with you. You do right by her, or you'll have to answer to me."

He chuckled. "I ought to be apologizing to you. She always was my favorite. I'm afraid I spoiled her rotten, and that will make her hard for any man to live with."

Hesitantly, Jake took Smith's hand and shook it. "I appreciate it, Mr. Smith. I love Nancy, and I'll do my best to see to it that I make her happy."

"Are you Mormon?"

"No, sir. I was raised Baptist, but I have to admit it's been awhile since I was to services. Nancy's got me saying grace before meals, so I'm making progress."

Smith laughed. "You're welcome to join us at the church." He hugged Nancy. "All right, then. We'd best be moving on, or it'll be pitch-dark before we get home." He kissed Nancy on the forehead. "You come into town with him and visit your mother. She's going to be awful glad to hear that you're alive."

Nancy laid her head on her father's chest. "I will, Daddy."

He took his hand and tilted up her chin. "I do have one thing to ask of you."

"What's that?"

"I have eight granddaughters. Not one of my children has been able to give me a grandson. They only make girls. I want you to have some boys, and when the first one comes along, I want you to name him after me."

"I will. I promise. The first boy I have will be Lucas Smith Belk."

"And you two bring him to see us as soon as you're able."

"We will."

Smith led his horse to the steps for help in mounting it. Once he huffed on top of the animal, he gave Nancy a small smile and touched the brim of his hat. "See you two another time."

Nancy grabbed his stirrup. "Daddy?"

"What is it, child?"

"Could I send Jake to get my clothes and things?"

Lucas pursed his lips and then nodded. "I'll tell your mother to pack them up for you. He can get them at the store the next time he's in town." He turned the horse toward the path. "Come along, Abner. We're finished here."

Abner's horse started to follow without being prompted, but Abner jerked back on the reins. "You may be finished, but I'm not. You promised her to me, and he stole her away. I won't have it. Now you're even helping them out. It isn't right. No man steals from me and lives to tell about it. I'll get even with both of them."

Smith put his hand on his Colt. "I said, let's go."

"You won't shoot me."

Smith leveled a purposeful gaze at Abner. "I'll shoot anyone who harms Nancy in any way— or harms someone she loves."

A twinge of fear showed in Abner's eyes, but as he turned to leave he directed his horse close to Nancy and Jake, who stepped in front of Nancy protectively. Abner leaned over as he passed them and hissed, "This isn't over yet." He stared at Jake. "It won't be over until you're dead and she's where she belongs."

Jake took a step forward and growled, "You stay away from here, stay away from me, and stay away from my wife."

Chapter 9

Nancy and Jake didn't go back in the cabin until her father and Abner were both out of sight. With one arm around her waist, he held her close to his side. "Abner means it. I told you, I know his kind. He'll be back, and he'll be coming to kill me."

"What are we going to do?"

"I'll think about that later." He put both arms around her and drew her to him. She stiffened at first, but then relaxed against him. He tilted his head, grinned, and asked, "I heard you tell your father that you loved me. Is it true, or did you just say that to save him from killin' me?"

She felt a blush work its way over her face. "It's true."

"You called me your husband in front of two witnesses, and I called you my wife. In Nevada, that makes it so."

"What about Vanessa? Did she divorce you?"

"I don't know, prob'ly, but even if she didn't, most every man around here has more than one wife. My being married before doesn't matter in Smithville, does it?"

"But you aren't Mormon."

"I don't see how that would make any difference."

"I guess it wouldn't." Her heart started beating faster. She stepped away from him. "I suppose that means I have to let you—you know."

"You don't have to, but I sure am hopin' you will. I'd have a hard time tellin' you how much I'm hoping you will."

She took a deep breath and exhaled slowly. "Could you do one thing for me first?"

He threw back his head and laughed. "I'd do just 'bout anything for you right now. What do you want?"

"You've waited all these weeks. I want you to wait one more day. Even though I said I'd never get married, a girl dreams about her wedding from the time she's small. All of that was taken away from me when Daddy said I had to marry Abner. Now, I can have it back. I'd like us to have a ceremony."

"You mean go into town and get the bishop?"

"No. I'm afraid that if we went into town, we'd run into Abner. Let me think a minute how we could do it. Uh, first, we'll both take our baths and get dressed up."

He grinned at her. "Take a bath in the middle of the week?"

She poked him in the chest. "Yes, the middle of the week. I used to dream that someday I'd be rich enough to take a bath every day."

He shook his head. "You sound like my mom. She said one of the happiest days of her life was when Dad put running water inside the house."

"Here's what we'll do. We'll get our baths. You put on your best outfit from the trunk, and I'll wear Lucy's yellow dress, the one you were saving, if that would be all right with you?"

"It'd be fine with me."

Nancy began to get excited as the ideas came to her. "We'll stand facing each other and read passages from the Bible and make our promises. Then we'll write our names in the Bible and we'll be married in my heart, not just in Nevada law."

He smiled his crooked smile and she knew he was about to make one of his jokes. He said, "We won't have any witnesses unless I bring Charlie and Pete inside to watch."

She laughed. "I'm not cleaning up after those two. They aren't exactly housebroken, but they are our best friends, though. I suppose Charlie could be your best man and Pete could be my bridesmaid. Maybe we could do it out on the porch so they can see us. "

"Since in Nevada you're legally my wife, can I at least kiss you?"

"You can kiss me all you want--if you wait until tomorrow for the other thing."

"I think I'll kiss you one time. I don't know as I could stand more than that and keep my promise."

He cupped her chin. Nancy closed her eyes and tilted her head back. His lips were warm and lingered on hers for a long time. The touch of his mouth on hers thrilled her so strongly she grew light-headed. *Tomorrow, I'll find out about the rest of it tomorrow.*

When he ended the kiss, he took a step away from her and huffed out a long breath. "One more day."

She grinned at him. "One more day."

"I have some work to do if I'm going to keep us safe tonight."

"Safe?"

"In case Abner tries to sneak up on us in the dark. That'd be like him. His kind are cowards at heart. They don't want to meet a man head on unless they somehow or other have an advantage."

He went in the shed and came out carrying several lengths of rope. He tied the end of one around the base of one of the trees that circled the clearing, about a foot up from the ground, then went to the next tree, looped it around that one, and the next, and the next. It took two more coils of rope to make the circle complete. Nancy watched him work. "What are you doing?"

"He'd probably get off his horse a ways away and sneak up on foot. If he shows up at night, he won't see this, and he'll trip over it. That ought to make enough noise to wake the horses and give me a chance to protect us."

"I hope he never comes back. I hope I never see him again."

Pete whinnied loudly. Jake said, "He's wanting me to unload him." While Nancy put dinner on the table, Jake put away the supplies he brought from town.

When they sat down to eat and she put her hand in his for the blessing, he held up her palm and kissed it the way he had before. This time, she didn't draw it away from him. He held his lips on her hand until she said, "I bet the chicken stew tastes better than that."

He chuckled. "I didn't actually taste your hand, but I don't see how it could." He ran the tip of his tongue across her palm and the feeling that ran through her was like an electric shock. She gasped and pulled her hand away from him. "I said, tomorrow."

"I know, I know."

After dinner, they talked for a while by the light of the lantern until he stood up and stretched. "I guess we better turn in."

That night, Jake slept in the shed with the horses, and Nancy alone on the cot for the last time.

Chapter 10

When Jake came in the cabin for breakfast the next morning, Nancy was already up and dressed. She flittered about, chatting rapidly as she put their breakfast on the table. He sat down and watched her without speaking. When she finally sat down and he took her hand to give the blessing, she jumped. He grinned at her. "Nerves?"

She laughed weakly, "I suppose. I didn't get much sleep last night, thinking about the wedding and all."

His eyes crinkled up, and he grinned at her. "I didn't get much sleep either, but I can't say I was thinking 'bout the ceremony. I was thinking on what comes after."

She blushed, bit her lip, and looked down. "I had that on my mind, too, but probably not in the same way you did."

He raised her hand to his lips and kissed it so softly she could barely feel it. "I'll do my best to see that you don't need to be afraid."

She managed a small smile. "I know you will."

As soon as they finished breakfast, he built up the fire and arranged her bathtub. "I'll see if we can heat up enough water to give you a special bath instead of a lay down and splash around one."

When the tub was assembled, he filled all of the buckets and pots with water, hanging the buckets on the cooking rod, and placing the pots next to the burning logs to heat them. When the water was hot enough, he poured it into the tarp and sat down to watch her bathe the way he had since that first time. "It's too cold for me to go to wash by the creek. You take your bath first, and then I'll jump in."

She stood by the tub but didn't move to take off her dress. He tilted his head. "What's wrong?"

She fluttered her hands in front of her. "I don't want you to watch me this time. I want this whole day to be different from any other day in my life. Would you wait outside until I call you?"

He stood, smiled, and scratched his head. "I reckon I can do that. I can do just 'bout anything right now."

He left her alone and she slipped out of her clothes and stepped into the tarp. When she slid down to the bottom, the water came all the way up to her chin, a wonderful luxury. She soaked for a while before she lathered up and rinsed. When she dried herself, she wrapped her body in a blanket, but took Lucy's dress and laid it out on the cot instead of getting dressed. She took Jake's best clothes and hung them on the row of pegs that lined the opposite wall.

Opening the door a crack to keep the cold from rushing in, she found him sitting on the top step of the porch. She said, "I'm all done."

He stood and came inside, holding one hand behind his back. When he saw her, he creased his brow. "Why are you wearing a blanket?"

"I didn't want you to see me in the dress yet, not until we start the ceremony."

"Well, all right, if that's the way you want it. This being the first time I took a bath inside the cabin, you're 'bout to see me ever' which way."

"Oh, no, I'm not, not yet. I'm going to turn this chair around backwards and look up the Bible verses I want us to read." She nodded at his clothes. "I hung your clothes over there. When you get out of the tub and start getting dressed, I'll get dressed, too. I want you to promise me you won't peek."

"I promise. I'll keep my back turned 'til you say the word for me to turn around."

She frowned at him. "Why are you holding your hand behind your back?"

He brought his arm forward. He was clutching a bunch of blue asters in his fist. "These were the only things I could find blooming. They were in that spot that gets the most sun and the frost hasn't got to 'em yet. I thought they would do for a bouquet."

She took the flowers from him, leaned her head on his chest, and looked in his eyes. "They're perfect. Thank you."

He kissed her forehead. "I better get to it 'fore the water gets cold." Still wrapped in the blanket, she arranged the chair so her back was to him when she sat down and picked up the Bible. She could hear him splashing around for a while and then he said, "I'm done washing up. I'll get myself dressed now."

"All right. I will, too. Don't look."

"I promised I wouldn't, and hard as it will be, I won't. I always keep my promises."

"Yes, you do. That's a wonderful thing, I think, to have a man who keeps his word."

They kept their backs to one another as they dressed. She slipped into the yellow lace dress and tied the satin sash around her hips. It fit her perfectly. She brushed her hair and wove the aster with the longest stem through the locks over one ear. When she was finished, she said, "I'm ready."

They turned to face one another. When he saw her, tears came to his eyes. "You're beautiful, 'bout the most beautiful thing I ever saw."

She almost asked him if he thought she was as beautiful as Lucy but held the question back. *What if he says no, or maybe he would say yes, but doesn't really mean it and is only saying it to please me? I'd rather not know.*

He held out his hand to her. "How do you want to do this?"

She picked up the Bible and beckoned to him over her shoulder as she walked toward the door. "It's going to be cold out there and I don't want to cover up my dress, so we'll have to do it fast. I've been thinking about what you said, about Charlie and Pete being our witnesses. I think they should. Let's bring them out of the shed to watch."

"Since this is sort of a second Sunday, I already let them out to graze."

They walked out to the porch. Charlie and Pete were munching the greens that still grew on the edge of the clearing. He called to them, "Come on over here, boys. We got something we want you to see."

The horses' heads came up, and they ambled over to the porch. Nancy pulled a flower from her bouquet and wove it into Pete's forelock.

Jake asked, "Doesn't Charlie get one too?"

"No, silly. Pete is my maid of honor, so for the next few minutes, he's a girl. As best man, Charlie is still a boy." She pressed her hand against Jake's shoulder to direct him to the top of the steps and stood next to him. "I'll say my part first."

She opened the Bible to the book of Ruth and read, "Entreat me not to leave thee, or to return from following after thee: for whither thou goest, I will go; and where thou lodgest, I will lodge: thy people shall be my people and thy God, my God: Where thou diest, will I die, and there will I be buried: The Lord do so to me, and more also, if ought but death part thee and me."

She smiled up at him. "And I promise to love you and do my best to make you happy."

She turned the pages of the Bible until she came to the passage she selected for him and handed him the book. She pointed to the verses she wanted him to read, Ephesians 5: 25-33. He nodded and, following the words with his finger, began reading, "Husbands, love your wives, even as Christ also loved the church, and gave Himself for it; That He might sanctify and cleanse it with the washing of water by the word, That He might present it to Himself a glorious church, not having spot or wrinkle, or any such thing; but that it should be holy and without blemish. So ought men to love their wives as their own bodies. He that loveth his wife loveth himself. For no man ever yet hated his own flesh; but nourisheth and cherisheth it, even as the Lord the church: For we are members of his body, of his flesh, and of his bones. For this cause shall a man leave his father and mother, and shall be joined unto his wife, and they two shall be one flesh. This is a great mystery: but I speak concerning Christ and the church. Neverthless, let every one of you in particular so love his wife even as himself; and let the wife see that she reverence her husband."

He looked up at her and smiled. She said, "Is there anything else that you want to promise me?"

"I promise to love you and protect you and take care of you the best I can. I wish I could give you a castle with running water to live in and a whole roomful of fancy clothes and pretty jewelry and such. All I have is this cabin and the little furniture in it and these horses."

"This cabin is the happiest place on earth for me. It will do just fine."

"Can I kiss you now?"

"Yes! Yes, yes, yes."

He took her in his arms and kissed her until her head was swimming. Then he laughed and scooped her up and carried her in the cabin. Once inside, he stopped abruptly. "Uh, oh."

"What's wrong?"

"I'm afraid I can't get to that being one flesh part of my promises on a cot made for one person."

"Put me down."

He set her on her feet. She took the blankets from the cot and spread them out one on top of another in front of the fireplace. "We can sleep here. I'll wash up the blankets you've been using in the shed, and we can put them on the pile, too."

He grinned at her. "There won't be any sleepin' 'til tonight, but that will serve the purpose for now."

He walked to her and wrapped his arms around her. Her old fear jumped up inside and she stiffened. He looked her in the eyes. "Don't be afraid."

"I'm sorry. I can't help it."

"I understand. I'm a little afraid myself."

"You? Why would you be afraid?"

"Well, Lucy and I grew up together, and we learned about this part of life together. I told her what pleased me, and she told me what pleased her, and after a little while, we did right well at it. She liked it almost as much as I did." He smiled crookedly. "Well, maybe not so much first thing in the morning, but other times. It was different with Vanessa. I never made her happy, not once. Maybe that's the reason she didn't want me anymore. I'm praying it will be really good with you and me. I want it to be the way it was with Lucy, and that makes me afraid it won't."

His confession that he lacked a bit of confidence was endearing. Nancy relaxed and leaned against him. "If it took a while with Lucy, it may take a while with me."

"Is it all right to go ahead?"

She nodded. He undid the buttons on her dress and she helped him pull it over her head. She draped it across the back of the chair and faced him. He slipped out of his jacket and tie and tossed them on top of the dress, then began unbuttoning his shirt. She pushed his hand away and undid the buttons for him. She ran her fingers through the patch of chest hair. "You aren't wearing your long underwear."

He grinned at her. "Takes too much time to get out of 'em. I put on my summer drawers."

She took the shirt off and tossed it onto the chair. He said, "My turn." He pulled her chemise over her head and she was wearing only her step-ins. She felt the blush that began at her feet creep up to her face.

He held out his hands. "Now I'm going to touch you more than just washing your back." He pulled the step-ins down to the floor and she stepped out of them. In a repeat of that first time he had watched her bathe, she stood frozen in front of him as he ran his hands over her entire body, this time letting them touch her skin. His palms were rough, and for some reason, she found that appealing. As he walked behind her and ran his hands over her back and buttocks and the back of her legs, the heat that had merely radiated close to her before when he was so careful not to touch her skin, now almost burned her.

She stood there naked while he caressed her body and felt no shame, and more importantly, no fear. When he came around to the front of her, she gazed in his eyes and reached out to unbuckle his belt and unbutton his trousers. He stepped out of the pants. He stood still and waited. She slid down his underwear and looked at him. When she raised her eyes back to his face, it amused her to find that he was blushing. She laughed a little. He frowned. "This isn't the right time for you to be laughing."

"I'm not laughing at you, I'm laughing at me."

"What's so funny?"

"I guess it's one of those nervous laughs. All this time, from the first day my sister told me about what married people do, I've been afraid of—" she pointed at his member—"of those. It's like I have two things going on inside me right now. Part of me is still afraid, and part of me wants to go ahead and find out."

He chuckled. "Then let's go ahead. I like that curious part of you the best." He took her hand and led her to the palette she made in front of the fire. She waited to see what came next. He lay down next to her and kissed her, first on her lips, then her neck, and worked his way down her body. Shivers of pleasure ran through her. For the next few minutes, she tingled at the sensation of his mouth on her breasts and his hands touching her in places where she had never been touched.

Her breath was coming in short gasps, and he shifted himself over her. His voice was hoarse when he finally whispered in her ear, "Are you ready?"

"Yes," she said, as she wrapped her arms around him and pulled him to her. "Yes."

Chapter 11

She couldn't get enough of him. Not only the lovemaking, which was a revelation and a delight to her, but of Jake's presence, and especially the feel of his nude body pressed against her in the night. "I want you to get some more blankets," she told him a few days after their wedding.

"More? We have four already."

"When it gets to be really colder, like in January, I don't want us to have to sleep in our clothes to stay warm."

He grinned at her. "No arguing with that, and I'll make us a proper bed so we won't be on the floor."

"How do you make a bed?"

"Pretty much the same way I made the rest of what I call furniture in here. The trunks of pine trees 'bout three inches thick ought to be strong enough. It won't be fancy, but it'll do the job."

The next Monday, he went into town to deliver his pelts. When he came back, Pete was loaded with the usual supplies, along with an extra-long hank of rope, more blankets, and a length of canvas. More things were tied behind Charlie's saddle. She pointed at the colorful rolls. "What's that?"

"Some of it's your clothes. Your mother had them ready, and she said to tell you there's a surprise or two inside. She put 'em on rag rugs so they wouldn't smell like horse by the time I got 'em here."

When she unrolled the rug, Nancy's heart pounded at the sight of the bundles from her mother. They were wrapped in pieces of fabric from her father's store and tied with ribbons. She knew the new fabric and ribbons were her mother's idea, and it made her fight back tears. Jake helped her carry them into the cabin. She laid the things meant for her on the cot and went back outside to help him with the rest of the load.

As he took down what he had brought home, he told her what each thing was for. He held up the rope. "This'll make us a good foundation for the bed," he said. He showed her the canvas. "This is for a mattress."

After they ate, she opened the bundles from home one at a time. The first held her dresses, four of them, a quilted robe, and four nightgowns, two flannel for cold weather, and two made in light cotton for summer. *I'm never going to sleep in a nightgown again. I can use these to make something else.* The second was stockings and underwear. When she opened that one she laughed. "Look! My underwear! Who would have thought

I'd be so happy to have them. Now I won't have to wash out my things every day."

The last parcel had her sweaters and a winter coat with a pair of gloves stuffed in the pockets. In the middle, was an oilcloth in a print of red roses on a white background. Last was the boots she used to wear in the yard and the shoes she wore to church. Tucked into one of the shoes was a small, paper-wrapped parcel. Nancy opened it to find a dozen or so licorice sticks. She started sobbing. "Look what father sent."

Jake scrunched up his face in the expression common to men when around a crying woman. "I think he wanted to please you, not make you cry."

"I can't help it. This is happy crying." She sniffled and wiped her cheeks with the back of her hand.

When her clothes were stored in the trunk, she turned her attention to the pieces of fabric. She spread out the oilcloth first and held it up. "Look at this. It's cut to a square and big enough to make us a nice tablecloth." She immediately spread it out on the table. "It's so pretty, isn't it?"

He was watching her with a big smile. "It is that. It sure looks better than those rough planks did."

When she held up the lengths of fabric, she measured them by holding out one end in her hand and the other to her nose. She made no effort to hold back the tears any more. "Mama sent me five yards of each one. That's enough to make myself almost anything I want. This fabric and my licorice is their way of showing us we have their blessing."

"Your licorice? Am I getting left out of that?"

She laughed and went to him, sitting on his lap and wrapping her arms around his neck. "No, Mr. Belk. I will never leave you out of anything."

"I see how you work to make the cabin more like a regular home, and it makes me feel bad. I wish I could give you a proper house, but there's no way to build one out here. I'd need more money than I can make from trapping, and I'd have to hire a real builder to do it. If we lived in town, I could maybe get a regular job and get you a nice house."

"I don't care about a house. I have everything I need to make me happy right here. I have a good roof over my head, plenty to eat, a very, very nice bed to sleep in, and the man I love to sleep next to me. What more could I ask for?"

"I been thinking whilst I watched you with your things. Would it be easier for you if I joined up to the Mormon Church?"

Nancy's mood changed in a flash. She jumped up and stomped her foot, her fists clenched at her side. "No! Don't you ever say that again!"

"I didn't mean to upset you. I thought you might like it."

"I'd hate it! If you were a member, in no time at all, the other men would be badgering you to take another wife."

"I don't want another wife. I got my hands full with the one I already have, and I just got that one last week. I'd just tell 'em no."

"They'd never leave you alone about it. As a member of the church, you'd have to go with their way of living and do what they do, or they'd take it as disapproval from you. Even my father bows down to pressure from the rest of them."

He grinned. "Well, if that's the way it has to be, maybe I'd have to go along with it, for your sake."

She got right next to his face and hissed, "Listen to me. I couldn't stand for you to be with another woman the way you are with me. I won't have it. I'd kill you in your sleep before I let that happen."

He jerked back his head and blinked. "Whoa! I believe you mean that."

Her eyes became slits and she said between clenched teeth, "I do mean it."

"All right, then. I'll have to go on being a backslidden Baptist."

She huffed out a long breath and leaned her head on his shoulder. "A Baptist, backslidden or not, is fine with me."

He kissed her along her neck and she shivered, and then kissed her mouth in earnest. He murmured, "It does me good to see you this happy."

"I am happy, so happy. I never dreamed it could be like this."

With one hand, he undid the buttons on her dress and when he slid his hand inside and caressed her, she forgot all about folding the pieces of fabric and putting them away.

In the morning, when he was ready to leave to cut the trees for their bed, she put on her winter coat. "Where are you going?" he asked.

"I'm going with you. I can help now. There wasn't much I could do in the cold wrapped in a blanket."

She went with him into the woods and watched when he cut the trees and then helped him drag them home. She held the trunks steady while he trimmed them, and looked on in fascination while he bored the holes and made the pegs on the ends to fasten them into one another. She and Jake worked together without him needing to tell her what she should do. She instinctively knew when to hand him the hammer or when to hold tight to the end of the log to steady it.

"I'll tell you what," he said, "you're a right good helper, and a lot better looking than Henry, my Paiute buddy."

115

"I love doing this. It's a lot more interesting than sweeping the floor."

When the headboard and foot board were ready, he cleared a place for the bed to stand to the right of the fireplace and carried in the sections. She helped him fit the side pieces to the ends and then held the rope, unwinding what he needed and keeping it taut while he looped it over the logs and tied it in squares. When he finished, the frame had a checkerboard pattern of interlaced rope that would support the two of them.

"Now what?" she asked.

"Now we take that canvas and sew it into a mattress."

"What?" The mattresses at her home were box-shaped, with a quilted top. They came from her father's store, shipped in from back east. "How on earth do you make a mattress?"

"We make a bag a little bigger than the bed frame and we stuff it with corn shucks and pine needles for the time being. I made the pillows we're using now from flour sacks and chicken feathers. I'm sorry I didn't save more feathers all along. We'll have to start keeping 'em so someday we can have a proper feather bed. This will have to do for now."

Assembling the bed, sewing the canvas in the right shape, and gathering and washing enough pine needles to make the mattress took two days.

When it was finished, and the pillows and blankets were in place, they stood in front of the bed with their arms around one another's waists, pleased with the result of their efforts. He nuzzled her neck. "What say we test it and see how it holds up?"

She hugged his waist so hard he had to catch his breath. He lifted her off her feet and dropped her in the middle of the bed. It made a little creaking sound, but held firm. Grinning at her, he said, "So far, so good--" and he pulled his shirt over his head.

Chapter 12

Over the next few months, their lives settled into a comfortable rhythm. She cleaned the house, sewed, and cooked. Tuesday through Saturday, Jake either tended to his traps and cured the hides, or did repair work around the clearing. On Sundays, they rested. On Mondays, he went into town with his hides and bought what they needed for the cabin. He delivered letters Nancy wrote to her mother and brought back the replies. When it was time for him to leave, he would ask, "Is there anything partic'lar you want me to bring back?"

One time she would say something like, "Needles and thread, one spool of blue and two of white, oh, and a tape measure, the sewing kind." The next time she might ask for a spatula or a paring knife. Her requests were never expensive, and he brought her back whatever she asked for, mostly things to make the cabin homier, or cooking staples.

One time, he brought a small package. When he handed it to her he said, "Your father gave this to me and said, 'Nancy's mother wants to send her this."

She took it and put it in the trunk. He raised an eyebrow. "Aren't you going to open it?"

She pressed her lips together to hide a smile. "Nope, I already know what's in it."

"Keeping it a secret, are you?"

"A girl has to have some mystery about her, doesn't she?"

"It's been my experience that everything 'bout a woman is a mystery."

One day in late December, he asked her, "Don't you want anything for yourself?"

Her eyes lit up. "I have everything I need."

"There isn't anything?"

"Well, I have everything I need--except a chair to sit on when we eat. I'm getting tired of the bucket."

His face turned red. "I was thinking 'bout that. I figured on making one for you for Christmas."

"That's only a week away. You better get busy on it."

A few days before Christmas she said, "I would like to have a little Christmas tree."

He nodded. "I think we can find the right one out there."

Jake brought an ax from the shed, and they went into the woods. After tramping through the snow for a while, she selected a young fir about five feet tall. He chopped it down, and he carried the end while she held the top as they took it home to the cabin. He nailed it to a square of wood and

119

set it inside, where she decorated it with the ribbons her mother sent and ornaments made of fabric scraps from her sewing.

On Christmas morning, when he finished taking care of the horses, he brought in her new chair. Like the other, it was made from pine branches, with a seat of woven ropes, but he had removed the bark and sanded down the wood to make the surfaces smoother. She clapped her hands together. "How wonderful. It's a very nice piece of furniture."

He blushed. "I don't think it's all that fine, but I made it the best I could."

"I love it." She went to the trunk and took out a bundle wrapped in blue cloth and tied with one of the ribbons. "I made these for you."

"What is it?"

"Silly. Open it and find out."

He pulled the bow open and unfolded the fabric, and then another piece of fabric and another, and found a shirt inside. He held it up in front of him. "This is beautiful. How could you make something like this?"

"That package my mother sent had the pattern and the buttons. I used one of the pieces of fabric from before, and I made you three handkerchiefs from the leftovers."

He took her in his arms and kissed her cheeks, forehead, and neck. His voice was hoarse when he whispered in her ear, "Did I ever tell you that you're my dream come true?"

"I believe you did, but it never hurts to hear it again."

"After Lucy died and things with Vanessa went so bad, I didn't have much hope of ever finding this kind of happiness again, but I never quit longin' for it. You brought that back in my life. That's what I mean when I say you're my dream come true."

On one Monday trip into town, he came home carrying a bundle from her parents. It was a half-dozen books and a set of terrycloth towels. When she opened the package, she shrieked, "Something to read!"

"I know you'll like them. You been wearing out that Bible."

"And look at these. Real towels! Now we can save the flour sacks for other things."

Smiling at her happiness, Jake sighed in satisfaction. "I think this may be the best time of my life."

"Really? I'm so glad, because that's exactly how I feel. Up to now, my happiest time would have been—oh—the year I got a room all to myself, when I was sixteen. My sister married Abner on Christmas Day and moved out to live with him. Mama made me a new quilt and curtains for my bed. I felt like a princess. If I had known what Linda would be suffering from living with him, I wouldn't have been happy about it at all. What was your best Christmas before this?"

"I was twelve and Mom gave me a horse to raise and train. I grew up with dozens of horses on the place and helped her with them all along, from the time I was big enough to hold a lead, but this was the first one that belonged to me."

He had never talked much about his parents, and had shied away from her earlier questions about his childhood until she stopped asking. *Maybe he's ready to talk about them now.* Nancy tilted her head. "You and your mom took care of all those horses? What about your dad?"

"He worked in town. Mom and my great-grandparents ran the ranch."

"You knew your great-grandparents?"

"Sure did, leastways, when I was a boy. They both passed when I was in France, first one and a few days later, the other, like they couldn't live without one another."

Nancy grew wistful. "It must have been so wonderful to have great-grandparents. I never knew my own, or even my grandparents. My father being older, they were gone before I was born, and I was still little when my grandparents on my mom's side died."

"That's too bad. I loved mine something awful."

After months of domestic life, the rough cabin that once had only the most necessary furniture and items for survival was more like an ordinary home. They had regular dishes and utensils for both of them, hemmed napkins Nancy made, and real sheets on the bed. She loved it. "This is what I call luxury, cotton sheets instead of sleeping between wool blankets."

"I thought the blankets were all right."

She kissed him quickly. "They're more than all right if you're in there with me, but these will be even better."

"This cabin sure is getting civilized. I reckon that's what happens when you let a woman move in."

"Don't you like it that way?"

"I do. It's like I have a new life now, and it's sure a sight better than the old one."

Before the deep snows and below zero temperatures that would come in January, he brought home enough supplies to see them and the animals through the coming three months when they might be snowed in so deep there would be no way to go into town. Wood for the fire was stacked up all around the shed, the house, and the outbuildings. The smokehouse hung full of muslin-wrapped meat.

The cold settled down on the cabin like a heavy weight. Jake seldom left except to take care of the horses and chickens, and he couldn't go into town for the whole month of February. Bringing in enough water for a real bath became too much of a problem. They resorted to washing out of a bucket of water warmed over the fire.

One day in late March, Nancy was undressing for bed when he looked at her and asked, "Nancy, when was the last time you had your monthly?"

She felt her face redden. In her family, men didn't talk about such things. In fact, they acted as if they didn't even know about them. "I don't know. Uh, I don't think about it much. Why?"

"Unless being cooped up in this cabin and not getting any exercise is making you gain weight, it looks to me as if you're expectin' a baby."

"What?" She pressed both hands over her abdomen and found a distinctive bulge. "A baby?" She threw back her head, closed her eyes, and laughed. "Yes. I may as well confess. I haven't had my monthly since we were married. I think you're right. I think I am going to have a baby!"

When she looked at him, instead of joy, his face was puckered in fear. *He's thinking about Lucy dying.* She ran to him, sat on his lap, and wrapped her arms around his neck. "Don't worry about me. I'll be just fine. When Daddy used to call me chunky, Momma always tried to make me feel better by saying that someday I'd be glad of it, because I was built just right for having babies, and when my time came I'd have it easy. I'll be all right. You'll see."

He shook his head. "Of course, I knew this could happen and part of me is happy, but the other part of me is scared to death. When Lucy and little Timothy died, I thought I would go right ahead and die along with 'em. Now I have you in my life and it's like a miracle. If anything went wrong and I lost you, I don't know as I could go on livin'."

She rubbed her cheek against his. "Nothing will go wrong," she vowed, but deep inside a quaver of doubt ran through her. She'd helped her mother deliver several babies, and no matter how strong a woman was, sometimes things did go wrong. She shoved her fears aside. *It won't do for both of us to feel anxious.*

Jake rested his chin on the top of her head and said, "When it gets close to your time, maybe we should go into town to stay near your mother 'til the baby comes. There's no way I could get someone out here to help you."

She was comforted by the idea that her mother would be with her. "I think that's a good idea. We could stay in my old bedroom."

His expression relaxed and he ran his hand over his face, as if wiping away his fear. He seemed more confident. "Yep, that's what we'll do, but how will we know when it's time?"

"Well, I must have conceived in the middle of November." She held up her hand and counted to nine on her fingers. "That would make him or her due to be born around the middle of August."

"We should go into town a little early, maybe at the start of the month, but I wish we knew exactly."

"Momma always said that you could tell when a baby is coming, because a week or so before it's born, it drops down. So I'll look for that as a sign that it's getting to be time."

He kissed her under her earlobe, something that always sent shivers of pleasure through her. "If it's a boy, I suppose you have to keep your promise to name it for your father."

"I do."

"It's just that every man wants a son named after him. When Lucy died, I wasn't even in my right mind to give the baby a name. Her mother called him Timothy. She said I'd be glad of it later. Now I know what she meant."

"We'll name the next one Jacob, Junior after you."

"The next one?"

She grinned at him. "The lovemaking isn't going to stop because I had a baby, is it?"

126

"No. Long as you still want me, the lovemaking won't stop 'til old age makes it stop."

"There will never come a time when I don't want you." She leaned her head on his shoulder and they sat there silently for a moment. She thought ahead to when she would have a baby to love and hold, and said, "I need some things from the store to make a layette. Don't you say anything to my mom right off. I want to be the one to tell it. I'll write Momma and Daddy a note. Momma wrote me that since I left the house, she spends a lot of time working with Daddy at the store, so she should be there when you go in. You give it to her and let her read it before you say anything."

"All right, I can see how you'd want to be the one to spread the good news. If I didn't need Pete to carry the furs there and the supplies back, I'd take you into town with me."

"Maybe someday we'll have enough money to buy another horse. Then I could make up a papoose sling for the baby and we could go show him off."

"I don't think we'll ever be able to afford that. It isn't only the cost of the animal. Another horse is another mouth to feed."

Her face fell. "Oh."

"I tell you what. After the baby comes and you're all healed and feel up to it, we'll make an extra trip into town once a month or so for you to visit your family. That way your mom and dad will be able to see little Lucas grow up."

She squeezed him. "I would love that so much. I love you more than my own life, but sometimes a woman needs to talk to another woman."

He chuckled. "You mean sometimes a woman just needs to talk. I know I'm not much to carry on a conversation."

"No, not since that time you told me about the war."

"I guess I got out a year's worth of words that day. I'm sorry."

She shrugged. "It's all right."

"Really? You wouldn't just be saying that, would you?"

"Well, I guess I am just saying it. I would like to know everything about you from the day you were born, but when I asked you questions, you always acted like you didn't want to talk about it, so I quit asking."

His face turned red. "I'll try to do better the next time."

"Is there some awful family secret you're keeping hidden?"

"No, no secrets, at least none about anything that happened recently. One of my grandfathers was a hell-raiser. We won't go into it right now, but someday we'll sit and talk, and I'll tell you so much you'll want me to shut up."

"Hah! I'll believe that when it happens."

He crossed his heart with one finger. "I promise."

"I'm going to hold you to that."

"All right."

He kissed her forehead and put his hand over her abdomen. "It's exciting,' isn't it, to know that our little boy is growing in there?"

"Very exciting, but it could be a girl, you know."

"That's all right, too."

Nancy patted her lips with one finger. "Oh, and I need to have you bring me some things from the store. I can make a lot of little clothes out of the scraps of fabric I saved from what Momma gave me when she sent my things here. I want a stack of flour sacks for diapers, and a bolt of flannel for blankets. I can make a list. Oh, do we have enough money for all this?"

He nodded. "I have some set aside for a special occasion, and I do believe a new baby fits the bill. I'll get you everything you want. Maybe your father will even give us a discount. He never offered one before, and I would never ask, but seeing as it's for little Lucas, maybe he'll shake loose a bit."

She threw back her head and laughed. "Ha! I wouldn't count on it. He has the reputation for being the toughest businessman in town. He'd give you something as a gift before he'd give it to you at a discount. I don't mean that he's stingy, but he looks on it as being a good businessman. He always did have a soft heart for me and Momma. Look at all the fabric and things Momma sent. He knew about all of them and if he didn't say it was all right, she couldn't have given them to me. Daddy always said that if you give a discount to one person, even family, then everyone else would expect it. When you live in a place where just about everyone is related, it can drive you right out of business."

She tapped his chest with her finger, "But my Momma might see things differently. She's his youngest wife and she has her way of getting what she wants."

He reached behind her and squeezed her backside. "That must be where you got it from."

She showed her dimples. "I don't know if Daddy was talking about the same thing you are, but that's what Daddy always said. He would tell me I looked like him, but I got my disposition from her."

"How old is your mom?"

"Thirty five. She was only seventeen when I was born."

"How old is your father?"

"Seventy."

Jake let out a low whistle. "I guess it's true."

"You guess what's true?"

"What that philosopher man said, what doesn't kill you makes you stronger."

Chapter 13

The winter seemed to drag on, but when April arrived, spring began teasing them with brief appearances, darting in for an afternoon and skittering away in frosty nights. Wild flowers began popping up from the ground. Nancy was still sleeping when Jake came into the cabin the last Monday morning of the month to say goodbye before he left for town. She hugged him. "The sun's barely up yet. Why are you leaving so early?"

"I never know what I'm going to run into at this time of year, trees down and such."

"You haven't even had your breakfast."

"I ate some cornbread and cheese and put one of the last two apples in my pocket. I'll be fine."

She got up and put on her coat. "I'll come out and see you off."

She walked to the porch with him. Charlie and Pete, shaggy with thick winter coats, waited at the bottom of the steps. An ax and a short-handled shovel were tied to Pete's tack. She hadn't seen him take those with him before. "What's the shovel for?"

"We've been holed up in this cabin for three months. There's not much snow piled up around the clearin' 'cause it gets a lot of sun, but you never know what's out there. That last storm was one of those heavy, wet ones that sometimes get a layer of ice on top when it freezes. I might have to work my way through some drifts."

"Maybe you should wait and go later."

He shook his head and looked up at the sky. "It's pretty clear today, but there's just about always a spring blizzard. I need to get in supplies whilst I have the chance."

"Are you sure it's safe?"

"Sure as I can be."

She frowned and bit her bottom lip. "Well--"

"Don't worry. Charlie always takes good care of me. He brought me home after dark more than once."

She grinned at him. "He does take care of you, doesn't he?" She handed him a list of baby supplies. "These are things I'll need for the baby."

He tucked the paper into the saddlebag. She hugged him again, kept her arms around his waist, and looked up at him. "The ground is starting to thaw. I asked Mama for some cuttings from her rose bushes. I'd like to plant them in front of the cabin, and I wrote down some seeds that I want. I can start them inside and set them out when there's no danger of frost. The ground will be soft enough soon that we can work on the garden. Ask Daddy if we can get some saplings for more fruit trees.

133

This fall, you can get us some Mason jars, and I can do some canning so we can have beans and such through next winter."

"You sure are thinking ahead."

"Yes, I am."

"Don't go lifting anything heavy or doing too much, especially while I'm gone."

"I won't. Remember what I told you? I'm as strong as old Charlie there."

He kissed her quickly. "And a sight better looking, not to mention better smelling. I'll try to get back early."

She tightened her arms around him. "Give me a proper kiss and get going."

"There you go, acting like your momma. You're starting to give the orders around here. Let's hope I like all of them as much as I like that one." He put his hand under her chin, tilted back her head, and kissed her passionately.

When she broke away from him, she fanned herself with her hand. "The temperature out here just went up twenty degrees. You keep doing that, and you'll have to go into town another day. Seeing that you already saddled up, you don't want to disappoint Charlie and Pete. I know they're just as happy that the winter's about over as we are. You hurry home so I don't worry. I wouldn't want anything to happen to the horses."

"The horses? Aren't you going to worry about me?"

"Maybe a little."

He put his foot in the stirrup and swung himself up into the saddle. "I'll get back as soon as I can."

She took a step back. "I'll be looking for you."

With a final smile, he clicked to Charlie, and they set off for the trail into town. As she always did, Nancy watched them until they were out of sight. Instead of going back inside, she walked around the clearing, enjoying the feeling of the spring sunshine on her face and thinking of how she could make more use of the open space.

Along with her mother, Nancy had successfully tended to the garden at home since she was a little girl. *It would be good to make the garden bigger, plant the vegetables that needed more sunlight closer to the inside of the circle, and the ones that liked shade on the outside.* She envisioned the row of roses growing along each side of the footpath that led to the cabin.

A cold wind sprang up just as a cloud passed under the sun and cast a shadow over her. She shivered and hugged herself. *I better get inside. I don't want to take a chill.*

She was up the stairs and on the porch when a strange sensation came over her. There was a fluttering in her abdomen. *What is that?* She stopped still and waited. *There it is again. Oh! It's the baby!* She laughed aloud. "Hello, little Lucas or Linda."

Standing in front of the cabin door, she slid her hands under her coat, pressed her palms flat against her belly, and waited. The fluttering came again, but she couldn't feel anything with her hands. A feeling of joy and fulfillment that she had never imagined came over her. *This is what life should be about, having a man you love, a home of your own, and bringing new life into the world.* She thought about her sister. *I wish Linda could have married someone besides Abner. Her life is so terrible, and there's no way for her to get away from him.*

To pass the time until Jake would be home, she busied herself around the cabin, cleaning, sewing, and reading her books. In the late afternoon, she took a nap. As she dozed off, she thought, *Why am I so sleepy all the time? Is it because of the baby? Maybe I'm only getting fat and lazy. I haven't been sick to my stomach at all, like a lot of women are. Will wanting to sleep a lot be the only thing I'll go through, or am I going to start doing all sort of strange things, maybe eating chalk, the way Marylou Jones did? Silly.*

She drifted off to sleep with a smile on her face. When she awoke, she went out on the porch to see that the sun was fading. She looked in the shed to see if Jake had come home while she slept. It was still empty. There was no sign of him. *He should be home by now. Well, I won't worry about it. He's been later than this a lot of times.* But the worry refused to be held back. Her stomach became queasy. *Is that because of the baby, or am I getting upset because he's not here?*

She started dinner and, for a while, was able to keep her anxiety under control. As she cooked, she strained to hear the sound of the horses coming home, but there was nothing but the trilling of the birds and the rustle of the bare branches in the wind that teased them. Every few minutes, she went out to the porch and peered at the trees where the trail emerged into the clearing.

This is like the time when Daddy and Abner came here thinking they were going to rescue me. Jake got home this late and he was just fine, safe and sound. Don't worry so much. It isn't good for the baby. All kind of things could be keeping him. Maybe Charlie or Pete came up lame again and he had to walk and lead them, or maybe something else is holding him up. She paced the length of the porch several times and stared at the trail.

Dear God, please let him be all right. Please don't let anything bad happen to him.

Soon, the sunlight was almost completely gone, and the shadows took control of the forest, stretching across the ground like tentacles. She lit a lantern, put on her coat, wrapped a scarf around her head, and sat on the top step, hugging herself and slowly rocking back and forth as she stared at the opening in the trees where he would appear. The birds took to their nests for the night, and only an owl and a few bats cut raggedly through the sky. *Thank God for the moonlight. I hope it's bright enough that he'll be able to see his way home, but even if it isn't, Charlie knows how to get here.*

With the sun completely gone, a chill settled on her. It was still only very early spring. She looked up at the moon and stars that sparkled overhead. *The sky is clear, so at least there won't be any snow.* Unable to keep warm, she got the other lantern from the shed, lit it to take inside, and left one sitting on the porch to guide his way. *I don't care how expensive lamp oil is. Maybe it will help him get home safely.*

Since her first day in the cabin, she had never eaten an evening meal without him, but the demands of her encumbered body wouldn't let her miss dinner. She brought in wood to build up the fire for the night, prepared her plate, and sat at the table, where she whispered her blessing. *Dear God, Thank you for this day and for this food. Bless it to the use of our bodies. Please, God, please, please, please, let him be all right. Bring him home to me safe and sound. In Jesus's name, amen.*

She ate mechanically, without tasting, feeding her baby more than herself. Her mind was on Jake, where he might be, what might have happened to him. She was washing her plate when she heard a horse whinny loudly. She ran out onto the porch. Charlie and Pete were standing in front of the steps. Jake was slumped over the saddle, his head resting on Charlie's neck. His face was dirty and bleeding from a cut over one eye, and he had bloody scrapes that disfigured his cheek. She flew down the steps to Charlie's side and grasped the denim of Jake's jeans. "Jake! What's wrong? What happened?"

He didn't move. He had passed out. *I have to get him into the cabin.* The reins were looped loosely over Charlie's neck, and both of Jake's hands were gripping Charlie's mane. It took all her strength to pry his fingers loose, but she finally managed to get them open. She shook his leg. "Jake! Wake up."

He stirred a little, turned to look at her through bleary eyes, and fell sideways out of the saddle, landing face down on the ground with a thud. Charlie whinnied nervously and stepped away to get clear of him. She knelt and wrapped his arm around her neck, keeping it there by holding tightly to his hand, and tried to lift him.

"We have to get you into the cabin. Lean on me." She tugged at him until he was on his knees. He managed to get one foot under himself and with her pulling, got to his feet. He staggered almost out of her grip. She put as much of his weight onto her side as she could, and they struggled up the steps and in the cabin. She dropped him on the bed.

"Horses," he gasped, "take care of--"

"I'll take care of you first," she said.

He pushed her away with his hand. "Horses."

"Oh, all right." She went back to the porch and picked up the lantern. Charlie and Pete followed her to the shed and waited while she opened the door for them. Both horses stopped just inside, making no effort to go in their stalls. She held up the lantern. "I guess I have to take off Charlie's saddle and unload Pete before I put you to bed," she said.

With no former interest in horses, she had only a rough idea of how a saddle stayed on. She picked up the stirrup and leaned over to look at the girth. It seemed simple enough. She'd seen it done many times. Nancy put the lantern on the ground-- close enough to give her some light, far enough away that it wouldn't get knocked over and maybe start a fire. She hooked one stirrup over the saddle horn and unbuckled the girth. Charlie stood completely still, as if he knew she needed all the cooperation he could give her.

When the buckle was open, she grasped the horn and cantle, took a deep breath, and pulled it toward her. The saddle slid off Charlie's back and Nancy jumped back, getting out of the way as it plopped on the ground. Charlie turned to look at her and tossed his head. "What now? Oh." She pulled his bridle down and dropped it on the saddle. He ambled into his stall.

She looked at Pete, who was loaded high with the supplies, which were covered with a canvas and strapped on his back in two places. *Should I try to take things off one at a time, or pull it all off at once? I have to get back to Jake.*

Nancy walked around Pete, examining the load on his back. *Oh, dear. I hope there's nothing in there that will break.* She unfastened the straps, took a deep breath, then pulled at the bulky load until it slid to the ground the way the saddle had. When she took off Pete's bridle, he followed Charlie in the stall.

I have to feed them and get them some water. She gathered armloads of hay and dropped it in front of the horses and went and drew water for them from the well. Those chores accomplished, she picked up the lantern and hurried right past the saddle and supplies. *They can wait to be put away until morning. I have to see to Jake.*

He was lying on the bed with his eyes closed and breathing in puffs, as if he had been climbing a hill. In the light of the lantern, she could see more clearly that his face was bloody and both his eyes were swollen and bruised. "Jake! What happened?"

He managed to open one eye a slit and said, "Abner."

"Abner? What did he do to you?"

"He tried to kill me by beating me to death. Would have done it, too, if your father hadn't stuck a shotgun in his back and told him he'd pull the trigger." Jake smiled weakly and frowned, as if the effort to speak were painful. "I believe he meant it, and so did Abner. He got off me and let me go."

She picked up his hand and started to kiss it but stopped. The skin on his knuckles was scraped, bleeding, and dirty, and she didn't want to cause him more pain. "What can I do for you?"

"Let me sleep. Tell you—'bout it in the morning." He closed his eye and exhaled a long, slow breath. In a moment, he was sleeping.

Nancy put her palm on his forehead. He was warm the way he always was, but didn't seem to have a fever. She took off his shoes and belt and pulled off his jeans before covering him with the blankets. *I'd like to get a cloth and wash his face, but I don't want to wake him. Maybe it's better to let him sleep. Momma always says the body heals while it's sleeping.*

Thinking about his usual bedtime routine, she banked the fire so it would last the night and fastened the bar on the cabin door. Next, she put out the lantern, took off her clothes, and got into bed next to him. She moved over and pressed her body against his.

Nancy awoke as soon as the sun came up. Jake was still sleeping, so she stepped out of bed and dressed as quietly as she could. She built up the fire, brought in two buckets of water, and put one over the flames to heat. She went back outside to see to the horses, and led them out to the clearing so they could graze on the grass buds pushing their way up through the ground. It took all her strength to lift the saddle from where she had let it fall and heft it on the rail where Jake usually left it. Then she got the rest of the tack and hung it on the pegs. She cleaned out the stalls, put down hay for the horses, and drew more water.

When she was finished, she went to the yard and wrapped her arms around Charlie's neck. "Thank you for bringing him home to me." Charlie nickered softly, and she laughed. "Is that your way of saying, 'You're welcome'?"

The pack Pete carried home was still lying on the ground in the shed. She unfastened the straps and un-wrapped the canvas from around the load. The bolt of white cotton flannel she'd asked for to make the baby clothes was on the top of the stack. It was wrapped in a piece of butcher's paper to keep it clean, and Nancy smiled. *That's probably Mama's doing.*

She held it to her cheek to feel the softness of the fabric and imagined how her baby would find comfort in its touch. That, and the other items that would go into the cabin, she stacked on the porch. She dragged the bag of corn for the chickens and one of oats for the horses into the shed. That accomplished, she tried to be as quiet as possible when she went back in the cabin.

Jake slept until well into the morning. When he opened his one good eye, she was sitting in a chair by the bed with the Bible in her lap, watching him. At first, he seemed disoriented. He moved his head and looked around the cabin. "When did I get home?"

"I don't know for sure what time it was, but it was past dark. You couldn't talk much. As soon as I got you near the bed, you passed out, and you've been sleeping ever since. I wanted to clean you up, but I didn't want to wake you. Tell me what happened."

He struggled to a sitting position. "I'll go see to the horses and then I'll tell you 'bout it."

"I already did that."

"You took care of them?"

"I did. I unpacked them and put them away last night. They helped me get it done. Charlie stood real still while I took the saddle and bridle off, and Pete did the same with the supplies. They went right into their stalls all on their own. It was like they knew I needed them to cooperate. I got their hay and water for them, and this morning I fed them again."

"They were prob'ly just as tired as I was. What 'bout Pete's load? There's no way you could carry that."

"I just unstrapped it and let it fall. This morning, I unpacked it and put it away one thing at a time. Getting the saddle up off the ground took some doing, but I finally got it hung up where you always put it, on the rail in the shed."

"You shouldn't be lifting heavy things like that."

"I took care of the chickens and cows at home. I'm used to it."

He turned his head to look at the fire. "I see you already got the fire going, and I smell coffee."

"I'll start breakfast if you're ready. I thought you should have meat and eggs instead of only oatmeal. It will help you heal."

"First things first. Let me see if I can get to the outhouse." He swung one leg over the side of the bed and groaned loudly as he tried to sit up. He made it only half-way before falling back down. "Lord Almighty, I feel like I been run over by a train."

"Abner's as big as a train. Let me help." Nancy put her arms under his and he wrapped one of his around her. She pulled him upright, and he groaned again, but was sitting up. He swung his other leg around and managed to get both feet on the floor. "Let's see if I can stand up."

She hugged him to his feet and he leaned against her, his cheek on her head. "As bad as I'm hurting, it's sure good to be home. I was afraid I'd never see you again."

"Do you think you can walk all the way to the outhouse? I can get you a pot to use."

The parts of his face that weren't black and blue turned red. "Not if I can help it. I got 'bout all the vinegar I had stomped out of me yesterday, but I still got a little. I'm tryin' to hang onto what dignity is left."

"I'll help you. We better get our coats. It's still cold in the mornings." She helped him into his jacket and then put on her own coat. With her arm around his waist and his around her shoulders, he limped to the door.

She waited while he took care of his needs and then helped him back to the cabin. She said, "You lie down while I get something to clean those cuts and scrapes on your face before they get infected. Do we have any iodine or anything with alcohol in it?"

"There's a bottle in the shed. Look in the wooden box under where the tools are hanging."

In the shed, she opened the box and dug around until she found the iodine. She was about to close the lid when she noticed a scrapbook. The edges of the paper were dotted with mildew, but the bulk of them were still in fairly good condition. She leafed through a few pages. There were pictures, newspaper clippings, ribbons that looked like awards from a county fair, and other things whose presence surprised her.

Her thorough investigation of the cabin when she first arrived hadn't included the shed. She'd glanced around inside that first day and assumed it held only work supplies, which didn't interest her at the time. She put the book back in the box. *I wonder why he keeps it out here instead of in the cabin where it would be out of the damp. I'll look at this later.* Nancy stood looking down at the book. *Maybe I should ask him permission first. He must have some reason for keeping it here instead of inside.*

Back in the cabin, she asked him again, "Are you sure you don't want to lie down for a while?"

He shook his head slowly, as if moving it faster would be painful. "If I lay down, I don't know if I could get back up. I'll sit here in the chair and watch you cook."

"All right. First let me take care of that cut on your face." She wet a cloth in the bucket of cold water and wrung it out, placing it over the cut on his swollen eye. "Hold this one here while I get another one." She wet another cloth and pressed it against the scrape in his cheek. "Hold that one there. The cold ought to bring down the swelling so we can see how bad it is. Now, tell me everything that happened."

He held the compress to his eye with one hand and the cloth on his cheek with the other. Looking at her through the one eye he could open, he made a twisted smile. "It's a good thing I'm not one of those fellas that talks with his hands. I wouldn't be able to say a word."

"Never mind that. How did you run into Abner?"

"I thought I had plenty of time to make it home 'fore dark. Your father wasn't all that busy, so I spent some time talkin' to him and your mom 'bout the baby and what not. He came out of the store to give me a hand wrappin' the things I bought in the canvas and tyin' it to Pete's back. I'd

148

said goodbye and had my foot in the stirrup to get up on Charlie when Abner grabbed me from behind and lifted me right up in the air. I never even heard him comin'."

Nancy snarled. "He always was sneaky. More than once, I saw him standing outside our house in a place where he could look in. It made the hair on the back of my neck stand up. I always made sure that my curtains covered every inch of the windows when I went to bed at night."

"Well, he threw me halfway across the road, and I landed on my back. It knocked the wind right out of me. Before I could catch my breath, he sat plop down across my stomach and started punching me in the face, growlin' like a grizzly bear, and sayin' how he would kill me. I reckon he would have, too, if it hadn't been for your daddy."

"What did he do?"

"He musta run back in the store and got his shotgun. You know, the one he keeps under the counter in case someone passing through town takes a notion to rob him. Well, he run up behind us and pushed the barrels of that gun right into Abner's neck, and I heard the hammers click when he cocked 'em, and Abner prob'ly did, too. Your daddy said, 'Stop it right now, Abner, or so help me God, I'll blow your head off.' Anyone could tell he meant to do it if he had to, so Abner stopped hittin' me. He bounced his knee on my chest 'fore he finally got up. I heard a cracking sound. He must weigh as much as a plow horse. I think he broke some ribs."

Nancy clapped her hand over her mouth. "Oh, Jake! It must have hurt something awful when I hugged you."

"I hurt so much all over I didn't much notice it."

"What happened then?"

"Your father kept a bead on him and told him to get on outta there. By then, a crowd had gathered and some of them were startin' to yell at Abner to leave me alone. He looked around at them real slow, like he was trying to memorize their faces, and then he stepped back. 'Fore he left, he pointed his finger at me and said, 'Sooner or later, I'm going to kill you,' and then he strolled off like he was going to a picnic."

"I'm not surprised people took your side. He's been bullying everyone in town for years. There's not a man in Smithville that hasn't had a run-in with him. They're all afraid. What surprises me, is that they let it show that they were backing you up."

Jake held the cold cloth against the gash in his head. "I'm grateful they did. If people stand together they can put a stop to the likes of him. I've faced down enemy soldiers and Grizzly bears, but I don't believe either one of 'em wanted me dead as much as that cousin of yours does. He meant what he said."

His eyes were full of sorrow, and he heaved a sigh and winced from pain as he exhaled. "I thought when I left France that the ship was taking me away from killin', but now I know sooner or later, I'll have to kill him or he'll kill me."

Nancy shuddered. "You're right. I've never seen Abner back down from getting what he wanted. The sheriff is the only man in town that Abner shows any respect. Did he see any of it happen?"

"Not that I know of. After Abner left, your father got me to my feet. He could see I was hurt pretty bad and offered to let me stay in town with them for the night. I told him I'd be all right, that I didn't want to leave you home wondering what had become of me."

She kissed his cheek. "In the morning, I would have had to set out walking to find you."

"I had to lead Charlie to the mountin' block to get on him. I knew he would get me home if I was able to stay in the saddle, even if I passed out, and I knew Pete would follow Charlie wherever he went, so I left the reins over their necks. I told Charlie it was time to go and he set out walkin' slow, like he understood that every step he took was a pain to me. Pete came right behind him."

He smiled and shook his head. "They were knickerin' back and forth like they were talkin' to one another the whole way. After a while my head started spinnin' and I knew I was going under, so I wrapped both hands in Charlie's mane and told myself that no matter what happened, I had to stay on his back."

"You were still hanging onto his mane when you got home. I had a hard time getting you to let go. I was beginning to think I'd have to give Charlie a haircut to get you off him."

That brought a chuckle from Jake. "I don't know how he'd feel about that, it not being all that warm yet."

"Well, you're home now, and you're safe. You rest up for a while. I'll take care of you."

He smiled weakly. "Darlin' girl. As long as Abner's alive, I'm not safe anywhere."

Nancy wanted to hug him to her but was afraid of hurting his broken ribs. She put her arm lightly around his shoulders and put her cheek on his undamaged one. "I want you to show me how to shoot a gun. I'll kill him myself if he shows his ugly face around here."

"Ammunition's too expensive to use it up practicin' shooting at trees." He hesitated, pursed his lips, and nodded. "It wouldn't hurt, though, for you to know how to fire a gun if you had to."

I'll fire it all right. There's enough of my daddy in me that, if I get the chance, I'll blow Abner's head off, just like he said he would do.

As gently as she could, she washed the dirt off his face and used the glass rod in the iodine bottle to dab the brown liquid into the scrapes on his cheek. She peered at the cut over his brow. "I should sew that up or it'll leave a scar."

"If it's all the same to you, I'd just as soon leave it be. What would one more scar mean to someone as cut up as I am?"

When she dabbed the iodine into the cut, Jake winced and shifted his weight in the chair. He moaned loudly. It hurt Nancy to hear his pain. She asked him, "Is there anything we can do to help with a broken rib?"

"It should be wrapped up tight, to make a kind of support. Take one of those pieces of cloth and tear it into strips about six inches wide. If you wrap it around me like a mummy in a museum, it should help."

Fabric was dear to Nancy, but she took a long piece and tore a strip off one side of the length. Jake raised his arms and she wrapped it around him and fastened it with several safety pins. "Will that do?" she asked.

He nodded. "It feels fine. The only thing that could make it better is if it was wrapped around a big breakfast. I'm so hungry I'm seeing light bread floating in the air."

"What? What does that mean?"

He chuckled and winced again. "I'm not sure. It's something my great-grandpa used to say when he came in for dinner."

She kissed his good cheek. "It's a good sign that you're hungry. I'll make you two breakfasts."

It was three days before Jake could walk without holding onto Nancy, and two weeks before he could take care of his traps. He still winced every time he stood up. It was another two weeks before he had enough pelts to make the trip into town. She knew he had to go, but when he brought the horses out of the shed wearing their tack, Nancy's stomach churned and turned sour. She ran to Jake and grabbed his arm. "Do you have to go into town?"

He shrugged. "Got to earn a living. Out here, trading pelts is the only way for me to do that. Got to get supplies. We need salt and flour. Sooner or later, there's other things we couldn't get by without. Got to live my life, same as always, and I can't do that without going into town."

She sobbed, "Maybe we could go live somewhere else."

"I thought you loved this cabin."

"I do. I've been so happy here. I love it more than I can tell, but what good is it if you're not here with me?"

His face was set when he looked at her. "I take a lot of pride in this place. I built all of it, the cabin, the shed, and the rest, with my own two hands, and I did a good job of it, too. Except for you and our baby, this is all I have in the world. What kind of man would I be if I let Abner run me off from my own home?"

Nancy felt the strength drain out of her. "I guess it's no use arguing with you?"

"None a'tall. What else can I do but stand my ground?"

She blinked back tears, pressed her lips together hard, and nodded. "I don't know. It's only that I'm so afraid."

He patted the Colt in its holster. "I got this, the little Smith and Wesson on the other side, and the rifle. I'll be all right. Don't worry."

"I can't help it. I wish I could do something to help."

He wrapped his arms around her and kissed her softly, a kiss that she found comforting. He tilted up her chin with his hand. "My momma always said that the best cure for worry was to talk it out with God. I reckon that's the best way for you to help me, pray that I make it home without runnin' into him."

"I will! I'll pray every minute you're gone until you come home."

She sat on the porch step and watched almost without blinking as he went through his usual routine of loading the furs onto Pete's back and tying them into place. The last thing he did was check his rifle and handguns and slide them back into their holsters. Nancy went to him and asked, "In the army, were you a good shot with that rifle?"

"I was pretty good in basic training. I don't know how well I did in those battles. I hope I missed everyone I aimed at. I'll be all right. I learned how to handle a rifle from my daddy. He sat behind a desk all week and on the weekends he liked to get out in the woods and stomp around. We went huntin' all year and I learned how to use it, not as good as he did, but all right for a boy."

"What about the pistols?"

"Haven't had much practice with the side arms. I carry those more for snakes, but I think I could hit a tree trunk if I set my mind to it, and that's about Abner's size."

She wasn't much comforted. "Take extra bullets with you."

"I already thought 'bout that. If it comes to a shootout, it'd be a good thing to have extra ammunition. Do you know anything about how well Abner might handle a gun?"

She thought about his question. "I never heard of him hunting, or even firing a gun, and I never saw him carry one. He always depended on his size to get what he wanted."

He patted his holster. "That's comfortin' to know. I'm not a small man, but I could never beat a mountain like him in a fistfight. There's a good reason a Colt .45 is known as the Great Equalizer."

He took Charlie's rein and led him to the porch. "I'm still a little sore." He used the end of the porch as a mounting block to get onto Charlie's back.

Hating to see him leave, Nancy clung to his pant cuff and walked alongside Charlie to the edge of the clearing. "You've already seen that Abner is the type to sneak up on you if he can. He probably knows you come into town on Mondays and may be watching for you. It will be the most dangerous when you leave. He could follow you and try to get at you outside of town."

He nodded. "I'll be lookin' out and listenin' for him, and Charlie will let me know if he hears anything unusual. It's times like these when I wish I had found myself another dog after old Dutch died." He smiled down at her. "You didn't ask me for anything from town. Can I bring somethin' back for you?"

"Just yourself."

He gave her a brief salute and headed down the trail. She stood looking after him, and as he disappeared into the forest, she sank to her knees. She bent over and sobbed a prayer. "Dear God, please don't let anything bad happen to him. Please bring him back to me."

Chapter 14

As soon as Jake left, Nancy went to the shed and brought the scrapbook into the cabin. She studied everything in it, only turning the pages after she absorbed every bit of information from whatever was pasted on each one. There were photos of what she assumed was Jake's family, an older couple that must be the great-grandparents he talked about a few times, and a middle aged man and woman. Jake was a younger copy of the man, tall and sharp faced. The woman was petite and slender, and her hair framed her face with tight, dark curls.

There were pictures of a boy and girl, she a few years older than he, that Nancy was sure was Jake and probably a sister. There were several pictures of the mother and children at various ages, sitting on horses and holding ribbons that looked as if they had won some sort of competition. On some pages, she read newspaper articles about prizes won at county fairs and news of high school graduations.

When she finished reading the last item, she closed the book, but didn't take it back to the shed. She laid it on the bed. *I'm tired of waiting for answers about his life. Tonight he'll just have to tell me about all of this and who these people are.*

The day dragged slowly by. As much as she could, Nancy kept busy, cleaning things that didn't need cleaning, sewing baby clothes from the scraps of fabric she had saved, and cooking.

It was thrilling, each time the baby moved inside her. *My little butterfly.* Throughout the day, she prayed hundreds of times, sometimes just murmuring her prayer as she worked, and sometimes kneeling at the side of the bed. It wasn't a lengthy or complicated prayer. "Dear Lord, Please watch over Jake. Please bring him home safely. In Jesus's name, amen."

Nancy was setting the table when she heard the horses coming and hurried out to the porch to meet Jake. He was a little early. *God answers prayer. Yes, He does.* Jake was still in one piece and didn't look as if he'd had any trouble along the way.

She held Charlie's reins while he put his right leg over the back of the saddle and slid carefully off the horse, grunting when his feet hit the ground. He winced. "That first step's a tough one."

"Are you all right?" Nancy asked.

"I'm good, better than I was a few days ago--just wore out, I think."

He pointed at her stomach. "You shouldn't be rushing around like that. You're liable to scramble that baby's brains."

She laughed. "I'm only about four or five months along. I'm all right, and so is he."

"I hope so, but just in case, don't be runnin' like that anymore. I want him to be smarter than his old man."

"I'll help you unload Pete."

"You'll do no such thing."

"I can take the small things and carry them inside."

He nodded. "All right, but don't you go straining yourself."

Jake took Pete's reins and they led the horses into the shed. While he stowed away the salt, lime, and heavier things, she carried the kitchen supplies in the cabin. By the time they were finished, he was breathing heavily, and even in the chill air, his head was covered in sweat.

When he came in the cabin to put away one of the heavy bags meant for the kitchen, she carefully wrapped her arms around him and laid her face on his chest. "Did you see Abner?"

"Not hide nor hair'a him, thank God. I took care of my business and got out of town as soon as I could. I kept an eye out for him the whole time. When I looked back to the store whilst I was riding away, your daddy was standin' out front with his shotgun in his hands. He was looking out for me, just in case Abner did show up."

He took a slow, deep breath and puffed it out. "I kept one hand on my pistol until I was half-way home. I have to admit, I was so jumpy, every twig that broke made me flinch and squeeze my gun. I must 'a held my breath the whole way here."

She clung to him. "I was so worried. I prayed every minute you were gone that God would bring you back to me."

He kissed her forehead. "Looks like He was listening. Here I am, safe and sound--well, more or less sound."

"I'm glad you're home early so I can stop worrying. Dinner's cooking, but it isn't ready yet."

"You go ahead and get it on the table whilst I take care of the boys."

She kissed him quickly. "It'll be ready by the time you're done."

When he came back into the cabin for the last time, he was carrying a sack of flour and the bag of table salt. A bundle wrapped in white cloth and tied with a ribbon sat on top. "Your momma sent you a present."

"Momma?" She took the package and hugged it against her breast.

"Yep, we were packing up when she brought it outta the back room. Said she'd been working on that ever since she heard 'bout the baby. Didn't say what was in it."

"I think I know." Nancy untied the ribbon and unfolded the fabric wrapper. Inside was a stack of baby clothes, little gowns in white, blue, and yellow flannel. She held one up and admired it. "Oh, look. Momma put lace around the hems and even embroidered little flowers on the sleeves and neck."

Jake crinkled up his face and scratched his jawline under one ear. "I don't know how little Luke will take to flowers and lace."

"He won't know the difference, and for all your talk of a boy, it could still be a girl."

"Well, whatever we get, it'll be the best dressed baby in the country."

Nancy frowned and asked, "Would you be disappointed if it turns out to be a girl?"

"Every man wants a son, but a girl will be fine with me. My mom always said that it's a good thing she had a girl first, so she could help take care of me, 'cause couldn't no one person keep me in line."

"You never told me you had a sister."

"I do. Her name is Shelby, and I thank God for her." He glanced at the scrapbook on the bed. "I see that you've been out in the shed."

"Jake, why can't I get you to talk about your life? Whenever I ask, you act as if it upsets you."

"Back when you first came, I didn't expect you to be here very long, and it was private. After a while, you stopped asking and I let it go. I suppose I didn't want to talk about it 'cause I did things when I was a boy I'm not proud of--acted out a lot, brought shame to my parents."

"Why would you misbehave? From what I saw in that book, you had a nice, happy family."

"I can't explain it. My mom said I was born screaming and didn't settle down until high school when I fell in love with Lucy, not puppy love, but grown-up kind of love, and she got me under control." His stomach growled loudly. "Let's sit and eat. I'll try to answer all your questions."

Nancy's mother had once told her that a man with an empty stomach couldn't think about anything else, so she waited until Jake had a few bites of the stew before she started. "You said you were from some place named Manhattan, Kansas. Tell me about that."

He grew misty eyed, and shook his head. "Manhattan. It's 'bout the prettiest place there is. Lots of trees, not like the rest of the state. The rivers come together there and we have hills and all sorts of things that flower. In the spring, when the fruit trees and the redbuds break out, the color is everywhere. The prairie gets a little brown in the summer heat, but the sunflowers don't mind. They bloom all through 'til fall. Then the trees turn and there's color in the leaves. My family owns about two hundred acres outside of town, not far from Pillsbury Crossing."

"What's Pillsbury Crossing?"

"It's a spot in Deep Creek a little ways down from the waterfall where the creek bed is flat rock and mostly shallow, unless there's been a lot of rain. The pioneers moving west in their wagons crossed there. It's part of the Oregon Trail."

"That's in American history books."

"It is."

He took another forkful of meat and she let him chew before she asked, "Tell me about the people that live there."

That brought out a smile. "They're Westerners, not like folks in the east. If you go to their home, they make you feel welcome, and feed you even if you aren't hungry. Manhattan was settled mostly by abolitionists, educated folk. They built the state university there. It was way ahead of its time. My mom graduated with a degree in animal husbandry, something that wasn't thought proper for a woman back then, but she did it." He chuckled. "You don't want to tell my mom she can't do something once she sets her mind to it."

"Your mother went to college? I used to dream of going to school. I was always the smartest in my classes here, but of course, none of the girls in Smithville ever went. Daddy said it was a waste of time and money to send a girl to school since all she was going to do was raise a family."

Jake made a low whistle. "If he ever said that in front of my mom, or just 'bout anyone else in Manhattan, he'd get a right loud argument started. They're all big on education, and that includes girls. Kansas State's first graduating class was half women, way back in 1863. Even the big schools back east couldn't say that."

Nancy grew wistful. "That makes me wish I had been born there, too."

"I'll take you there someday."

"Promise?"

"I promise."

She cocked an eyebrow. "Tell me about the trouble you got into."

His face reddened. "Well, it wasn't anything big. I never went to jail for more than one night. I 'spect I got off real punishment sometimes 'cause my dad was a lawyer and worked with all the judges. They all grew up together."

"What did you do?"

"This and that, mostly just mischief. One time, when I was 'bout nine or ten, I snuck out of the house and took a half-dozen horses from different neighbors then switched them around and left them in someone else's barn."

"How did you keep them quiet so they wouldn't wake the owners?"

166

"Held my hand over their nose 'til I got them settled."

"I'm surprised the horses didn't raise a fuss."

"I picked horses that were raised right on my place over the years. They knew me since the day they were born, so me coming into their stall or paddock wasn't anything new to them. All the noise they made was just like a nicker, saying hello to me."

"Is that what got you in jail?"

"No. I didn't get caught doing that, but my mom figured out it that I was the one who did it. She had me saddle up two horses and went with me to go 'pologize to the owners for the confusion."

Nancy moved her hand in a winding motion. "Tell me more."

He grinned at her. "My friends and I would sneak around at night and tip over the outhouses. We did that off and on, 'til the time Joey Heatwohl got to laughin' so hard he backed up and fell right into the hole. Wouldn't none of us pull him out. I got a rope and tied it to a tree and threw him the end so he could pull himself up. When he finally did get out, he was covered in—you know. That was the end of movin' outhouses for all of us. Try coming home in that condition and 'splainin' it to your folks."

"He had to go home like that?"

"Nah. He went down to Deep Creek and dunked himself 'til he was clean, but he did almost freeze to death. It was a Halloween stunt and that water can be awful cold come October. It was a wonder he didn't catch his death of cold, but he came out of it all right--if you don't count the whippin' he got for it."

"He got caught?"

"His daddy heard him sneakin' back into the house soakin' wet and gave him a shellackin' for it."

Nancy giggled. "Poor Joey, he had quite a night, falling into the outhouse hole, getting all wet in cold water, and then getting a spanking on top of it."

"We did a lot of stuff like that, harmless, mostly only things to aggravate people. Three of us spent one night in jail for paintin' dirty words on the schoolhouse fence."

"I wouldn't think they would put you in jail for that."

"Normally they wouldn't, but when the sheriff showed up, we all ran, and when he came out after us, he tripped on the paint can and fell, and the paint got all over him. It ruined his clothes, so he rounded us up and tossed us in a cell."

"He kept you for one night?"

"Yeah. The two other boys got sent home and got off with a whippin', but my dad made me paint the whole fence by myself, two coats, and he made me do extra chores for a month to pay for the paint and to buy a new outfit for the sheriff. That was the last time I did anything that involved paint."

"What was the worst thing you did?"

Jake looked as if a cloud had fallen over his face and he dropped his head. She could barely hear him when he said, "When I was fourteen, I got into a fight and nearly beat a boy to death."

"Lord have mercy! Why on earth would you do that?"

He looked up at her and nodded. "See, that was the question what should'a been asked right off."

"What happened?"

"My mom raisin' and trainin' horses put me around them all my life. I admit I love 'em almost as much as she does. Back then, it wasn't unusual for boys to ride their horses to school and leave 'em tied outside while they had their lessons. Some still do today. I owned my own horse since I was a kid. He was a gelding named Mashcinge."

"That's a funny name. Say it again."

"Mosh-cheen-gah. It's Kansa language for rabbit. Most of the time, I just called him Mosh. My grandma Mimi named him that 'cause as soon as he was born, he got to his feet and 'stead of walkin', he started hoppin' around. Anyway, he was always a little skittish."

"Like his name."

"This one day, he was tied next to Junior Wilkins's horse. Junior was out of the door a few hundred feet in front of me when school was over, and when he went between the horses to get to his, Mosh kicked him. He didn't get him hard enough to hurt him bad. Any fool knows you don't walk up on a horse from behind, but that's what Junior did. When Mosh kicked him, Junior ran 'round in front of him, doubled up his fist and hit him right between the eyes. He could have killed him. Horses are funny that way. They look so big and strong that you would think nothin' could hurt 'em, but hit one in the right place, and you can take him right down."

"So that's why you were fighting?"

"I saw red for sure. I wanted to kill him. I took out after him on a run. He didn't see me comin' and I took him down with my first punch. I jumped on top a' him and kept sockin' him 'til one of the teachers pulled me off. I don't know how many times I hit him, but even in the war, when I was in France, I was never in such a state. His nose was gushin' like a fountain. I remember the sight and smell of blood, and that egged me on. They

170

told me later, ever' time I hit him, I kept yellin', 'How does it feel?'"

"But he didn't die?"

"No, but he might have if that teacher didn't come along. No telling what would have happened to me if he died. I could'a gone to prison for sure. They had to haul him off to the hospital. He was unconscious. The doctor said he had a concussion. The principal got hold of my arm and dragged me all the way to the sheriff's office. I had to stay there overnight 'fore I could even see the judge."

"What did your parents say?"

"I got a big lecture from my mother 'bout fightin', and my dad told me I ought to be glad I was too big for a whippin' or he'd take my britches down just like he used to. Both of them went on and on and never even asked me why I did it."

"When did the sheriff decide to let you go?"

He chuckled and rested his chin on his hand. "We all went to court the next mornin' and my dad was going to act as my lawyer, but that's not how it turned out."

"What happened?"

"Well, Junior and his parents showed up. His mother was yellin' and goin' on, sayin' how I was dangerous and they ought to send me to the reform school in Kansas City. They didn't even get the hearin' started when Junior jumped up and shouted, 'You can't kill a person just 'cause they

171

hit your horse.' When he said that, everything in the courtroom got real quiet. Kansas is still western enough that a man's, or even a boy's, horse is still his most valuable thing."

Nancy put in, "That's still the way it is here, too."

"The judge asked Junior, 'Did you hit this boy's horse?' and Junior stood up and said, 'Yes, sir, but I was only acting in self-defense. He kicked me.' Then the judge looked at me and asked, 'What happened?' so I told him 'bout Junior walkin' up from the back on Mosh with no warnin' and how Mosh kicked at him, then Junior went 'round in front of him and hit him as hard as he could right between the eyes. My mother jumped up and said to the judge, 'It doesn't sound to me like there was any self-defense involved. If he walked around in front of the horse to hit him, his life wasn't in any danger.'"

Jake chuckled. "Then Mom looked at the judge and said, 'Matt, I mean, your Honor, you think right highly of that Quarterhorse mare, Alberta, that I sold you. I've seen you cutting up apples and feeding her out of your hand before you come in to court. What would you do to Junior if he hit Alberta in the face like that?' The judge looked at Junior for a long time, a stare that could cut through sheet metal, and then he banged his gavel on his desk and shouted, 'Case dismissed.'"

"So that was the end of it?"

"It was for me. Junior's mother didn't like it much. She started yellin' again and the judge had to threaten to throw her in jail for contempt of court if she didn't be quiet. She snapped her mouth shut like a river turtle. She got Junior by the hair of the head and dragged him out of there. You could hear her yellin' all the way down the street."

"Did you do anything else that put you in jail?"

"No. I was still up to boy-type pranks for a while after that, but we didn't do anything to land us in trouble with the law."

"So, you were growing up and getting some sense."

"Not really, but that was 'round the time I started lookin' at Lucy different. I saw the woman she was growing into. It 'bout struck me dumb. We'd been sweethearts from the time we were toddlers, but she told me she didn't fancy my playin' the fool and that was the end of it. I took some ribbin' from the guys 'cause I didn't want to go out with them and act up anymore, but I cared a whole lot more 'bout what Lucy thought of me than I did 'bout what they had to say."

Nancy put her hand over his. "I suppose I owe her a debt of gratitude."

He smiled and nodded. "She straightened me out when my parents and my sister Shelby

173

couldn't make any headway at all. I behaved myself pretty well after that, at least 'til Lucy died, and I started drinkin' and actin' out again. Goin' to war stopped that."

Chapter 15

Allowing his body time to heal from Abner's beating, Jake didn't set his traps for several weeks. With the worst of winter over and the cabin still stocked with supplies, he didn't need to make many trips to town. Those he did make passed with no sight of Abner. One mid-morning in May, Jake was in the shed brushing down the remnants of Charlie's winter coat when Nancy came in eating a cheese sandwich. He grinned at her. "You're a might early to be having lunch, aren't you?"

Without swallowing, she said through a mouthful of bread, "I'm so hungry I can't wait for noon. I can't seem to get enough to eat."

"I s'pose that's cause you're eating for two."

She rubbed her free hand across her stomach. "This baby will probably weigh twenty pounds. I don't ever remember any of the women in town being this big when they still had four months to go."

"You go ahead and eat as much as you need. Who knows? I heard of a woman once who had three babies at one time."

"Three? Heaven help me! One will be a handful."

By the first of July, Nancy's stomach was so big she couldn't see her feet. Jake cut some sections of deerskin into the right shapes, and she made herself slippers she could get into without having to bend over to tie laces.

At the dinner table one night, she was nodding her head and having trouble keeping her eyes open. He kissed her cheek. "Why don't you go ahead and get to bed? I'll clean up."

"I don't know what's wrong with me. All I want to do is sleep and eat."

On a late July visit to town, Jake came home all excited. "Your daddy told me that my Paiute friend, Henry, and his wife were in the store buying supplies. They told him they spent the last year tending to her sick mother down by Paradise, and once she died, they decided to come home. They had a baby with them. Your daddy said it must be three, four months old."

"Henry?"

"The Paiute friend I told you about, the one who helped me build the cabin. They only live 'bout a mile from here."

"Oh, yes. I remember. Maybe once I'm delivered and back on my feet, we can go visit. It would be nice to have another woman to talk with."

He took her hand, turned it palm up, and kissed it. "I'm sorry. I know I'm not the most talkative man on earth."

"You have your moments, like when you told me about your wicked childhood, or when you talked about the war, but that's not what I mean."

"What, then?"

"Oh, it's hard to explain. A woman gets hungry to talk with another woman. There are things you can't talk about with a man."

"Like female plumbing and stuff."

She blushed. "Yes, and cooking and sewing and babies. Since Henry's wife already has a baby, like I will in another month or so, I imagine she can help me with knowing what to do."

"I thought you had lots of experience with your family's babies."

"I did, but--never mind. Maybe it's only a female thing. Don't you ever get to wanting to talk to another man?"

"I talk to them every time I go into town."

"That's not the kind of conversation I need."

"I guess I know what you mean. Tell you what, if you're feeling all right in the morning and think it'll be all right for me to leave you alone for a few hours, maybe I'll ride over to Henry's place and see if they can come for a visit."

"That would be so wonderful."

The next morning, Jake saddled up Charlie and rode off into the woods. He arrived home around dinner time. Expecting that he would only be gone a few hours, Nancy had been growing more anxious as the day went on. She didn't greet him with a smile. "I thought you'd only be gone a few hours. I've been worried sick. I was afraid Abner got hold of you."

"No, no, I'm all right. I was helping Henry fix up his cabin. I don't know why it is, but a place will get messed up more when you're gone than it does when you're living in it."

"What did they say about the visit?"

"Henry and his wife will be coming by in a few days."

"That's wonderful. What day?"

"I don't know, two or three, he said, whenever he gets the work done on the cabin."

"I need to know what day so I can make a nice meal for them. Now, let's see, I imagine they'd start out early and have to be home before dark, so it would be the noon meal."

"Well, I know it won't be tomorrow, he has to get up on the roof and patch that. Plan on the day after, or the day after that. The garden is full of things ready for harvest. You won't be caught without enough to make a meal."

Nancy bit a lip. *Men don't understand anything.* "All right."

It was two days later when Henry and his wife arrived. Nancy heard their horses and called Jake from the shed. They went to meet their guests.

Henry slid off his horse and helped his wife down from her's. He was short and stocky-built, with straight black hair tied back with a rawhide string. He was dressed in white man's clothing of jeans and a plaid shirt. His wife was slim, and wore her long, black hair loose, kept in place by a headband across her forehead. The baby in the sling across her chest was plump and had thick, black hair that stuck out in spikes. Jake grasped Henry's hand and shook it. "I'm right glad you could make it. Did you get that roof done?"

"It's good as new."

"If there's anything you need some help with, just let me know."

Henry tied the horses in front of the water trough and nodded. "I will."

"Let me make the introductions." Jake wrapped his arm around Nancy's waist. "This here's my wife, Nancy. Nancy, this is my friend Henry that I told you about, and this is his wife, Taima."

Nancy's smile stretched all the way across her face. "I'm so happy to meet you. Your baby is so beautiful. What's his name?"

179

Taima smiled. "I named him William, after my grandfather, but his daddy calls him Big Willy because he was so fat when he was born."

"Let's go inside so we can sit and talk."

Henry said, "Jake, how 'bout I get a look at the smokehouse you built since I was here?"

Jake nodded. "Sure thing, it'll give these women time to complain 'bout how useless we men are."

Nancy laughed. "If we talk about all of that, lunch is going to be late."

"My stomach's growling already. Talk while you put it on the table."

"I will."

The men went off toward the outbuildings, and Nancy and Taima went in the cabin. When Taima laid the baby on the bed, Nancy stood next to her and they gazed down at him. Nancy said, "He hasn't made a peep, even when you got off your horse. Is he always a good sleeper like this?"

"He'll sleep like an angel until his stomach gets empty and then he'll make a terrible racket. That ought to be any minute now."

Nancy nodded. "My sister used to have an awful time of it. When her baby cried to be fed, her body would get all excited and half the milk would run down her dress before she could get him latched on. She was always afraid she wouldn't have enough."

"At least that's one thing I don't have to worry about. I could feed a whole village of babies with how much milk I've been making."

Since they only had two chairs, Jake pulled the table over next to the bed so two people could sit on it to eat. The women set up a summer mid-day meal and when it was ready, called the men inside. After they ate, Jake stood and stretched. "That was really a fine lunch, ladies. You outdid yourselves. Now, us men will go out on the porch and sit for a spell, and you women can talk about your secret things in here."

Nancy tsk'd and waved a hand in the air to shoo them out. "Fine, get on out of here."

She and Taima cleared the table, and as they were washing the dishes, the baby woke and let out an ear-splitting scream. Taima looked at Nancy and laughed. "What did I tell you?"

She sat on the bed, picked up the baby, untied a flap on her dress to expose a breast, and held the baby against it. He shook his head back and forth a few times, making little grunting noises, slapped at her with his little hands, and started nursing.

Nancy sighed. "I'll be so glad when my baby finally comes. This summer heat is getting to me."

"How much longer do you have?"

"I think I have more than a month."

"More than a month? Are you sure?"

"That's just it, I'm not sure of anything. I know when I had my last monthly, and that would make it the end of August, but I hope I'm wrong. I hope it's earlier."

Taima beckoned her with a wave of her hand. "Come here."

Nancy went to the bed and stood in front of Taima, who ran her free hand over Nancy's stomach, pressing slightly, and going from side to side and then up and down. "You have two babies in there."

Nancy gasped, swallowed hard, and choked. *Oh, dear God!* She fought back her terror and tried to sound normal when she said, "Two? We joked about how big I was getting, but I didn't think I had more than one baby."

"I'm pretty sure. Pick out more names."

"Oh. More names? I had Lucas already picked out, after my daddy, for a boy, and Linda, after one of my sisters, for a girl. Now, I'll have to think up some more. I like your name. I never heard it before. What does it mean?"

"My given name is Sara, after a great woman of my tribe. Henry is the one who started calling me Taima."

"Why is that?"

"In my language it means, 'Thunder.' He says that when I lose my temper, I sound like the Great Spirit is sending in a storm."

"That's a good name. I like it."

Henry stuck his head inside. "It's getting late, Taima. We best be going."

"In a minute. William isn't finished with his lunch." The women talked for a while longer, and when the baby was back asleep, Taima stood. "I guess we better go. It was very nice to meet you, Nancy."

"I'm so happy you came. Please come again."

"We will, and when you are well, you come to visit us."

"I will, I promise. I can hardly wait."

The women walked arm in arm to the horses. Once she was in the saddle, Taima looked down to Nancy, and with a sincere note in her voice, said, "If you need me when your time comes, send Jake and I'll come right away."

Nancy felt a wave of relief come over her. "Thank you. I will. I can't tell you how much better that makes me feel, to have a woman close. We talked about me going into town to be with my mother, but I don't think I could ride a horse that far." Nancy didn't mention the trouble with Abner.

She and Jake stood with their arms around one another until Henry and Taima were out of sight. She leaned her head on his shoulder. "I'm so glad to have a friend now."

"I'm your friend, aren't I?"

"Not that kind of friend."

"What kind is that?"

"One who can sympathize completely if I laugh and pee my pants."

He kissed her forehead. "Oh, that kind of friend."

When they went to bed that night, he held her in his arms and asked, "Are you content to be living out here in the wilderness? I can see how you must get lonely."

"I'm not lonely. I was only missing having another woman to talk to. Now that I know I can visit Taima, and that she'll visit me from time to time, I have everything I need."

"I'd do whatever you want to make you happy. You know that, don't you?"

"I do, and knowing you feel that way is one of the things I love about you. As much as my father loved my mother, she still always had to let him have the final say-so because he was the head of the house. He used to talk about spoiling us because he gave us licorice sticks and extra clothes, but Mom never got to decide anything important. He didn't even ask her what she thought. She wasn't held much higher than us children."

184

Jake propped himself up on one elbow. "I know that there'll be times we don't agree, but I promise you, you'll always be the most important thing in my life."

Nancy fell asleep thinking about how happy she was. She didn't tell Jake about Taima's prediction that she was carrying two babies. He was worried enough about her safely delivering one without giving him twice as much to fret about.

Chapter 16

August came, sticky and hot. Nancy's clothes clung to her, and perspiration constantly trickled down her body. The fireplace was stacked with logs, but Jake built a rock pile outside, and she did the cooking there so as not to heat up the cabin. In the early spring, Jake had cleared more land for the garden and plied it with horse manure before he planted. Now they were enjoying the early fruits and vegetables. He'd put out a row of strawberries, and when the fruit began to turn pink, covered them with a mesh he brought from the store to keep the birds out. Now they were hanging with fat, ripening berries.

The tomatoes were producing a half-dozen red ones a day, and soon there would be so many, Nancy would have plenty to can for winter. The corn was as high as her head. There were beans and turnips and potatoes. "Look at it, Jake. Isn't it beautiful? You know just what to do to make it all wonderful. A person would think you were a farmer instead of a trapper."

"I ought to know. I was raised on a farm. I only started in to being a trapper to make a living up here."

"I forgot about Kansas. Do you miss it?"

He didn't answer her right away, but knelt and picked up a handful of dirt, smelled it, and then let it run through his fingers. "I do. I miss Kansas, and I miss being a farmer. Funny, I didn't know that until you asked me just now. There's something wonderful about plantin' a seed and watchin' it turn into food for your table or even flowers to make the world prettier. Mom was always so crazy about the horses, she didn't pay much mind to the farm part of it, but I always loved it."

The sweet, crisp lettuce was leafing out faster than they could use it, so they ate mostly salads and fruit during the day. Jake joked, "I'm eating so much salad, I'm likely to start hoppin' 'round like a rabbit."

"It's good for you, good for the baby, too."

At night, he would lay his head against her stomach and talk to the baby as if it could understand what he was saying. Every now and then, she would see fear pass across his face and know that he was remembering losing Lucy and their son. She never told him that Taima had predicted twins. It would only have made him more afraid.

Most of Nancy's waking hours, she sat on the porch with her sewing on her lap, either dozing or rocking slowly in the shade of the overhang. She used some of the flour sacks to make a loose shift and took to wearing only that when she was inside. When she protested that she could help, Jake refused to let her do any work at all. "You need your rest, darlin', and I did it all before you came here."

"There wasn't so much to get done before I came."

"Don't you worry 'bout it." He sat on the porch step in front of her as she rocked in the chair behind him. Swatting at flies with a thin branch that had a cluster of leaves on the end, he said, "I been thinkin' that your time must be getting' close."

"Are you saying that because my belly button has turned inside out, and I'm so big it looks like I'm going to pop open?"

He chuckled. "No, I'm sayin' it because we were sort of countin' the time going by and it seems to me we figured on the end of August."

"You're right. It won't be much longer now. The way this baby runs around in there, he's doing his best to get out right now. Look at this."

He turned to look at her. She pulled her shift tighter across her stomach and he could see the outline of a little foot pushing against her from the inside. He put both of his hands on her belly and laughed as the movement ran back and forth under his fingers.

"What I was about to say is that I think maybe I ought to see if I can get your mom to come and stay with us until it's time."

Nancy shook her head. "As much as I'd like that, I have no idea how she could get away. Even if we had one of my sisters, who knows when my time would come? Where would they sleep? I'll be fine. I helped deliver a few babies at home."

"I'm afraid for you to try to do it all alone."

"Women have been having babies since Adam and Eve. Most of the time, it comes out fine."

His face was drawn in a combination of fear and sorrow when he said, "Sometimes, it doesn't come out fine."

"I helped Momma bring babies into the world. Sometimes, it doesn't come out fine, and having a doctor or someone else there doesn't make any difference."

He shook his head and turned away from her. She held him closer. "Taima said she would come if I needed her. I know the signs to look for when it's time. The baby drops down a day or so before. When that happens, you can go get her to help me."

She could see the relief that flooded over him. He even managed to force a smile. "That's right. She'll come. She'll help us."

Chapter 17

By the end of August, Jake wouldn't put out his traps. If he set them, he'd have to leave Nancy alone while he went and emptied them. Afraid to be gone even as far as the shed for more than a few minutes, he was underfoot all the time. Wanting him out of the way, she told him, "You should take Charlie and Pete for a ride so they can get some exercise."

"They're free to roam around the clearing if they want."

"That's not the same thing. They'll get all out of shape and won't be able to do what you need—if you ever go back to work, that is."

He grinned at her. "Are you telling me that I'm getting on your nerves?"

"I don't want to hurt your feelings, but it's the way you're watching me every minute. When I go to the outhouse, which is every ten minutes these days, you're standing outside when I come out. If I open my eyes in the middle of the night, you're staring at me. Stop worrying. I'm fine. If I need you, I'm sure that I can holler loud enough for you to hear me from anywhere in the clearing."

"I know. It's not only that I worry about you, it's the other thing, too."

"Other thing? What other thing?"

"You done got so beautiful I can't take my eyes off you."

She pouted. "You shouldn't tease me like that. I can't help it if I'm as big as a house. I'm hungry all the time, and I can't move around much to burn up what I eat."

He nuzzled her neck and ran a row of kisses down into her recently ample bosom. "I'm not teasing you. You are beautiful. Your skin is like a porcelain doll, and you got a glow about you. I never saw anything like it, even on Lucy. When I was in France, I saw that painting in the museum in Paris that they made a big fuss about, the Mona Lisa. She wasn't anywhere near as good-looking as you are right now."

"I'm going to hit you in the head with the frying pan and see if you come to your senses. Go see to the horses. When you go into town the next time, get a dog to play with you and keep your mind busy. In the meantime, maybe you can teach Charlie to fetch a ball."

Jake scratched his chin. "I think I will. He is about the smartest horse I ever saw."

"Good. Now get on out there before I get that pan."

He hugged her loosely and nibbled on her earlobe. "Things sure have changed around here. A few months ago you were begging me to let you stay, and now you're ordering me around like I was hired help."

Her face lost its smile and she swallowed hard. Her voice was husky when she asked, "Are you sorry you let me stay?"

"Sorry? You being here saved me. I was living like a hermit, and now my life is so full of happiness it just naturally busts outta me from time to time. How can you even think I'd be sorry to have you here? Do I make you feel like I don't want you? I love you more than my own life."

She wiped away a tear. "I don't know what's wrong with me. I'm happy one minute and get sad all of a sudden for no reason at all."

He kissed her cheeks and forehead and then placed a series of light kisses on her lips. "I've heard that's a common thing in women carrying babies, to have their moods go up and down. It'll pass in a few more days when this baby comes."

She sniffled. "I hope so. I am so tired of peeing when I cough or even if I laugh. Most of all, I'm tired of looking like this. I hope it comes soon or you'll have to go into town and get a wheelbarrow for me to rest my stomach on when I need to walk around. I'm sorry I'm so flighty."

"One or two more days and we'll have our little Lucas and you'll be your old self again, all sweet and happy."

"Was I sweet and happy?"

"Not all the time. Not at first you weren't."
He wiggled his eyebrows at her. "Once you found
out how much fun I could be in certain situations,
you were about the happiest girl I ever saw. Made
me feel right powerful. I reckon maybe missin'
that is what's making you flighty."

Nancy couldn't stop the blush that exploded
across her face and neck. *He's right, but it
wouldn't be ladylike to admit how much I miss us
being together that way.* She pushed him away
from her. "Sounds to me like you're getting what
Daddy used to call the big head. Get on out of here
or I'll have to get that skillet and take you down a
peg or two."

He held up his hands in surrender. "I'm
goin' right now, but I'll be just outside if you need
me."

Jake went out to the yard and a few minutes
later, Nancy looked out to see him and Charlie
playing tag while Pete stood at the edge of the
grass having lunch. *I guess he's right. Charlie is
about the smartest horse I ever saw. Of course, I
only know one other horse to speak of, and that's
Daddy's, and he doesn't have any sense at all.*

She busied herself making lunch, waddling
slowly around the cabin with her toes pointed
outward to help keep her balance. It had rained for
hours the night before and the air was thick with
humidity. Sweat ran down her body and she was

chafed under her breasts. *After we eat, I'm going to ask Jake to go down to the creek with me and help me get in the water all the way up to my chin. The water is always cool. That would feel so good.*

She was standing at the table slicing a loaf of bread when she felt a popping sensation in her lower back and a gush of water ran down her legs. She gasped in shock. Nancy knew what it was, but at first was so surprised, she couldn't move. She caught her breath and bellowed, "Jake! Come here."

Wild-eyed, he ran into the cabin. "What is it? Is it time? Are you all right?"

Nancy sucked in a long breath. "I'm fine. My water broke is all. Help me get to the bed."

He wrapped one arm around her, helped her get to the bed and lie down, and slipped off her shoes. "Are you having pains?"

"Not yet. It may be a while before they start in. Sometimes it takes a long time between when your water breaks and the pains come. Slip the tarp under me to save the mattress from getting wet, and then fold up a blanket and get it down there to soak up the water. We have to get ready. I want you to fill up everything we have that holds water. Get all the flour sacks and towels down from the shelf and put them by the bed, and leave me a knife before you go, just in case it comes fast and I need to cut the cord before you get back."

"I can cut the cord."

"No, you likely won't have to. I said, just in case, but I don't expect to need it. This will probably take all day and maybe all night, too."

Jake looked so frightened, she felt sorry for him. She put aside her own panic and tried to sound calm. "Don't worry. My friend Emmalou was three days birthing her first baby and it all turned out fine, even though she did handle some language a good Christian girl shouldn't even know. Momma always said I would have an easy time of it because I'm built natural to birth babies, but I still want a woman here with me. When you get finished with getting the water and things, go tell Taima it's time to come."

He nodded slowly, as if he were in a daze, held up one finger to make some sort of point, opened his mouth and closed it without saying anything. He put the tarp and blanket under her. That accomplished, he wheeled around and ran out of the cabin. In a few seconds, Nancy could hear the water pump working. Jake drew the water, filled every vessel he could find, and lined up the buckets and pots along the wall by the bed. He brought the cloths from the shelf, and laid a sharp knife on the little bedside table.

He grasped her hand so tightly it almost hurt, but she didn't flinch. He kissed her cheek. "Are you sure I should leave you here alone?"

"You'll be back in less than two hours. I'll probably be eight hours or more once my pains start, and I haven't even had the first one yet. Go! Get Taima for me."

He kissed her again. "I'll get back as fast as I can."

"Take your time. There's no need to push Charlie into a lather. That trail is hard enough as it is."

"All right. You lay there and rest."

"I will. If there's one thing I've been good at for the last nine months, it's taking a nap."

He nodded, swallowed hard, and said, "I'm going now." He stood there staring down at her and made no move to leave.

She waved a hand toward the door. "Go!"

"All right." He raced out of the cabin and in only a little while, she heard Charlie's hoof beats as he trotted into the woods. *Lord God, please don't let Jake fall off and hurt himself.*

She took another deep breath. *All in all, I feel fine. I should have had him bring me the Bible or one of my books so I'd have something to read and help me pass the time.* Nancy said another prayer and, in a matter of minutes, drifted off to sleep.

She was lying on her side facing the window when the sound of footsteps woke her. She opened her eyes to see that the sun had sunk below the tree

line. *How late is it? It's getting dark already.*
Awkwardly trying to turn over onto her back, she
said, "What took you so long? Are you all right?"

When there was no answer, she turned her
head to find the massive bulk of Abner looming
over her, his face twisted with hatred.

Chapter 18

Abner's rage seemed to seep out of him, as if he were oozing venom. Nancy wanted to get as far away as possible and tried to scoot to the far side of the bed. He threw back his head, roared like a wounded bear, and then pointed a finger at her and bellowed, "You harlot! That should have been mine."

He doubled up his fist and his arm plunged down like a jackhammer into her stomach. Nancy screamed as a pain flashed over her that was so intense she almost lost consciousness. When she was able to open her eyes, Abner was drawing back his fist for another punch. Behind him, Nancy saw Jake run into the cabin. He launched himself through the air and wrapped his arms around Abner, who shook him off as if he were a child.

Jake flew across the room and smashed against the wall. His head hit one of the logs with a loud crack, and his body sank down, flopping against the floor with a thud.

Abner strode over to where Jake lay, knelt down on one knee, grasped Jake's shirt to pull him up, and began punching him, his fist smashing into Jake's face, over and over. Not able to defend himself against the monster, Jake's head snapped first one way and then the other, bouncing against the logs of the wall with each hit.

Nancy screamed, "Stop it! You're killing him." Abner stopped with his fist in mid-air. He turned slowly to look at her and his mouth twisted into a satanic grin. "Kill him? You're right. I don't want him to die so fast."

He let go of Jake's shirt and Jake fell into a heap. Abner lumbered to his feet and walked over to the fireplace, where he tossed a handful of kindling onto the logs stacked there. He picked up the long matches and struck one, holding it against the chips of wood until they burst into flame.

Nancy was trying to get to her feet when another pain enveloped her, different than the last. This one was in the small of her back. It knocked her back on the mattress. She pressed her palms against her stomach. It was as hard as a rock. She could feel something hot and wet gush out of her and then she could smell the sharp, coppery smell of blood. She struggled to catch her breath.

She watched as Abner poked at the smoking logs and then picked up one that had caught the flames. He held it up like a torch. "The two of you are going to rot in hell," he snarled, and then he stomped out of the cabin.

Nancy's whole body was in agony. She thrashed on the bed, trying to get up and go to Jake, but her pain was so intense she thought it would rip her apart, and she couldn't make it. Through the window, she saw Abner walk past, holding his torch up to the underhang of the roof, the only place where the wood would be dry after the storm of last night. After another minute, she heard the sound of his horse galloping away and through the window, she could see little flames running along the eaves.

Abner's gone. Jake needs me. I have to help him. Nancy made another effort to get up, but the best she could do was to inch her body to the edge of the bed. In a minute, the worst of the pain ebbed a little, leaving only the throbbing in her abdomen from Abner's punch. Before she could get to her feet, another spasm enveloped her.

She was covered in sweat, blood, and fluids. The heat from the spreading fire seemed to swallow her. She panted several times, and then drew in a long breath before swinging one leg over the side of the bed and getting a foot on the floor. Clutching the log headboard, she was able to pull herself to a sitting position.

The heat, the wracking pain, and the thickening smoke creeping into the cabin, combined with the effort to sit up, exhausted her.

She rested there for a few seconds, wheezing and trying to gather her strength, and then swung the other foot to the floor. Putting both hands to her side, she tried to push herself to her feet, but couldn't make it.

There was a crackling sound coming from outside, and the musty odor of burning wood wrapped around her.

Oh, God! Help me! Help us! With tremendous effort, she used both hands to push herself up and managed to get to her feet. The pain tore through her, and she rocked back and forth, trying not to fall over.

Nancy reached out, grabbed the back of the chair, and dragged it to her. She leaned on it for support, and then pushed it toward Jake, took a few steps, stopped and rested on it for a moment, then pushed it a little further, repeating the process until she made her way across the cabin to where he lay.

Grasping the chair for support, she stood looking down at him. *I have to get him out of here.* Holding on, she leaned over him and shouted, "Jake! Jake, wake up!"

He didn't move at all. *Oh, God! He's already dead.* She stared at his chest and saw a slight rise and fall. *No, he's alive!* She reached down, grasped his shirt, and tried to drag him toward the door.

With the struggle, another pain washed over her and her legs gave way. She fell next to him, where the air near the floor was clearer of smoke.

After a deep breath, she rolled over and struggled to get up, but the pain was slicing her in two, and the effort was wasted.

She fell back next to Jake and surrendered to her fate. *We're all going to die here, me, Jake, and our babies. We're going to burn to death.* Calm came over her and she straightened her body next to Jake's and wrapped her arms around him.

The smoke began to fill the room and floated overhead. The wall where the bed stood had flames licking from between the logs to the inside. The wood popped and hissed, and cracks like gunshots echoed around the cabin.

One spasm of pain had barely receded before Nancy felt another wave washing over her. *Will I live to see my babies' faces before the fire gets me?* She closed her eyes, laid her head on Jake's chest, and began to sink into oblivion.

She felt someone grasping her under her arms and lifting her up. When she looked up, she saw Henry backing out the door as he carried her along. "Jake," she screamed. "Get Jake out of there."

"I'll get him next," Henry shouted over the roar of the fire. When they reached the porch, he carried her away from the cabin and laid her gently on the ground. He then turned and ran back inside the inferno.

Nancy could see Taima, with little William still in his sling, come out of the shed leading Charlie with a feed sack pulled over his head. She tied him to a tree at the edge of the clearing and went back to get Pete.

Two sides of the cabin were covered with flames, and they were moving around to the front, running along the porch eave as if they were liquid. Henry came out with Jake thrown over his shoulder and ran right through the fire and down the steps. He laid Jake next to Nancy and she rolled onto her side so she could see him. "Is he still alive?"

Henry put his cheek next to Jake's mouth and, after a moment, said, "He's alive, but he's in trouble."

"Can you help him?"

"I can try," Henry said. He went to the shed, came out with a bucket, and started drawing water from the well.

Taima tied Pete to the tree next to Charlie and came running to Nancy's side. She knelt down and pressed her hand against Nancy's stomach. "When did the pains start?"

"When Abner hit me there, but that was a different pain from the next one. That was only a few minutes ago, and they keep coming in waves. As soon as one stops, the next one comes."

Taima glanced up at Henry and Nancy saw them exchange a knowing look. Nancy tugged at Taima's sleeve. "Did he kill my babies? Is that why it hurts so much?"

Taima patted her on the shoulder. "We'll see. It won't be long until we know."

Nancy had opened her mouth to ask another question when the worst pain she could ever have imagined took hold of her, and she felt herself sinking into a black pit.

Chapter 19

Through a thick fog, Nancy could hear a voice calling her name and then felt someone shaking her shoulder. "Wake up, Nancy. Your baby needs to eat."

Nancy pushed herself out of the mists and opened her eyes to see Taima looking down at her. Her first thought was of her husband. "Jake? Is Jake alive?"

Taima waved a hand toward the corner of the shed. "He's alive, but not awake yet."

Nancy lifted her head and saw Jake lying there. He was safe. She asked, "Is the fire out?"

"Yes, but the cabin is almost gone. The fireplace can be used when you rebuild. You've lost almost everything. Henry was able to save your trunk, but the fire was too high by then for him to get anything else. I imagine your cooking pots and such will be all right. It's a good thing we had the storm the night before, or the fire could have spread. The shed and the other buildings are all right."

"How long have I been sleeping?"

"Since yesterday afternoon. It's almost noon today."

Somewhere Nancy could hear babies crying, and the sound made her body tingle inside. She looked down at her now-flat stomach. "My baby?"

"Your little girl needs her mother, and my William wants me, too."

My little girl? Nancy snapped to full consciousness and looked around. She was lying on one of the horse blankets that had been spread over a pile of hay. Taima held out a tiny bundle wrapped in one of the quilts Nancy had sewn. Some of the crying was coming from inside it.

Nancy pushed herself to a sitting position and took the bundle. When she pulled aside the cover, she looked down into the face of her daughter. The baby had a perfectly round head with thick auburn curls. "Look at her," Nancy exclaimed. "She's going to have Jake's hair."

She examined the perfect little body before re-wrapping her and then looked at Taima. "She's so small. Is she all right?"

"She's very good size for a twin and very hungry, too. You need to nurse her. It will help you heal."

"I don't know how."

Taima smiled. "I've already fed her a few times while you were sleeping. You don't need to know how. If you get her close enough to you, she knows how."

"I'm so thirsty. Can you get me some water?"

While Taima brought Nancy a cup of water, she unbuttoned her dress and held the baby in the crook of her arm with its face against her breast. The baby shook her head from side to side until her mouth found the nipple. She latched on and began sucking frantically. Nancy looked up at Taima in awe. "You're right! She does know how."

Taima unbuttoned her own dress. She took a piece of cloth from her pocket, and placed it under her breast before she picked up her William and began nursing him. Her milk flowed so freely, the boy couldn't drink it fast enough, and some ran down onto the cloth.

Nancy looked at Taima, and then down at her own breast. "I don't have any milk yet."

"No, that will come tomorrow or the next day"

Her little girl was sucking harder. "Ow!" Nancy said. "That hurts."

"Only for one or two times, and then it will be all right. Let her try for a while, and then I'll feed her."

"You and Henry saved our lives."

Taima nodded. "We were riding only a few minutes behind Jake on the way to your cabin. What happened here?"

"Abner did this."

"Who is Abner?"

"He's the man who wanted to marry me before I came here. He promised he would kill Jake, and he already tried once before. He got Jake in town and would have beaten him to death if my daddy hadn't stopped him."

Taima gasped. "That's terrible. He set the fire?"

"Abner came into the cabin only a minute before Jake got back from your place. He hit me in the stomach really hard with his fist, and then, when Jake ran in and tried to stop him, he beat Jake something awful. He must have thought Jake was dead, and then he started the fire. He wanted us and our baby to burn to death."

"He's an evil man, this Abner."

"Yes, he is. He pretends to be a Christian, but if there was ever anyone possessed by demons, Abner is."

Taima fell silent and the two women nursed their children. Nancy felt an overwhelming rapture as she watched her baby try to eat, and after a while she said, "You said twins. So you were right about there being two of them. Is the other one sleeping?"

Taima's face grew sad and she looked away. "I'm sorry, Nancy. The little boy didn't make it. The damage was too great."

"Damage?"

"He—his ribcage was caved in, probably from your being hit in the stomach. I think he also was hurt inside, maybe his heart."

"Where is he?"

"He is over there." Taima indicated the far corner of the shed with her head. "We didn't want to bury him until you woke up."

As tears trickled down her cheeks, Nancy looked down at her baby girl. "After what Abner did, it's a miracle this one survived. Would you bring my son to me so I can see him?"

"Are you sure? It may be very difficult for you."

"I'm sure."

"I will bring him to you when your daughter is finished with her dinner."

Taima put a now-sleeping William down and took the baby girl from Nancy. Unfastened from her mother, the baby let out a cry so loud it made both of them laugh. Taima gave her a breast and she settled down and had her meal.

When the baby girl had finished eating and gone back to sleep, Taima brought the little boy to Nancy. He was wrapped in another of the quilts Nancy had made and stored in the trunk. Taima laid him in Nancy's arms and she pulled the wrap aside to see her son. He was a copy of the little girl, with the same auburn curls. Nancy pulled the cloth further down and gasped at the baby's smashed torso.

Sobs from deep inside wracked Nancy's body and she wailed, "Oh, God, oh, God! Look what Abner did to him!"

Almost whispering, Taima said, "We should bury him as soon as possible."

Nancy looked up at Taima and pleaded, "We have to wait for Jake."

Taima bit a lip and patted Nancy on the shoulder. "Jake is very badly hurt, and we don't know when he will wake up. We won't be able to wait in this heat. It may be a long time before Jake comes to—if he does."

Nancy gasped, "What will we do without him?"

"If he doesn't make it, Henry and I will take care of you until you can go back to your father's house. Will he take you in?"

"He'll take care of us. I know he loves me, even if I didn't always do as he said. He'll love my baby, too."

"When we talked, you said you were going to name your baby after one of your sisters. Have you decided which one?"

Nancy reached out and took Taima's hand. "I'm naming her after my new sister, too. She will be Linda Taima Belk."

Taima asked, "So her middle name will mean thunder? Are you sure she will like that?"

Nancy wiped away a tear and managed a wistful smile. "I know I do. I like Taima for one of her names because she should learn to stand up for herself, and Linda because that means beautiful, and this precious baby is the most beautiful thing on the earth."

Henry came in the door and took off his hat. "How are you doing, Nancy?"

"I'm alive. Jake's alive, and I still have one of my babies. I guess I should give thanks for that."

"I have to be gone for a while. When we got here, I had to get you out of the cabin, and I didn't take time to tie up our horses. Both of them ran away from the fire. They're back home by now. I saddled up Charlie, and I'm going to go get them and some supplies from our cabin. There's no telling how long it will be before we can get you and Jake into town. Is there anything you need before I leave?"

Taima told him, "You should build a small fire outside so I can prepare dinner. I'll go into what's left of the cabin and see if I can find some pans to cook in among the ashes."

Henry nodded and went out.

Little William was sleeping soundly on the blanket next to Linda. "The babies should both sleep for a long time," Taima told Nancy. "You should get some more rest yourself."

"All right," Nancy murmured, but her mind was running ahead. She knew what she was going to do, and she wasn't about to tell either of her friends or they would stop her.

When Taima left the shed, Nancy got awkwardly to her feet and went to where Jake was lying. He was worse this time than he had been the day Abner beat him in town. His face was so bruised and swollen she wouldn't have been able to recognize him if it weren't for his copper-colored hair and beard. She knelt next to him and brushed his hair off his forehead. "Wake up, Jake. Please, wake up."

There was no response. Nancy took his hand in hers, and it frightened her how cold it was, even in the midday heat. She pressed her ear against his chest and was slightly comforted by the sound of his heart beating rhythmically. She kissed his lips softly and whispered, "I'll be back as soon as I can."

The sling Taima used to carry William was hanging on a rail. Nancy drew it over her head and adjusted it. She picked up the body of her son and nestled it in the sling. At the door to the shed, she peeked out. None of the outbuildings had been burned. The smoke house, outhouse, and mercifully, the shed, had been spared. All that was left of the cabin was the fireplace and one charred wall. She felt a pang of sorrow at the loss of the place she had come to love so much, where she had been so happy only a few days earlier.

Henry was on the other side of the clearing with his back to her. The circle of rocks where she cooked summer meals had been scattered, and Henry was re-shaping the circle. There was no sign of Taima, but Nancy could hear sounds coming from the cabin and assumed Taima was in there looking for what she could save.

Good, the noise Taima is making will keep Henry from hearing me.

Only a few feet away from her, Charlie was saddled and tied to the rail. She looked for something to wear on her feet, but there was nothing she could use in place of shoes. Hers had burned with the cabin. Nancy slipped barefoot out the door, went to where Charlie was standing, and untied the reins. With her hand over his muzzle so he wouldn't whinny and draw Henry's attention, she led the horse a short distance into the woods, to where she knew there was a stump that would serve her purpose. Once there, she climbed on the stump, put her foot in the stirrup, and managed to get on Charlie's back.

"Take me to town, Charlie," she whispered, hugging him with her knees. Charlie shook his head up and down as if he were saying "Yes" and started off at a fast walk. Nancy had no idea if he was going in the right direction and trusted that he had made the trip often enough he could take her there without guidance.

After a while, her head began to swim, and she didn't know if she were only sleepy, or if she were going to pass out. She remembered how Jake had managed to stay on Charlie's back the time Abner had beaten him in town, and twined her fingers into Charlie's mane with both hands, gripping the hairs as tightly as she could before she slipped into unconsciousness.

Chapter 20

The sound of Charlie neighing loudly drew Nancy back into the world. Her eyes fluttered open and she struggled out of her fog. Charlie was standing in front of her father's store, his head over the hitching post rail as if he were waiting to be tied there. Lucas came out of the store. When he saw Nancy, his face lit up for a split-second before his forehead creased with anxiety. "Nancy! What are you doing here?"

She rasped, "Help me down."

Lucas came to Charlie's side and held up his hands. Nancy kicked free of the stirrups and tried to lift her leg over the back of the saddle, but couldn't. She fought the blackness coming over her.

One way or another, she was determined to complete the task she had set for herself. "Catch me, Daddy," she said. She tossed the reins over Charlie's head and let them drop to the ground so he would stay put, and let herself fall into her father's arms.

He carried her into the store, laid her on the counter, and bellowed, "Wilfred!"

One of Nancy's younger brothers came running out of the back room. When he saw Nancy lying there he skidded to a stop and his mouth fell open. Lucas pointed to the door. "Run and fetch your mother," he shouted. Wilfred spun around and ran out.

Lucas held Nancy's hand against his chest. "What happened? Where is Jake?"

She struggled to sit up, but was too weak. "Abner may have killed him. He's been sleeping for a two days and we can't wake him. Help me sit up, Daddy."

He put his arm under her shoulders and lifted her. When she swung her legs down, blood ran down her calf and dripped from her foot. She opened the folds of the sling, took out the body of her son, and held it out to him. "This is your grandson, Lucas Smith Belk. We named him after you, just like we promised. Look what Abner did to him."

Lucas took the baby and unwrapped the covering. When he saw the tiny, crushed body of the grandson he had craved, he put back his head and screamed a long, piercing cry, so loud it shook the merchandise on the store shelves.

Nancy's mother, Rebecca, came rushing into the store. "Nancy! What on earth?" She hurried to her daughter's side and wrapped her arms around Nancy's shoulders.

Lucas handed the baby to Rebecca and said, "Take care of them." He strode to the row of rifles hanging on the wall, took one off its pegs, and cracked it open. He began jamming shells into the housing. Finished, he snapped the barrel into place. "I'll be back in a bit," he told his wife.

Nancy's mother looked at her grandson and sobbed, "Oh, Nancy! What happened to him?"

"Abner killed him."

"Abner? How did he do this?"

"My water broke yesterday morning, and Jake went to get the neighbor woman to help me. While he was gone, Abner came into our cabin and hit me as hard as he could with his fist, right in my stomach."

Rebecca gasped, and Nancy went on, "He was getting ready to hit me again, but Jake came home just then and jumped on him. Abner forgot about me and beat Jake something awful. I still don't know if he's going to live or die. Abner set the cabin on fire before he left. He wanted us all to die in there. If Jake's friends hadn't shown up and dragged us out, we'd have burned alive."

Nancy coughed and swallowed hard. Her throat was still feeling raspy from the smoke she had inhaled. "Mom, could you get me a drink of water?"

Rebecca brought a cup of water from the back of the store, stopping at the sugar barrel to scoop a handful of sugar in it and swirl it around. As Nancy drank, Rebecca paced back and forth in front of the counter, wringing her hands. "God help us! Your father is going to kill Abner."

Through gritted teeth, Nancy said, "Good, that's why I came here. I want him dead."

"Nancy! You must forgive. The Lord expects it. It's in the scripture."

Nancy looked away from her mother's reproving face. "An eye for an eye, Mom. That's scripture, too. I want Abner dead, and I want him to suffer before he dies."

Rebecca began wringing her hands. "But you can't hold hatred in your heart. It will kill you. Pray for the Lord to help you forgive him."

"I'll pray about that another time. Abner swore he would see us all dead, and he meant it. When he finds out we're alive, he won't quit trying to kill us until he's done the job. He proved he'd even murder a baby. Shooting him is the only way to stop him from killing me and Jake and little Linda. I only wish I could be the one to do it."

"Linda?"

"I had twins. I have another baby, Mom, a little girl."

Rebecca fluttered her hands in the air. "I don't understand. Where is she?"

"I left her with my friend. Her own baby is still nursing, and Taima can take care of her until I get back. I have to go home now."

Rebecca looked down at the growing puddle of blood on the floor. "Nancy, you're in no condition to go anywhere but to bed. There's no telling when you'll be able to travel, especially on horseback. It will be two or three weeks at the earliest."

"I can't wait that long. I have to go home now and take care of Jake and my little girl."

Rebecca shook her finger at Nancy and said, "You'll do no such thing. It won't do your family any good if you kill yourself. Your friends will take care of them for you. You sit right there until I get back, understand? I'm going to go home and get your bed ready. I'll find one of your brothers to carry you to the house and get you to your room."

Nancy started to reply, but knew there was no point in arguing with her mother. She sat still and nodded. When Rebecca left the store, and Nancy was alone, she rolled over onto her side and slid down from the counter until her feet were on the floor. A wave of dizziness passed over her. She grasped the side of the counter and slowly made her way around to the ledger where her father wrote down his accounts. She opened the book to a blank page, found a pencil, and wrote:

Mama,

I have to go back to my baby girl. Bury little Lucas next to Grandma.

She left the book open on the counter where her mother would see it as soon as she returned to the store. Holding the counter's edge for support, she made her way around the store. At the end of the counter, she walked unsteadily to the door.

Out front, Charlie was standing where she had left him, his nose deep in the water trough that stood in front of the hitching post. She clutched the stirrup. Charlie looked enormously tall to her. *How will I ever be able to get back on him?*

She looked around and saw Mr. Blevins, one of her father's customers, coming toward the store. Making her best effort to act as if there were nothing wrong, she went to Charlie's head and picked up the reins. When the man came near, she said, "Good afternoon. Mr. Blevins. Would you be so kind as to give me a boost onto my horse?"

He looked at her oddly and frowned. Nancy could see disapproval on his face, but he said, "All right."

He stood at Charlie's side and laced his fingers together. She took a deep breath, grasped the saddle horn, and with his assistance, managed to lift herself onto the horse's back.

Her head was spinning. She clung to consciousness and made an effort to appear as if she were fine. "Thank you so much," she said with a weak smile, and turned Charlie toward home. She gave him a little kick, and he started to walk.

Grasping Charlie's mane, Nancy drifted in and out of consciousness as they made the trip back to the cabin. The sun was setting before they finally reached the clearing. She could see that while she was gone, Taima and Henry had been working. A pile of household goods had been salvaged from the cabin and lay scattered on the ground. There were pots and pans, metal cups, some tools, and other things that fire couldn't harm.

The wooden box where the layette she had made for her baby, and where Nancy and Jake's extra clothes were kept, was there. She wondered if the contents, especially the Bible, were unharmed.

There was no one in sight. Charlie walked up to the shed and whinnied loudly, the way he had in town. Henry and Taima came out together. Taima put her hands on her hips. "Nancy! What have you been doing? You scared us half to death. We didn't think you would live to make it back. Where did you have to go that was so important you sneaked away like that?"

Ignoring Taima's question, Nancy asked, "How's my baby?"

"She's fine. She has a good appetite."

"Jake?"

"Still sleeping. Now tell me where you went in your condition."

"I took my baby boy to his grandfather so he could get justice for him."

Henry pointed to a mound of freshly turned soil on the edge of the clearing. "We were going to bury him there."

"No. I wanted my father to see with his own eyes what Abner did to him. It wouldn't have been the same if he was only told about it."

"But what about his burial?"

"I left a note for my mother asking her to bury him next to my grandmother. She'll see to it that he gets a proper Christian service, and my father will see to it that Abner pays for what he did."

Henry nodded. "As a father, I know you are right. What did your father do when he saw the baby?"

"He took his rifle and went to look for Abner. I don't know if he found him or not. I snuck away while I was alone 'cause I knew they would stop me if I tried to leave."

Taima jabbed her forefinger in Nancy's direction. "They were right, and I would have stopped you from leaving here if I had seen or heard you when you left."

"It doesn't matter. I'm home now." Nancy took her feet out of the stirrups. "Henry, would you help me down?"

He held up his arms. With great effort, Nancy was able to drag her right leg over the back of the saddle and let her body slide down Charlie's side. Henry held her under her arms until her feet touched the ground, and then he scooped her up and carried her into the shed, placing her back on the bed of straw where she had awakened only that morning. So much had happened since then it seemed to have been a long time ago.

When Henry left the shed, Nancy clutched Taima's sleeve. "Taima, I'm so embarrassed to tell you this, but I need a bath and I need clean clothes. I've been bleeding, and I don't even remember much, but sometimes I wasn't in my right mind. I must have peed myself on the way home."

"Don't be embarrassed. You've been through a great ordeal. I'll tell Henry to stay outside with Charlie until we're through, and I'll help you get cleaned up."

Taima brought a bucket of water, some soap, and a few of the cloths from the trunk. Nancy took off her soiled clothing, and Taima carried the pile to the stream to rinse it while Nancy washed herself from top to bottom. By then, Taima was back and helped Nancy into her fresh clothes. Finally clean and dry, Nancy looked around. "Where is my baby?"

"Sleeping next to William. She is a good baby and sleeps most of the time."

"Did she eat all right while I was gone?"

Taima chuckled. "That one has no problem with her appetite. She'll help you with that if you want to wake her."

"Help me with what?"

Taima pointed to Nancy's chest and Nancy looked down to where two damp spots showed on the front of her dress, right over her breasts. "Oh! I thought you said my milk wouldn't come in until tomorrow or the next day."

"Everyone is different. She was working very hard at bringing it in when you first nursed her. Maybe that makes a difference."

"Bring her here," Nancy said, unbuttoning her bodice.

Taima brought the baby to Nancy and she held her daughter close to her breast. Linda latched on immediately, sucking hard, waving her little hands in the air, and pounding one tiny fist on Nancy's breast. Nancy looked up at Taima and said, "It doesn't hurt this time."

"That's because your milk is ready for her. Let me get you some water. You need to drink more than usual while you nurse."

Taima dipped a cup full of water out of the bucket and brought it to Nancy. She hadn't had a drink since she left town, and almost slurped as she drained the cup. From outside, Henry called, "Can we come in yet?"

Taima said, "We're finished. Come on in."

Henry led Charlie to his stall next to Pete. "It's too late today to make the trip home. Our horses will have plenty of grass to graze on, and they're close to the stream if they need water. I'll wait until morning to go to our cabin and get supplies."

He gave the horses fresh water, a scoop of oats, and hay before he went back out.

Nancy watched, almost hypnotized, as her daughter ate greedily. She said, "Her official name is Linda Taima Belk, but that sounds so formal. I think I'll call her Tammy for short. What do you think?"

"Try it out for a while. You will know later if it's right."

Nancy stretched her neck to see Jake. He was still lying as she had left him. "Has there been any change in Jake?"

"Still sleeping."

"Oh. He hasn't shown any signs of waking up?"

"Not yet. Sleep may be the best thing for him. His body is healing itself."

When the baby was finished eating, Taima brought Nancy a dish with some chopped meat and a potato that had been baked in the campfire. Nancy didn't realize how hungry she was until she saw the food. When she had eaten, Nancy held out her hand to Taima. "Help me get to Jake."

Taima frowned and shook her head. "You should rest."

"No. I want to be next to him."

Taima helped Nancy to her feet and supported her while she walked to where Jake lay. She sat on the floor next to him, stretched out alongside his body, and put one arm over his chest. Jake had an unfamiliar, woodsy smell, and as she drifted off to sleep, she wondered what it was.

Chapter 21

During the night, Nancy was dragged from her sleep by the sound of her baby crying. She fed her, changed her diaper, and put her back in the little straw bed Taima had made.

In a matter of seconds after she lay down, Nancy went back to sleep holding Jake's hand. The next time she woke, it was morning and Tammy was crying again.

Henry was on the other side of the shed, saddling Charlie. She sat up. "Good morning, Henry. Where is Taima?"

"She's making breakfast. I'm going to my place to get a few things we need."

Nancy picked up the baby, and unself-consciously, held her to her breast the way she had seen Taima do with William in front of Jake. "Where did you and Taima sleep?"

"Outside."

"On the ground? I'm so sorry."

"It was no problem. We have slept on the ground many times." He gathered up Charlie's reins. "I should be back in a few hours."

Nancy looked at Jake to find no change in him. With Linda still eating, she cradled her baby in her arm, used a rail to pull herself to her feet, and followed Henry outside. Taima was bent over the campfire, stirring something in a pot. Dishes and spoons were lying on a big rock next to the fire. William was sleeping, lying on one of the horse blankets on the ground a few feet away. "Good morning," Nancy said.

"Good morning. How are you feeling?"

"I'm fine." Nancy's stomach rumbled and she asked, "What're you cooking?"

"Oatmeal."

"The oats didn't burn up in the fire?"

"The ones in the house did. This morning we're sharing some of the horse's breakfast."

Nancy hooted. "I guess it's all the same. We could probably live on hay if we had to. Isn't Henry going to eat before he leaves?"

"He already ate." Taima scooped some of the oats into a ceramic bowl that Nancy recognized as one from the cabin, and put a spoon in it. She handed it to Nancy and then filled a bowl for herself. Nancy sat cross-legged next to Taima and took a bite of the oats. "They taste just the same, only they don't have the same feel in your mouth."

"They don't mill oats for horses the same way they do those for people. These take a longer time to cook to soften them up, but we can live on them just fine."

When the rumble in Nancy's stomach began to quiet, she asked, "What's that funny smell on Jake?"

"Herbs. They will help him heal."

"What kind of herbs?"

"Mountain Goldenrod for the cuts, so they don't flare up, Rosemary to keep his passages open and help him breathe, others to ease his pain."

"We had all that growing around here?"

"Yes."

Half afraid of the answer, Nancy asked, "Do you think Jake will ever wake up?"

"I don't know, but his breathing is regular, and his heart sounds strong. I couldn't find any broken bones unless his ribs are cracked. He had a very large bump on his head, but the swelling seems to have gone down. Only time will tell."

Both Nancy and the baby finished eating and Nancy visited the outhouse. When she came back to the fire, Taima asked, "Are you bleeding much?"

"Hardly at all."

"Good. You are young and strong, and even though you had a horrible thing happen to you, and went to town when it would be better if you had stayed put, I believe you will be all right."

"I always was healthy. I got over a cold better than any of my family and, sometimes, when they all got sick I didn't catch it from them. I can help you with the work."

"Get as much sleep as you want, drink lots of water, and take care of little Tammy. Don't worry about helping me. There isn't that much work to do."

Henry returned with his own two horses, riding one, leading the other, and with Charlie following behind. He had food, clothes, and tools loaded on both Charlie and his second horse. Nancy watched while Taima helped him unload.

Taima cocked an eyebrow at Henry. ""This is a lot. Did you bring everything we owned?" she asked.

"Almost, I thought it would be easier to have things here than to run back and forth getting it when we needed something."

He unrolled a large canvas and stakes, and in only a few minutes, had put together a tent big enough for him and Taima to sleep in.

Nancy asked, "How long can you and Taima stay here with us?"

With his back to her, Henry unlashed a bundle from Charlie's back and answered matter-of-factly, "As long as it takes."

"Takes for what?"

He laid down a bundle and looked at her. "Until Jake wakes up or dies."

Nancy's mouth made a small 'o,' but no sound escaped her lips.

When Nancy lay down next to Jake that night, she put her head on his shoulder and whispered, "Please, Dear God, let him wake up, please, please, please. I need him, and I want him to meet his daughter. She needs her daddy to take care of her, the same way I needed mine."

When the baby woke her for a middle-of-the-night feeding, Nancy repeated her prayer, and said it again in the morning. All during the day, as she tended to her daughter and went about what few chores Taima would allow her to perform, she chanted a prayer or silently thought it to herself. Sometimes, all it consisted of was, "Please, God, help us."

Nancy was sleeping soundly, curled up with her back against Jake when she heard someone say, "Water."

Was that a dream?

He said it again, "Water." Nancy bolted upright. "Jake! Oh, Jake!" she yelled. "You're awake."

"And thirsty."

"I'll get you some water. I'll get you a whole bucket of water." She hurried out of the shed. It was still dark outside, but there was a full moon lighting the clearing and the campfire was burning brightly enough that she could see. Henry and Taima were coming out of their tent.

"Jake's awake," she shouted at them. She went to the pump and began working the handle furiously. "He wants a drink of water!"

Henry took the bucket from her and carried it to the shed. He slid his arm under Jake's shoulders and lifted him up a little. Nancy took a cup off a hook, dipped it into the bucket, and held it to his lips. He drained it. "Do you want some more?" she asked.

"Not right now, but that sure was good. I…" His head fell back, and he slumped back into unconsciousness. Henry carefully laid him back down.

Nancy's head swam. "What's wrong with him? Is he going to be all right?"

Taima patted her on the back. "He must rest as much as he needs. He woke up, that's the main thing. We'll see how it goes in the morning."

Henry and Taima went back to their tent while Nancy sat next to Jake and stared at his face. He was lit by the moonlight coming through the open door. She watched for a long time, looking for some sign of movement, but there was none. Tammy began to cry, and she fed and changed her daughter and then lay down next to Jake with the baby between them. She said softly into his ear, "This is your little girl, Jake. Her name is Linda Taima Belk, and her hair is the same color as her daddy's. She wants to meet you. Please wake up again so you can say hello."

A cloud passed over the moon and the light that had been shining through the window faded.

Nancy chanted over and over, "Please, God, let him be all right," until she went back to sleep.

It wasn't the baby who woke her in the morning. The rooster began crowing, and when she opened her eyes, the sun was streaming in. She sat up, stretched, and yawned. When she turned to look at Jake, his head was turned toward her, his eyes were open, and he was looking back at her. The gray in what part of his face that wasn't bruised and scabbed over had turned a better shade of pink.

"Jake! You're awake."

"More or less. The rooster woke me up. It was a bit of a surprise. I thought I was already dead."

"You were awake last night for a few minutes."

"I was? I don't remember it. The last thing I recall is when Abner had me on the floor screaming at me like a wild thing and beating me with those ham-sized fists of his." Tammy, lying between them, let out an ear-splitting cry. Jake raised his head to look at her. "The baby? When did it come?"

"Sometime during the fire, Taima delivered her."

"Let me get a look at her. Her?"

"Yes. We have a little girl and her name is Linda Taima Belk, but Taima and I call her

Tammy." She picked up the screaming baby and held her where Jake could see her face.

He gazed at her and then chuckled. "She has the Belk hair, that's for sure. She looks so small, and you were so big before she came. Did you have a hard time of it? Are you all right?"

Nancy unbuttoned her dress and let Tammy begin nursing. "I'm fine. Henry and Taima got here and dragged us out of the cabin. I passed out. I wasn't even awake when she was born."

Nancy helped him with her free arm and, moaning loudly, Jake struggled to a sitting position. "You said something about a fire?"

"After Abner beat you, he set fire to the cabin. He wanted both of us dead."

"How bad was the cabin burnt?"

"I'm sorry, Jake. There's nothing left but one wall and the fireplace. Henry managed to save a few of our things, metal cups and so forth, and the big box where we kept our clothes is all right."

"When I get back on my feet, I'm going to go kill Abner."

"My daddy probably has that taken care of. The last time I saw him, he had his rifle and was going to go looking for him."

"Your daddy? Was he here? Did Henry go tell him what happened?"

"No, I went into town and told him."

"You did? How long have I been out of it?"

234

"Three days now."

"You mean to tell me that you rode a horse all the way into town right after having a baby?" Jake was stunned and upset. "Are you crazy?"

"In a way I *was* out of my mind at the time." Nancy swallowed hard. She squeezed Jake's hand. "There were two babies, Jake, a girl and a boy. When you were gone to fetch Taima and Henry that morning, Abner came into the cabin screaming how our baby should have been his. I had already gone into labor and couldn't even get up to try to run away from him. He hit me in the stomach as hard as he could, and it killed our son."

Jake's face lost what little color it had. His hand under Nancy's clenched into a fist. "I hope your daddy didn't kill him yet. I want that pleasure for myself."

"I know how you feel. I really do, but we'll have to wait and see what happened in town. I couldn't stay around to find out. I had to come home right off to take care of Tammy."

"Where did you bury our boy?"

"I took him into town with me. I wanted Daddy to see what Abner had done. That's why I couldn't wait until I was healed to go to Daddy and had to do it right away. I asked my mom to bury him in the cemetery next to Grandma."

Jake leaned forward and moaned. He held out his hand. "Let's see if I can get to my feet."

Nancy took his hand and pulled as Jake struggled to get up. He managed to get on his knees first, put one foot under him, and pushed up until he was standing. "Ah-h-h-hgh! Lord A'mighty. He must have sat on me. I'm hurting all over."

"Maybe you should rest for a few more days. Henry and Taima are taking care of everything here."

Jake shook his head. "If I lay there any more, my muscles will shut down and I won't be any good to anyone. Help me walk a bit. I want to see what's left of our home."

He draped one arm over Nancy's shoulders. Carrying Tammy in one arm, she wrapped the other around his waist, and supporting as much of his weight as she could, led him out of the shed to the clearing. Henry was chopping firewood and Taima was cooking on the campfire. When they saw that Jake was up and about, they left what they were doing and came to greet him.

With a wry smile, Henry patted him on the shoulder. "Good to see you on your feet again, old friend. We thought you'd never wake up and start doing your share of the work."

Jake managed a small smile. "Why should I run around working? You're doing all right. It looks like you have things pretty much under way."

When Nancy walked him to the cabin, Jake groaned and pressed his lips together so tightly they lost their color. He blinked back tears. "I don't think I can stand to go inside and look."

Nancy laid her head on his shoulder. "Henry saved a lot of our things and all of the outbuildings are still good. The wind was blowing in the other direction and the fire didn't touch them at all. We can re-build the cabin. The fireplace is still standing. That will give us a head-start."

Jake held up a hand to stop her. "I don't know, Nancy. My heart isn't in it anymore."

"But what will we do?"

"I'll have to think about that for a while, I guess."

The sound of a horse whinnying drew their attention, and when they looked, a man was riding into the clearing from the trail into town. When he climbed down from his horse and took off his hat, Nancy recognized him. It was Sheriff Barnes of Smithville, and she had known him all her life.

Lean and slightly stoop-shouldered, Barnes had a drooping mustache and skin creased and brown from the sun. His gun belt carried a pair of Colt .45's in dual holsters, and there was a rifle in a saddle holster. He nodded at Nancy first, and then each of the others. "Good morning, Nancy, Jacob, Henry, Taima." The men shook hands and they all murmured their hellos.

The sheriff scuffed the dirt with the toe of his boot as if he were reluctant to explain the reason for his presence. Finally, he squinched up his nose and began. "Your daddy told me what Abner done, but I had to come ask you some questions to make sure I had all the facts of the case. Nancy, tell me what you remember."

Nancy recounted her story, and then the sheriff turned to Jake. "I can see from your face that you got the worst of the fight, and I'm not surprised, given Abner's size. What's your view of it?"

"When it started, I was gone to fetch Taima there to help deliver the baby. I was a few minutes ahead of her and Henry on the trail coming back, and when I got home, I found Abner in the cabin, beating on Nancy and screaming at her. I jumped on his back to try to pull him off her, but he's twice my size. He shook me off like I was a rag doll and jerked me up off the floor with one hand before he doubled up that bucket-sized fist of his and knocked me down flat with his first blow. He started in kicking me and cursing at me. The last thing I remember, was him picking up the kerosene lamp and throwing it at my head. It musta got me a pretty good lick, 'cause I passed out. I didn't come to until just a few minutes ago."

The sheriff looked at Henry. "What can you tell me? Did you see any of this?"

Henry shook his head. "Not really. We rode up just as the blacksmith was riding off toward town. He must have heard us, because he turned and looked back, but then he spurred his horse and took off at a run. The fire was starting to crawl around the overhang and we ran inside. I carried Nancy into the yard, and then I got Jake out. They were both out cold. I knew I didn't have a chance of putting out the fire, so I ran back in the cabin trying to save what I could from their things, but I could only get their trunk because the fire got to be too much for me. The babies were coming fast, so Taima had to tend to that. The first one, the little girl, was fine, started in crying right off, but it was a long time before the second one came. It was just as well Nancy wasn't awake."

The sheriff nodded. "Thank you. I'll be getting back now." He put his foot in the stirrup and swung onto his horse, but before he could leave, Nancy grabbed the horse's bridle.

"Wait, aren't you going to tell me what happened in town after I left? Daddy took his rifle and said he was going to find Abner and kill him. Did he?"

"No, Abner never came back from here. When your father couldn't find him, he came to my office and told me everything you said. I had the boys take turns watching Abner's house and the blacksmith shack until this morning, but he never showed up at either one of those. He probably thinks both of you are dead. No telling where he went. He has kin in Utah. I reckon he ran off there to hide out."

Oh, Lord! Abner is still on the loose! Nancy's throat constricted and she could barely speak. "Is there anything you can do about him?"

Sheriff Barnes shook his head. "Not with him in another state. If he comes back here, I'll throw him in jail, and I reckon to press murder charges against him."

"Murder?"

"Being the outcasts we are in Smithville, we tend to go by Bible law. Even if you and your husband made it through what Abner did to the two of you, he caused your son to die, and it's scriptural. I looked it up before I left just so's I'd know I was in the right of it. In Exodus 21, the Bible gives Jake here the right to say what kind of punishment Abner ought to get. I just figured he would want him dead." He looked to Jake to see his reaction.

Jake took a long, deep breath and winced. "I suppose it's a terrible, un-Christian thing to want someone dead, even if they did try to kill you, but as long as Abner's alive, I'll have to be afraid of him coming back here to kill me and my family. He swore he wouldn't rest until he murdered both of us. I'd just as soon see him hung. If what

240

happens to him depends on my opinion, I'd say the man has given up his right to live."

Sheriff Barnes nodded. "That's what I thought you'd say. It's what I'd say myself, but I hate hangings. I'm afraid I'll have to give Nancy's father the right to string him up."

"I don't have the stomach for it myself," Jake admitted. "Mr. Smith can do it if he's of a mind. Nancy's father wanted that baby as much as we did."

Barnes touched the rim of his hat with one finger. "I'll be saying good day to you then. Keep your rifle close at hand, and if you still have a handgun, I'd wear it."

"I will, Sheriff. Thank you."

They stood silently and watched as the sheriff disappeared down the trail through the woods. Henry broke the stillness by saying, "When you're able to ride, we ought to take what we can of your things and go back to my place. Abner can't possibly know where it is. You ought to be safe there."

Jake nodded. "We will, but we'll only stay for a few days. You said he saw who you were, and he's shod your horses for years, so he probably recognized you. If he has the least idea we might be at your place, he'll find some way to track us down. I won't put your lives in danger to protect myself and Nancy."

The baby in the crook of Nancy's arm was sleeping soundly. Nancy looked down at her beautiful face. "He'll kill all of us, Tammy and little William too, and he wouldn't think another minute after doing it. Jake, do you think you're up to riding today? I'm afraid to stay here any longer than we have to."

"I reckon I can stay on Charlie long enough to get us to Henry's. We'll have to leave our things for now."

Henry said, "Take what's most important to you. If Abner comes back here tonight or in the morning, he'll probably destroy anything you left."

Jake looked at Nancy. "What do you think we ought to take with us?"

"As many of our clothes as we can move in one trip, and the Bible, and your scrapbook."

"Let me rest a minute and we can get started packing up."

Taima shook her head. "I don't know if Nancy should be riding. It's only been a few days since she gave birth."

Nancy said, "I don't really have any choice, do I? I couldn't get any rest here, wondering if Abner was going to jump out from behind a tree and beat me to death and then kill Tammy and Jake."

"All right, then. We'll go slowly."

Jake sat on a big rock and rested while Henry saddled the horses and he and Taima packed the Bible, scrapbook, and the clothes into the saddlebags. When they were finished, Jake said, "We don't have a saddle for Pete. I'll ride him. Nancy, you can ride Charlie."

Taima made a sling for Tammy from a piece of cloth Henry had brought from her place, and Nancy slipped it over her head and placed her daughter in it. They led Charlie to a stump and Henry helped Nancy into the saddle.

Jake stepped up to Pete's side. "You're going to have to give me a boost up," he told Henry.

Henry pointed to the trees. "I'll steady you while you get onto the stump. It'd be easier for you to get on from there than it would be to get a boost all the way."

"Right, right. Okay, let's have a go at it."

Henry stood behind Jake and cupped Jake's elbows in his hands. He bent both knees. "Ready?"

"I'm as ready as I'll ever be."

Henry pushed up on Jake's elbows and lifted him high enough that he could step onto the stump and swing one leg over. He landed with a long, loud groan and huffed out several breaths.

Henry asked, "You all right?"

"Not all right, but I'll survive. Let's get going."

243

With Henry riding bareback on Pete and leading the way, and Taima bringing up the rear, the procession started out. They reached Henry's cabin shortly before dark, where Henry helped Nancy and Jake down from their horses and steadied them until they were inside the cabin. He led Jake to the bed, but Jake protested. "I can't take your bed. We can sleep on a pallet on the floor."

"Not for tonight, you can't. Taima and I can manage. We've been sleeping on the ground on a bedroll for the last few days, and we're fine."

Jake shook his head. "I don't know how I can ever repay you for what all you've done for us. We'd both be goners if you hadn't a drug us out of that cabin when you did."

"You would have done the same for us."

"You're right, I would."

"Then get some rest."

Taima brought a cup of water and handed Jake a small bunch of dried herbs. "Chew on these until they are finely ground, swallow them, and then drink the water. They will ease your aches and help you sleep."

Propping himself up on one elbow, Jake asked, "What are they?"

"Rosemary."

Jake followed Taima's instructions and then lay back on the bed. Henry stacked some blankets in a corner to make a bed for him and Taima, then he told Jake, "I'll ride back to your place in the morning, and if your other things are still unharmed, I'll load as much as I can on Pete and bring it back here."

"There's the tools in the shed, quite a bit of feed, and meat in the smokehouse, my traps and gear are still good. It'll take more than one trip. If I'm able to ride, I'll go with you."

"You won't be riding anywhere in one day. I can take Pete with me. Two pack horses will get it done faster."

"All right, but we'll only be stayin' 'til I'm able to travel."

"We'll talk about that tomorrow."

Nancy and Taima sat on the porch to feed their babies, then settled them side-by-side on a blanket on the floor for the night.

Jake was still awake when Nancy eased into bed next to him. She kissed him lightly on his lips. "I thought you'd be asleep by now."

"I been thinking. We can't stay here. Every minute we're with Henry and Taima, they're in danger just as much as we are. Abner could sneak in here and kill all of us, including Tammy and William."

"What should we do?"

"I know one way to get us out of Abner's reach permanently."

"What is it?"

"We're going home."

"But it's all burned up, and that's the first place Abner would come looking for us."

"No, I'm not talking about our cabin. We're going home to Manhattan."

"Manhattan?"

"Manhattan, Kansas. That's my real home. That's where we'll be safe."

"But we don't have very much money, only what you had in your pocket when Abner came. I know Kansas is too far away to ride the horses. How will we get there?"

"I'll think on it."

Nancy wanted to resist the idea of moving to a different place, to live among people she didn't know, but then she remembered the vows she had taken, vows she selected with no prompting from Jake or anyone else.

Whither thou goest, I will go, and thy people shall be my people, and thy God, my God.

Chapter 22

When Nancy woke in the morning, Jake was sitting at the table writing. She looked over his shoulder. "What's that you're writing?"

"A telegram."

Nancy read aloud what Jake had written on the paper.

To Emma Belk Manhattan Kansas

Coming home with wife baby two horses stop send enough money for train fare to Lucas Smith Smithville Nevada stop Jake

"That's a funny letter. Why do you write the word stop in it?"

"That's the way you do a telegram. It's sent over the wire with a bunch of dots and dashes. They don't have periods and commas and so forth, so you have to tell them to stop wherever a period would go."

"It's kind of short. Maybe you should explain things more."

"They charge by the word, and they charge quite a bit, so I kept it as short as I could." Jake read over what he had written one more time, nodded, and folded the paper in half.

A current of fear ran over Nancy and she bit her lower lip. "What if Abner is still hanging around and he sees you when you go in town to send it?"

"I already thought about that. Just 'cause Sheriff Barnes thinks Abner's in Utah doesn't make it so. Henry is saddlin' up his horse. I'll have him take this in town and send it for me."

"How long will it be before the money gets here?"

"Mom may get the telegram today. If I know her, when she reads it, she'll send the money out right away, so we can leave first thing in the morning. The money transfer will be waiting for us at your dad's house. We can get our things ready to go before we go to sleep tonight. "

"If we're both riding, how are we going to manage our things?"

"All we can take with us is what we need for the trip. It'll have to fit in the saddlebags. We can strap on our bedrolls, some food and a few other supplies."

"We have to take the Bible, and your scrapbook. I won't leave those behind."

Jake nodded. "All right."

"It all seems impossible. Reno is so far away. How do we get there to catch the train?"

"If we take the bus, too many people will know what we're doing. We'll ride. That's the only way. It will probably take us two days after we leave your father's house."

"Will you be able to stay on a horse that long after the beating Abner gave you?"

"I'm not worried about me, I'm worried about you. Are you up to it?"

"I feel strong enough. If I get tired, we can stop and rest along the way. We don't have a choice, do we? If we stay around here, sooner or later, Abner will find us. Even if he's in Utah now, he'll come back to kill us. He meant it when he said he wanted both of us dead and wouldn't stop until he got it done."

Jake stood and wrapped his arms around her. "All right, then. I suppose we'll do what we have to do."

He took the message out to Henry, who was waiting with Taima, and gave him the paper and all the money he had. "After you send the wire, stop by the general store and tell Nancy's father what we're doing, and that we'll be to his place tomorrow. I hope this is enough to pay for the telegram. I don't have any idea what it will cost."

Henry looked at the bills. "I sent a wire to Taima's family last year. This will be more than enough. I'll bring you back your change."

As usual, Henry was wearing his sidearm and had a rifle in the saddle holster. Nancy stood next to Taima, and they watched as Henry mounted his horse, tipped his hat, and trotted off into the woods. Nancy gulped down her fears. "I hope he doesn't run into Abner along the way."

Taima looked into Nancy's eyes and spoke with an air of confidence that calmed Nancy's fears a slight bit. "Don't worry about Henry. No one can sneak up on him. He has lived in the forest all his life and will know if there's anyone around. If Abner shows up, Henry will kill him."

"It's a terrible thing to say, but I hope so."

Henry was home later that day with the good news that his trip had been uneventful. He told Nancy, "Your father will be waiting for you."

Nancy and Jake packed their things that evening. Henry said, "Maybe I should ride to town with you. It never hurts to have an extra gun."

Jake shook his head. "You stay here with your family. I'll be all right. Use anything of mine you can."

Nancy told Taima, "The garden is full of fruit and vegetables, and there's a few apples on the little trees. Don't let them go to waste."

"Thank you. I won't."

After a tearful goodbye and promises from both couples that they would see one another again, Nancy and Jake set out the next morning as soon as it was light enough to see the trail. Jake led the way down the narrow path. Nancy followed, with Tammy sleeping peacefully in her sling, her little copper-colored head propped on Nancy's breast. They moved slowly. Jake groaned from time to time and often stopped Charlie and rested in the saddle a few minutes before moving on.

When they came to the clearing where the fireplace and one wall was all that was left of their former home, Nancy couldn't hold back the tears. She sobbed as she rode by, looking back over her shoulder as long as she could, remembering the day she first came there. *I was so happy here, so happy, and now I'm going to a strange place with people I don't know.*

Normally only a two hour trip, it was late in the afternoon and the sun was setting before they reached Smithville. Hoping they could reach Nancy's home without being noticed, Jake slowed outside of town, and instead of riding down the street, steered Charlie around to the rear of the buildings where they rode along the tree line to the Smith house on the edge of town.

They came to the back of the house and stopped. Jake helped her down. He held one hand over Charlie's muzzle to keep him from whinnying, and in a low voice said, "You go on in to your mother. I'll put the horses in the barn."

Nancy went in the kitchen door and found her mother cooking. Rebecca looked up and clapped her hands together. "Oh, my grandbaby is here at last!" She gave Nancy a peck on the cheek and took possession of Tammy. "Look at that hair!

There's no doubting who her daddy is!" She swayed back and forth, cradling the baby in her arms. "Did you have any trouble on the way here?"

Nancy sank onto a kitchen chair. "No. I'm a little tired is all."

"Well, no wonder. Look at what you went through, and it's only a few days since you had your babies. Where's Jake?"

"Bedding down the horses. He'll be here in a minute. We rode in the back way in case Abner was watching."

"Haven't seen hide nor hair of him. If he shows up, your father will shoot him on the spot."

"Is daddy at the store?"

"Where else? He thought it best to act as if everything was normal. It's just as well you stay out of sight. No matter what the sheriff says, Abner had kin in this town who would think he was in the right, doing what he did."

"Would you send one of the boys to the store to see if the money for our trip has come in?"

"I already thought of that. James is going to be there all day. He'll run home and let us know when it shows up. Meanwhile, I get to love on this beautiful, little copper-haired sweetheart. Tell me all about her."

"She sleeps most all the time, except when she gets hungry. Then she screams like a banshee until I feed her."

252

"What did you name her?"

"She's Linda Taima Belk."

"Linda for your sister?"

"Yes, and Taima for my Paiute friend who saved my life and delivered her and her brother. It means Thunder, because she can yell so loud when she wants something. I call her Tammy for short."

"That seems fitting."

"Mom, tell me about little Lucas's getting buried."

"We did it like you asked. The bishop read over him and we put him next to your grandma."

With the back of one hand, Nancy wiped tears from her cheeks. "I wish I could go visit his grave while I'm here, but I'm afraid to go out of the house. We're afraid to let anyone outside of the family know we're here."

"Your brother's been sworn to secrecy. It seemed to me the less said, the safer you'd be. I told him if he let on to anyone, even your sisters and brothers, your daddy would tan his hide good."

"What about Linda? How is she?"

Rebecca patted Nancy's shoulder. "She's so happy Abner is gone she could dance and sing. She's hoping he'll never come back."

"So am I. Did you tell her I'd be here?"

"Not yet. I didn't know if I should."

"I want her to see her namesake before we have to leave."

253

"I'll send for her in the morning and tell her I need to see her right away."

Jake came in and stopped at the door. He clutched the frame. His face was gray and he was breathing raggedly. "I think I need to lay down for a bit."

When Rebecca saw Jake's beaten and bruised face, she gasped. "I heard he beat you about to death, but I didn't know it was so bad."

"I'll take him to my room," Nancy said. She wrapped her arm around Jake and walked him slowly down the hall to the bedroom where she grew up. He looked around and smiled weakly at her. "This sure is fancy looking, what with a four poster bed and all."

"It isn't nearly as beautiful as our cabin was." She helped him to the bed and pulled back the covers. He almost collapsed onto the mattress. She pulled off his boots and socks, and then his jeans, and put the blanket over him. "Do you want something to eat, or a glass of water or anything?"

"Not right now. I think I'll just rest a bit." He closed his eyes and Nancy could see his muscles go limp. She watched him until he was breathing evenly, and then crept out of the room, closing the door softly behind her.

Holding her new granddaughter on her lap, Rebecca cooed and fussed over her as she and Nancy sat in the kitchen and talked. Nancy told her mother as much about Jake and the cabin as she dared, omitting the part about the baths, and stressed how happy she was and what a good man Jake was.

They talked until Nancy's father came home. He entered the kitchen door and propped the rifle he was carrying against the frame. "I didn't close the store until the regular time so no one would think there was anything unusual going on, but it was all I could do not to run home early and see my granddaughter." He took the sleeping baby from Rebecca and held her tenderly in the crook of his arm. "Lord Almighty, look at that hair. She sure is her daddy's girl."

"That's what Momma said."

Rebecca clapped her hands over her mouth. "I got so busy hearing Nancy's story I forgot all about dinner. Lucas, you get acquainted with that little granddaughter while I get a meal ready."

Lucas sat holding Tammy while Nancy repeated the stories she had just told her mother. This time she told her father the truth, that Jake had slept in the shed until after they had their ceremony.

He shook his head. "I suppose I ought to be disappointed with you for telling me a lie, but after what Abner did, I'm glad you didn't wind up with him. Lord willing, we'll never see his sorry soul around here again."

"Daddy, did the money for our train fare come today?"

"No, darling, it didn't. It'll probably show up tomorrow. Don't you worry about it, if it doesn't come first thing in the morning, I can give it to you."

Nancy heard the sound of Jake groaning and went to check on him. He had thrown off the covers, pulled his shirt off and tossed it in a corner, and was covered with sweat. Like his face, his torso was a mass of bruises, now turning a ghastly shade of yellow and purple. She sat next to him on the bed and put her hand on his forehead. It was burning hot, the way her little brother's was once when he had Scarlet Fever. She rushed back to her mother.

"Momma, Jake is burning up with fever. What should I do?"

Rebecca went to the cupboard, poked around a little, and took out a bottle of aspirin. "This is all I have in the house that might help. Give him two of these, and see if you can get him to eat a piece of bread and drink a glass of water to help them get where he needs them to be."

Nancy took her mother's prescription with her and sat down next to Jake. "Jake, wake up!" He didn't respond. She wanted to shake his shoulder, but it was as bruised as the rest of his body so she grabbed his ankle and shook it. "Jake?"

He opened his eyes a slit. She held out the aspirin. "Momma said you should take these and eat this bread and drink the water. It'll help with the pain."

Jake tried to sit up, but fell back. Nancy slid her arm under him and held him up enough that he could swallow the pills. He ate a few bites of the bread, and then she held the glass to his lips until he had swallowed almost all of it. He took a deep breath, winced, and said, "I didn't know I was so thirsty."

She laid him gently back on the pillow and he immediately fell asleep. She went to the kitchen where her mother was bustling about preparing dinner and her father was talking to Tammy. Lucas looked up at Nancy. "How is he?"

"Not good. He took the aspirin and drank the water and went right back to sleep."

"Sleep's the best thing for him. He'll be better in the morning."

Nancy began crying. "What if he isn't better? We can't take off for Kansas with him in this condition."

Lucas patted her on the arm. "Then you can stay here until he's able to travel. You could probably use some rest yourself."

"What if Abner shows up?"

257

Lucas's mouth twisted. "If he shows his face around here, I'll blow it clean off his head. I've been carrying that rifle with me everywhere I go since this started."

"You may not see him coming. He's sneaky."

"It's hard for a man that size to sneak up on anyone. Besides, he's probably gone to Utah and won't ever come back."

"Then why are you carrying a rifle with you?"

"Just in case, Nancy mine, just in case."

That evening, Nancy made a sleeping place for Tammy in an empty dresser drawer and slid into bed next to Jake, being careful not to wake him. She was somewhat comforted to lie next to him and hear his deep, regular breathing. His fever seemed to have gone down a bit. *I'll have to ask Momma if I can take that bottle of aspirin with me when we leave.*

When Tammy's demands to be fed woke Nancy in the morning, Jake was sleeping soundly. She pressed her palm against his forehead and was relieved to find that the fever had broken. She lifted Tammy from her drawer, went to the kitchen, and gave her breast to the baby. Her mother was already making breakfast. She turned and waved a spatula at Nancy. "How's Jake?"

"He's still sleeping. I thought it best to leave him be."

"You're right. He needs as much rest as he can get before you try to make that trip. Can't you change your mind and stay here?"

"We won't be safe here, Momma."

"You have the law on your side, and your daddy can protect you."

"I don't think anyone could protect us if Abner came back. He wouldn't care if it cost him his own life doing it. He's determined to kill all of us. I think he'd even murder you and Daddy, too, for helping us. We have to go."

"I just don't want you to leave."

Nancy sighed. "It's not only Abner, Momma, it's the other thing."

"What other thing?"

"Sooner or later, the other men in town would be after Jake to take another wife. I couldn't stand it, knowing he was with someone else. I might be moved to do murder. I'm afraid I'd kill Jake or whoever he married, or maybe even myself."

"Nancy! Don't talk like that. The Lord is like to strike you dead."

"I know it, Momma. I don't really mean it, but that's how strong I feel. I grew up watching your face when Daddy went off to spend the night with one of his other wives. I could see how it hurt you. I don't want to live like that."

Rebecca sat across from Nancy and took her hand. "You're right. I'm a very fortunate woman in some ways. I love your daddy, and he was always good to me. He didn't take any more wives after me, but it still hurt to think of him in another woman's bed, even if she may have had more right to him than I did, since she came before me. You go on to Kansas then. Be happy."

"I will, Momma. I'll be happy wherever Jake and Tammy are."

"Good. Let Jake get his rest before you leave, and you, too. I want you to promise me you'll come home to see me again when you're able."

"I promise. I hope to bring Daddy that grandson someday."

"That would make him very happy. I don't know when I'll see you again, but you can write me at least once a month, can't you?"

"I will, I promise."

Rebecca began setting the table, placing six plates on it.

"Six plates?"

"I sent Matthew to fetch Linda, but he's not to tell her you're here. I wanted it to be a surprise for her."

"I hope she'll be happy to see me."

"Good Lord, child! Why wouldn't she be happy to see her sister after you being gone for almost a year?"

"I've been thinking about her, Momma. I'm glad for her that she doesn't have to put up with Abner anymore, but what's going to happen to her now?"

Rebecca talked as she worked. "We talked about that. She's going to move back here. There's no need for her to stay in Abner's house with him gone."

"How long does he have to be away before she can marry again?"

"I doubt that anyone will ask. Her not having children makes her unattractive to men."

"She's a very pretty girl. I want her to find a man like Jake, a man who will love her for who she is. That isn't going to happen around here. Besides, if Abner does come back, he's likely to kill her simply because she's my sister and he hated her anyway, even before all this started. She can't stay here."

"What else can she do, Nancy?"

"She can come with us to Kansas."

"Have you talked to Jake about this?"

"No. The idea just now came to me. I'm going to go ask him about it."

"Well, I'm pretty sure Linda would jump at the chance to get away from here, and as much as I hate to see my girls go to a place so far away, it'd be the best thing for her. Don't bring it up to her until you know how Jake feels. He may not like the idea."

"You're right," Nancy said, handing the baby to her mother. "I'll go see if he's awake and ask him right now."

When Nancy went to her room, Jake was sitting up in bed. She sat next to him and leaned over to kiss his forehead, letting her lips linger. He chuckled. "You taking my temperature?"

"Yes, how did you know?"

"That's the way my mom used to do it when I was sick."

"How do you feel?"

"I just now woke up. How long have I been sleeping?"

"About fifteen hours."

His jaw dropped. "Fifteen hours! Good grief. I never slept that long at one time in my life."

"Momma is putting breakfast on the table. Do you feel like eating?"

"I could eat a cow."

She took his hand. "Good, but there's something I want to talk to you about first."

He frowned at her. "Oh, oh."

"Why, oh, oh?"

"You look pretty serious."

"It is serious. I wanted to ask you if Linda can go to Kansas with us."

He thought a moment. "What? Well,--yes. I don't think my mom and dad would mind a bit. I was afraid you were going to tell me you changed your mind and didn't want to go with me."

"I'll go anywhere you go. Remember what I said at our wedding?"

"I remember." He leaned forward and rested his arms on her shoulders. "Let's see if I can get to my feet without falling over."

She helped him to a standing position, and he took a few steps away from her. He turned and grinned at her. "I feel pretty good. Let's go see about that breakfast."

"Jake?"

"What?"

"Are you sure about taking Linda with us?"

"I'm sure. I know how much you love her, and I wouldn't want to leave anyone you loved here where Abner could come back and get his hands on her."

She threw her arms around his waist and hugged him. He flinched. "Ow! Stop that. I'm still sore there."

She let go of him. "Oh, I'm sorry. I was so happy I forgot. Get dressed and come get something to eat."

When Nancy went back to the kitchen, Linda was sitting at the table holding her niece in her arms. The two sisters hugged with the baby between them. Linda said, "She's beautiful, and look at that hair!" She twirled one of Tammy's auburn locks around her finger. "Momma said she gets it from her daddy."

"That's right. He tells me everyone in his father's family has hair that color."

Linda peered at Nancy. "Momma's told me everything that happened. How are you feeling? I was afraid you were trying to do too much so soon after the baby came, riding back and forth to town like this."

"I was only doing what had to be done. I needed to bring little Lucas here to show him to daddy like I promised. I couldn't wait. Then, when Jake woke up after three days, he said we had to go somewhere Abner couldn't find us."

Linda got a faraway look in her eyes and said, "I envy you. I wish I could go someplace where he could never see me again."

Nancy squeezed her sister's hand. "You can, Linda. Jake said you could go to Kansas with us."

Linda's face lit up. "Did he? Really?" She looked at her mother and her face fell. "But I'd have to leave Momma and Daddy."

Rebecca placed a platter full of biscuits on the table. "Go with Nancy and Jake, Linda.

There's nothing for you if you stay here but more heartache."

Linda thought a moment, then nodded. "You're right."

Jake came walking into the kitchen and Linda gasped, then laughed. "I know who you are—you're little Linda's father."

"Guilty as charged."

Nancy went to Jake and put her arm around his waist. "Jake, this is my sister, Linda. She's going to Kansas with us.

Linda's face became doubtful. "That is, if you really don't mind."

"I don't mind at all. My mom and dad's place has plenty of room, and you'll be away from Abner."

"It sounds like heaven to me."

Jake nodded. "All right, then. We'll be going to Reno on horseback to catch the train, so you won't be able to take much with you. You'll need a sleeping roll and a few changes of clothes."

Linda frowned and her face clouded up. "I don't have a horse." She looked about to cry.

Rebecca put a plate on the table and said, "You can ride one of Abner's horses, and I'll have one of your older brothers go with you. After you get there, he can lead the second animal home."

Linda immediately perked up. "That would work. I haven't ridden in a long time, but the road is in pretty good shape. I should be able to stay on a horse that long."

Rebecca said, "Have a seat, Jake. You look hungry."

Jake sat next to Nancy. "I am hungry, and whatever you're cooking there sure smells good."

Nancy asked, "Where's Daddy?"

Rebecca dropped her head, but not before Nancy saw the sadness on her face. "He spent the night at Elizabeth's house. Said he'd promised her, and he had to go, or she'd be all torn up about it. He'll go to the store from there. He said he'd let us know first thing if the money for your train fare came in today."

Nancy shot Jake a meaningful look. He cleared his throat and reached for a biscuit. "I do believe these are the lightest biscuits I ever saw."

Linda ate breakfast with them and then said, "I'll go pack my clothes. When are we going to leave?"

"After the money comes from my mom, we ought to sneak out of town at first light. I was hoping it would be here yesterday, but it ought to show up today, for sure. If it does, we can leave in the morning. I figure traveling with a baby, and with me all beat up like I am, it'll take two days riding, maybe three, to get to Reno. Then we catch the Western Pacific into Denver and switch to the

Union Pacific, and that will take us right into my home town. I sure will be happy to see it again."

The wire transfer arrived that afternoon with a telegram saying:

Emma Belk Manhattan Kansas,

To Lucas Smith Smithville Nevada

Am sending enough for you to take a compartment so you can rest stop can't wait to see you stop

Mom

Jake's mother, Emma Belk, had been more than generous. Cash would be the least of their worries. Lucas gave Linda a wad of bills as well. With the money they needed in hand, they began planning the last-minute details for their trip. Everyone went to bed early, intending to get plenty of rest, but Nancy had trouble sleeping that night. Abner's image never left her mind, and every creak and crack of the house jarred her.

It seemed she had barely fallen into a deep sleep before Jake was shaking her shoulder. "Time to get ready to go," he whispered to her. Nancy dressed quickly and pulled back the curtains to see that there was no sign of sunlight. Tammy was still sleeping when she lifted her out of her drawer and nestled her into the sling.

Her sister, Linda, was waiting in the kitchen with the rest of the family and one of Nancy's unmarried older half-brothers, Elizabeth's son,

Ethan. She greeted him with a quick hug and showed off the sleeping baby before she sat down.

"I know where she got that hair," Ethan said.

"Everyone who sees the two of them says that. Did you and Jake have time to get acquainted?" Nancy asked.

"Yep, a little. We talked a bit whilst we saddled up. I like him."

Nancy grinned. "So do I. We've been trying to keep all this a secret so Abner wouldn't find out we were here. Did Daddy tell you what we're going to do?"

"Not 'til this morning. All he told me last night was that I was to show up here before dawn, saddled up and ready for a four or five day trip."

"I'm surprised you didn't try to get it out of him."

"You know how he is," Ethan grinned. "It doesn't matter how old we get, we have to do as we're told. He explained it all to me this morning. I'm sorry it's come to this, where you have to leave your home to be safe from Abner, but I'm proud to help you out."

They had a quick breakfast and everyone assembled in the yard. Seven horses in all were saddled or bearing packs. Jake and Ethan were wearing their side arms, and all of the saddles had a rifle in the holster. Nancy's parents were waiting for them to say goodbye. Nancy looked to her father, who stood with a rifle slung in the crook of his right arm. "How did we get seven horses?"

"One for you, one for Jake, Ethan, and Linda, and three to carry your clothes and things."

"Where did you find all these horses?

"Charlie and Pete, and then, one's mine, one's Ethan's, and three of them are Linda's."

"Linda's? She doesn't have any horses."

"They're from the livery stable. She's still Abner's wife. If they belong to him, they belong to her."

"If he comes back, he'll say she stole them."

"Unless he's here right now, he'll never know the difference. When Ethan leaves you at the train station, he's bringing them back home with him. Not that it matters. If Abner comes back here, I'll kill him."

"No, Daddy, as much as I want him to be where he can't hurt anyone, I don't want you to go to jail."

"I wouldn't go to jail over it. The sheriff gave Jake here the right to say what happened to him, and Jake told him he wanted him dead. Since Jake will be out of town, I'd be acting in his stead. I already talked it over with the sheriff, and we have an understanding."

"Is that legal?"

Her father hugged her and kissed her on the forehead. "Lots of things are legal in Smithville

269

that may not be legal somewhere else. The sheriff would probably rather me be the one that faces Abner down. You best be getting up on that horse and on down the road before daylight comes and everyone can see you."

Lucas shook Jake's hand and patted his saddlebag. "I put extra ammunition in here and in Ethan's bags, too. I'll be praying for all of you."

There were hugs and kisses all around, with Nancy and Linda clinging to their mother and making no effort to hide their tears. The sun was taking the black out of the sky, and a rooster crowed. Finally, Lucas said, "That's enough now. You have to be going."

Nancy and Linda were boosted into the saddles, and Nancy was relieved to see Jake manage to mount his horse without assistance. As they rode away, Nancy turned to see her mother sobbing in her father's arms.

Nancy was going away from the only home she ever knew, leaving for a new life with strangers in a strange place.

They rode slowly down the road through town, trying to be quiet and not draw attention to the caravan. Jake and Ethan kept one hand on their guns all the way, and whenever there was an unexpected sound, drew them from the holsters. As they passed the cemetery, Nancy stopped Pete and called softly, "Jake."

He reined in Charlie. "What?"

"I can't leave without saying goodbye to little Lucas."

He nodded, and Nancy turned Pete in the direction of her grandmother's grave. When she found the right place, Jake helped her down and they stood in front of the tiny, unmarked grave. She leaned against him and sobbed. He held her for a few moments and wiped tears from his own cheeks before he said, "It's getting light, Nancy. We have to go."

She nodded. As they walked away, she told him, "Momma said Daddy ordered a proper headstone, but it won't be ready for a few more days."

"Good."

He boosted her back into the saddle and they resumed their quiet journey, the only sounds the clopping of the horses' hooves, Nancy's crying, and the crowing of town roosters. When they were farther out in the countryside, Nancy breathed a sigh of relief. She was aware, as her father had reminded her, that there were still some men in town who sympathized with Abner. Soon, she would be out of his reach and could live her life in peace.

Chapter 23

The trip to Reno took longer than the two days Jake planned. Both he and Nancy needed to rest along the way. Ethan knew the trail well and was aware of where they could find water, so they camped alongside streams, giving the horses places to graze and getting water to refill their canteens.

Still bleeding from childbirth, each night, Nancy and Linda would go downstream a bit from the campsite so Nancy could bathe and change her clothes. She tried to hide her exhaustion from Jake, and she had a suspicion he was doing the same for her, but neither of them spoke of it.

On the afternoon of the fourth day, they finally reached Reno. Nancy's hometown was much smaller in comparison. Smithville was a growing town with several two-story businesses and more and more homes, but it was a fraction of the size of Reno. Nancy was awed by so many tall buildings and the paved streets bustling with people. A trolley went by, and Nancy said, "That train is so small. It doesn't look like the pictures I've seen at all."

Jake smiled and said, "That's a trolley. It takes people around the city. The train will be way bigger."

Ethan had visited the city often and knew the way to the railroad station. The horses were tied at the front of the building, and bedrolls, extra gear, and saddles they wouldn't need any more were transferred to Abner's horses, leaving only their clothes and Charlie's tack to take with them on the train.

Inside the station, Jake bought their tickets and came back out with information on where to take the horses for loading. As luck would have it, a train was leaving for Denver in only two hours.

Nancy was awed by the size of the locomotive. As they walked along the side of the train, she noticed there were two engines at the front. She tugged at Jake's arm. "Why does it have two of those?"

He pointed at the crests of the Sierras in the distance. "It needs the extra power to make it over the mountains."

She watched as Jake loaded Charlie and Pete into the cattle car. Pete was skittish, so Jake gave his rein to Ethan and led Charlie, who had been on trains before and wasn't afraid, up the ramp first. Pete then followed without complaint. Jake tied them to a rail inside the car and then told Nancy, "I'll go back in a bit and bed them down."

Nancy and Linda hugged their brother goodbye. Jake shook Ethan's hand and told him, "I sure do appreciate you doing this for us. Come visit us sometime."

"I will. I always did want to see other parts of the country. I may be able to find myself a wife there. Where I live, all the women my age are already married."

"You do that, Ethan." Jake encouraged. "My mom will give you a job on the ranch. We grow some awful pretty girls in that part of Kansas. A handsome, healthy young man like you wouldn't have any trouble finding one to marry, but you'd have to settle for only one."

"I could do that. It sounds encouraging. I may show up on your doorstep right soon."

"You'll be welcome."

As the conductor called "All aboard," there were more goodbye hugs and tears from the women, until finally they boarded the train. A porter showed them where the ladies' room was, led them to their compartment, and explained how one bed pulled down from the wall. When they were settled in, Jake said, "I hope the crying part of this trip is over for a while. Can't stand to see a woman cry."

Nancy laughed. "You may as well get used to it. Your mother hasn't seen you in over three years. Unless I'm wrong, there'll be some crying when we reach your home."

Jake ran his hands through his hair. "Maybe this isn't such a good idea. I'll be going from living alone, where the only crying going on was the wolves at night, to living with a whole passel of women where there's likely to be one wailing about something just about every day."

Nancy asked, "How many women do you expect to be there?"

"There's the two of you, and my sister Shelby, our housekeeper, Brenda, and Mom, and the five of you'll be together all the time. Then, there'll be the neighbors, they're coming and going most every day, and the women at church. They're going to make a big fuss over you and the baby. Dad and I may have to go hide somewhere 'til the worst part of it's over."

"You may as well get used to it, since we expect most of it to be happy tears."

Jake exaggerated a shiver. "I'll do my best."

The train started moving, and Nancy and Linda watched from the window, o-o-h-ing and a-a-h-ing as it picked up speed. While Jake went to look after the horses, Nancy fed Tammy, then she and Linda watched the spectacular mountain scenery for a while. Jake came back and everyone grew hungry at the same time. "It's getting late." Jake said. "Let's go to the dining car and get us some dinner."

They were soon seated at a table with a pristine white tablecloth, dishes so thin they could almost see through them, and more knives, forks, and spoons than Nancy had ever seen on a table. She wanted to express her excitement over the dining car, the menu, and the sharply dressed waiters, but forced herself to act as though she knew what to do and how to behave. Her menu and Linda's had no prices on it. They told Jake what they wanted and Jake gave their order to the waiter. Each time the waiter walked away from the table, Nancy quietly asked Jake to explain things to her, and Linda would lean close to hear the answers.

When the bill came, Nancy asked, "Is it terrible?"

He nodded. "Yes, but Mom sent us enough money that we don't have to worry 'bout it."

"I feel awful, costing her so much."

Jake chuckled. "Nancy, darlin', we don't ever have to worry over money again."

"What do you mean?"

"My family isn't Wall Street millionaires, like my great-grandfather was before the stock market crashed back in '69, but both my mom and dad do well at their work. They're what you could call, right comfortable."

"I only now realized that you never talked about what they do for a living. I've had such a hard time getting information out of you about yourself, I didn't even ask. You talk like your mother works at a job somewhere. What do they do?"

"Don't you remember how I said my mother loves horses?"

"Yes, but a lot of people love horses."

"Did you ever notice what a fine piece of horseflesh Charlie is?"

"I'm afraid I wouldn't know what makes up a 'fine piece of horseflesh,' but he is prettier than an average horse."

"He's a registered Quarter Horse. My mother is a breeder, one of the first ones in the country. She delivered Charlie when he was born and raised and trained him herself. She gave him to me and Lucy as a wedding present when we were married. He was only three years old."

"She breeds horses? Is there a lot of money in that?"

"Not enough to make us filthy rich," Jake grinned, "but yes, on a good year she can make a right smart piece of money."

"And your father?"

"He's a lawyer. He has a pretty good-sized practice in town."

Nancy fell back against the seat. "I'm glad I didn't know this when I was worrying over asking you to make me a second chair, or I'd have wanted all sort of things. If you had told me your family was rich, you might have thought I was marrying you for your money. Why were you living as if you didn't have a penny to your name?"

"Cause I didn't have a penny to *my* name. That's my folks' money, and they're not what most people would call rich, but what I said was, we don't have to worry about money. I was living poor because when I ran away from Kansas and Vanessa, I had my mustering out pay from the Cavalry. It was enough to get me settled. After that, I put out traps and made what I needed to live on. I didn't need to ask Mom and Dad to support me."

Linda spoke up, asking, "Who's Vanessa?"

"It's a long story," Nancy said. "I'll tell you tomorrow."

When they returned to their compartment, the beds had been turned down. Seeing the crisp, white sheets, the energy drained out of them in one rush. Almost as soon as they lay down, they were rocked to sleep by the train's movement. Even Tammy slept through the night.

During the next few days, Nancy told her sister everything she could remember about Jake, his two wives, and the war. From their compartment window, she and Linda watched the western part of the United States pass by. Mountain ranges were conquered by the straining engines, flat grasslands rolled effortlessly by, and then more mountains challenged the coal-driven locomotives. Once they crossed the border of Colorado and were in Kansas, the American prairie lay before them. Seemingly endless acre after acre of wheat and corn bordered the railroad tracks.

They were having lunch in the dining car when Linda pointed out the window and said, "Look at that! The whole place looks as if it's been pressed by a giant flatiron!"

Nancy wasn't so impressed. "There are hardly any trees. I don't know if I'm going to like this place."

Jake patted her hand. "Wait until you see Manhattan. It's where the rivers come together and there's plenty of hills and trees. It's about the prettiest part of the country--to me, anyway."

Linda asked, "If it's so nice, why did you leave?"

Nancy made a move to shush her, but Jake held up a palm. "It's all right. After the war, I wasn't happy inside myself. I had to go somewhere and find peace."

Linda hooted as if to make a joke. "Instead you found Nancy."

Jake looked into Nancy's eyes. "Yes, I did, and that's when I found my life again."

Linda took in a sharp breath. "I hope someone feels that way about me someday."

Nancy pressed her hand. "Someone will. I've been praying about it, that somewhere out there in Kansas is a man who will love you and appreciate you and treat you the way you deserve."

Linda's eyes glistened. "Oh, I hope so! I hope so."

Nancy pursed her lips and poked Jake in the side with her elbow. "Maybe Jake can even help find a wife for Ethan."

Linda clapped her hand over her mouth. "What about Abner? Am I married to him or not?"

Jake asked, "Were you his first wife?"

"No, I was his third."

"Then in Kansas, you're not legally married to him."

Nancy felt a panic surging up in her heart. "What about us? We didn't have a preacher or a license or anything."

Jake whistled low. "I don't know. I'll have Dad look into it. He'll know what to do, and how to do it. My dad knows all about legal stuff."

Chapter 24

As they passed through Abilene, the women commented on the hundreds of cattle pens along the tracks. There was a short layover, and then the train started up again. Late in the afternoon, it came to a tall hill and chugged over the top. As it rolled down the other side, the whistle blew, loud and long. More trees than they had seen for over a day dotted the landscape.

"This is it," Jake said, his excitement showing in his voice. "This is Manhattan."

Nancy and Linda pressed against the glass, looking back and forth and commenting on the greenery and the clusters of trees. Jake leaned over them, looking at his home town. When he spoke, his voice was ragged with emotion. "I 'spect Mom will have given up waiting on us. I should have had Ethan send her a wire telling her when we'd be here. We'll probably have to hire a wagon to take us to the ranch."

Nancy said, "Hire a wagon? We don't have much to carry, and we have the two horses. Couldn't we ride? How far is it?"

"It's about five miles. We only have the one saddle now. I suppose you girls could ride double on Charlie, throw me over the luggage on Pete's back, and tie me on like a load of hay. Course, I wouldn't be able to see very far, but Charlie would remember the way home."

Nancy rolled her eyes and then tsk'ed in mock disdain. "Silly. I could ride Charlie and Linda could ride Pete, and you could either carry our things and walk, or wait until we sent Charlie back to get you."

Linda looked from one to the other. "You two are crazy. Did you know that?"

"Maybe we are," Nancy said, "but I'll tell you one thing, I feel like I've been set free. We're safe in Manhattan. Abner will never find us. We can be happy here and live out our lives knowing that he's part of the past."

Linda drew her eyebrows together in a frown. "I hope so, Nancy. I hope so."

The brakes squealed loudly, and the train slowed to a stop in front of the station. *Manhattan* was printed on a large sign over the door of the ticket office. They gathered their things and joined the queue of people waiting in the corridor to disembark. Jake went down the steps and held out a hand to help first Nancy, and then Linda.

Once on the platform, he looked over the top of Nancy's head, and his face lit up with delight. Nancy turned to see what brought such a smile and saw a slender woman in buckskin pants and shirt running at them with her arms outstretched.

Nancy had never seen a woman wearing trousers. When the woman reached them, Jake grabbed her and swung her up in the air, whirling her around in a full circle before he set her back down. Tears ran down her face and she was sobbing.

"Oh, you're home! You're finally home," she yelled. People turned to stare at her, but she either didn't notice them or didn't care.

She looked to be in her forties, with an oval face, deeply tanned skin that crinkled around blue eyes, and short, bobbed, dark brown hair that was threaded with gray at the temples. Her springy curls were sticking out from her head like Medusa's snakes. Jake put her back on her feet, and she pointed to the sleeping Tammy. "Is this a girl or a boy?" she asked, still shouting.

Nancy was dumbstruck, so Jake answered. "It's a girl. Her name is Tammy."

The woman held out her arms and commanded, "Give her to me! Give her to me!"

Nancy looked at Jake for guidance, and he nodded. Nancy lifted Tammy from her sling and handed her over. The woman took her, and without comment, turned and walked away, making cooing sounds like a nesting dove. Nancy stood there with her mouth open, speechless.

Jake chuckled. "That was my mother," he said, which explained it all.

Chapter 25

Jake picked up their bags and he, Nancy, and Linda followed his mother to a line of waiting automobiles, a few buggies, and one farm wagon. Jake greeted the speckled gray horse that stood harnessed to the wagon. "Hey, Concrete, how ya doing?" The horse seemed to recognize Jake and tossed its head and whinnied.

Jake heaved their belongings in the back of the wagon. "I'll go get Charlie and Pete. You all might as well go on ahead. I'll catch up."

He walked away, leaving Nancy standing next to his mother, her stomach in a knot. Jake's mother looked from Nancy to Linda and back. "Sisters, I see. Which one of you is my new daughter-in-law?"

Nancy timidly raised her hand like a sixth-grader. "I am."

"What's your name?"

"I'm Nancy, and this is Linda."

"Call me Emma." She threw one arm around Nancy's shoulders and pressed a kiss on her cheek that ended with a loud smack. "I can't tell you how much I'm going to love you. You brought my boy back to me when I didn't think I'd ever see him again, and you brought me this precious little girl when I didn't think I'd ever have another grandchild. I hope you'll come to love me right back. I'm afraid I'm a little eccentric, and you may have to take some time getting used to me."

The knot in Nancy's stomach loosened, and she smiled at Emma. "We both love Jake, so I'm sure we can love one another."

"Now, I don't know if I can let loose of little Tammy long enough to get us home. Can you drive a buggy?"

"I never did before, but I'll try if you want me to."

Emma sighed. "No, I better do it. Most everyone is driving automobiles these days, and Old Concrete here gets a little spooked if someone blows a horn."

At the sound of his name, the horse turned to look at them and whinnied loudly. Emma laughed and said to him, "Don't complain. You know it's the truth. Every time someone blows a horn, you act like you never saw a Buick before." She flapped her hand in the air. "You two go on and get up there, and I'll hand Tammy to you."

Nancy and Linda climbed on the wagon. Emma handed the baby to Nancy and then climbed up next to her. She picked up the reins, propped one foot on the wagon frame in front of her, and clucked to the horse. It started off at a walk.

Emma talked at a rapid fire pace as she drove. "We'll ride right through town along Poyntz

Avenue on the way to our place. We live about five miles to the southeast, down by Deep Creek." She went on and on, pointing out places of interest. There was the court house, the library, and various schools and important buildings.

Most of them were built from the same yellow stone, and Nancy asked, "What kind of rock are these buildings?"

"That's limestone. There's a quarry not far from here. Limestone is easy to work with and lasts for a long time. Once you get settled, Jake can take the buggy and show you the sights. My favorite place is Pillsbury Crossing. There's a waterfall and a lot of family history tied to it. I'll tell you more about that later. The country around here is beautiful."

"It really is," Nancy agreed. "Jake told me how pretty it is, but I was still surprised after riding all the way across the state. I was so glad to see the hills and trees again."

"Now, it's going to take us a while to get home, so I'm going to shut up and let you tell me all about yourself and your pretty sister there. I want to know where you came from and how you met Jake, how you fell in love, and how…" Emma stopped herself. "I said I was going to shut up, didn't I? You talk."

Nancy was surprised that she felt so comfortable telling her story to this strange, warm woman. She began with her childhood, described the town of renegade Mormons where she grew up, and finally reached the point where Linda was pushed into marrying Abner after Nancy refused him, even though he already had two wives. Then it was Linda's turn to answer Emma's questions, and she spoke even more freely than Nancy had. She told Emma what it was like being married to Abner when she was barely fourteen, the beatings, and the tortured sexual relations.

As she listened, Emma's face tightened and she shook her head. "I don't want to criticize, and maybe I shouldn't say anything against your father, but I don't understand him. How could he make you marry someone like that?"

Nancy said, "We love our daddy, but it's the religion. He was raised to it, just like we were. He honestly thought he was doing God's will."

Emma smiled and nodded. "I suppose I can understand how you do things for your religion you wouldn't ordinarily do. We Baptists probably have some things that seem strange to other people, too. Let's talk about something happier. How did you come to meet Jake?"

Nancy related the story about her running away from home and finding the cabin, how Jake let her stay, and how her father eventually found her and wanted to take her home, but gave his blessing to the two of them.

Emma said, "That changes my mind about your father. It seems he thought your happiness was more important than what his plans for you were."

"He did, but Abner wasn't going to go along with it. He's been trying to kill us ever since."

Emma's face blanched. "Kill you?"

"I don't want to upset you by telling you what happened after we married, but if you're going to take us in, you have the right to know."

Nancy explained the rest of the story, how Abner beat Jake in town, and his attempt to kill her and Jake on the day she went into labor with the twins.

She told her how Taima and Henry saved their lives and cared for them until they were able to ride. As she talked about her baby boy, and how he was buried next to his great-grandmother, Nancy and Emma both wiped away tears.

As Nancy went on, she could see that Emma became more and more angry. When Nancy reached the point in her story where her father took his rifle and went to find Abner, Emma's eyes blazed. She bared her teeth and growled, "I wish I could be the one that killed him."

"Daddy didn't find him that day. I went back to the cabin and, for a few days, all I could do was take care of the baby and wait to see if Jake was going to live or die. The sheriff came and told us Abner'd probably gone to stay with family in Utah, but he said that the law was on our side, and if Abner ever came back to Smithville, he'd be hung. I can't say as I find much comfort in that. Abner swore he'd kill us, and he meant it. Now he'll want to kill Linda, too, since she ran off with us. As long as he's alive, I'll be afraid of him."

Emma wrapped her arm around Nancy's shoulder. "Hangings better than he deserves. Don't you worry about him. You're safe here." She looked at Linda. "You, too, Linda. I doubt that there's any way for him to find you, but if he ever shows his face around me, I'll be happy to shoot him. It wouldn't be the first time I killed something ugly."

"I can't help it. I'll be afraid as long as Abner's still alive."

"I'll talk to our sheriff so he knows the story. From the way you described him, it wouldn't be hard to recognize this Abner. You don't see many men that tall and big. If he shows his face in these parts, he'll be sorry."

Chapter 26

It took almost an hour to reach the ranch. When Emma pulled the wagon up to the front of the limestone house, she swept a hand across in front of her. "This is our place. My grandparents built the house around 1850."

She pointed to an almost identical house across the road. It had the same front porch, picket fences around the yard, and rows of rose bushes filling the space on the side of the path to the front steps. "That one belonged to my husband's family. We had a foreman with a wife and children that lived there for a few years, but he left last year to work in Detroit. It's been sitting empty for a while. We call that one the Belk House, because it was Jake's grandfather's."

She pointed to the other house. "We call this one the West House, because that was built by my grandparents. My daughter, Shelby, still lives at home with us. There's plenty of room in our house, but the Belk House will be all yours. I thought you'd like to settle in tonight. I already had the housekeeper clean one bedroom and the bed is made up, but you'll have to get one ready for Linda. I have plenty of linens. The rest of the house will take some cleaning, and maybe you'll want to do some decorating, paint it different colors and such. It should be just fine for you and Jake. Brenda will help you."

Nancy asked, "Brenda?"

"She's our housekeeper, but she might as well be family. I don't know what I'd do without her. What with breeding the horses and running the business end of it, I don't have time for cooking and cleaning. I mean, I know how, but I'd rather train a colt than wash dishes. She'll help you with the work. I'm sure you'll love it. The house has five bedrooms, so if more grandbabies come along, you'll have someplace to put them. You'll have the whole house to yourselves."

Nancy gasped. "My own house? Jake and I have been living in a one-room cabin. I mean, I loved it because it was ours, but I never dreamed we'd have a whole house to ourselves."

"Not only the house. It has a barn and a very nice cabin out back that you could use for a workroom or something. Akecheta's maw used to live in it when she first came to the family."

"Akecheta?"

"Jake didn't tell you?"

"He really hasn't told me much of anything. Getting him to talk is like pulling teeth."

Emma nodded. "Hah! He gets that from his father. I think they invented the word 'stoic' just for them. Akecheta is what I call Jake's father."

"Is that an Indian name, like my friend Taima?"

"It is. He doesn't have any Indian blood, but he was raised by a Kansa woman. He has all kind of names. His Bible name is Isaac Matthew Belk. Most folks call him Ike, but his Maw called him Akecheta from the day they got him because it means 'fighter' in Kansa Indian language, and she thought it fit him. There's folks he met in New York back when he went to university there that call him Matthew. I took to calling him Akecheta when we were children and never stopped. I remember his grandpa used to always tell that old joke. 'You can call Akecheta anything, just don't call him late for dinner.'"

Nancy was startled when Emma threw back her head and bellowed, "Daniel!" and then leapt down from the wagon. She held up her hands. "Give me my granddaughter."

Nancy handed the baby to her grandmother, and she and Linda climbed down. A pack of dogs of varying sizes and types, ran around from the side of the house and swirled around Emma's feet. She reached down and scratched each one of them in turn, and having greeted her, they all found a shady spot to lie down. They were followed by a young man in his twenties, wearing jeans, a plaid shirt, cowboy boots, and a western hat, which he pulled off as soon as he saw Nancy and Linda. "Yes, Ma'am?"

Emma nodded at Nancy. "This is my daughter-in-law, Nancy, and her sister, Linda. Would you please carry their things into the Belk house and then unhitch Concrete here and see to him."

He swept off his hat to reveal a head of thick, blond curls and bright blue eyes. Emma said, "Girls, this is Dan Winslow. He's my foreman now." She looked purposefully at Linda, "He's still single so he sleeps in the bunk house with the other hands instead of taking up a whole house."

Dan nodded. "Pleased to meet you, Ma'am," he said to Nancy. His eyes went to Linda and he nodded. "Miss Linda." His glance lingered on Linda until Emma said. "Get to it, Dan. You and Linda can get better acquainted later."

Nancy was stunned. In all that had happened in the last few days, she had only thought about getting Linda to safety. Anything that might happen in the future was merely a distant possibility. Dan's attention to Linda filled Nancy with hope for her sister's happiness. She stared at him.

Maybe Linda can be free of Abner, and maybe someday she can find a good man who will love her. Maybe Dan here, or someone like him, could be that man. Oh, God, make it so. She's gone through enough hell and deserves some peace and happiness in her life.

Dan blushed at Emma's words and clapped his hat back on his head. "Yes, Ma'am." He went to the back of the wagon and began unloading Nancy and Linda's things.

Emma said, "Let's go inside so we can sit and talk a spell. I have a pitcher of iced tea that ought to taste real good right about now." Cooing to the baby, she led the way into the house. Nancy noticed there were electric lamps on the tables instead of kerosene lanterns. They walked right through the living room and into the kitchen.

It was the largest kitchen Nancy had ever seen, with a table already set for six, but that had room for four more than that. A woman, who looked to be in her sixties, wore a cobbler's apron, and had her gray hair pinned into a tight bun at the back of her neck. She was cooking at the stove.

Emma said, "Brenda, this is my daughter-in-law, Nancy, and her sister, Linda. Girls, this is Brenda Marshall. She keeps the house in order and keeps us from starving to death. I couldn't get by without her."

Brenda looked at Nancy and Linda over the top of wire-rimmed glasses and smiled. "Pleased to meet you. If there's anything you need, you just let me know."

Nancy nodded. "Thank you."

Brenda went back to tending the pans on the stove. Emma waved a hand at the big table. "Have a seat." Holding Tammy in one arm, she took glasses from the cupboard and set them on the table, opened the refrigerator, and came back with a pitcher of tea.

Nancy and Linda both stared at the refrigerator. They didn't see a block of ice, and when Emma opened the door, a little light had come on. Nancy said, "I heard about electric refrigerators, but this is the first one I've seen. Being so high up in the mountains like we were, we didn't have power lines in Smithville yet. Daddy fixed up pipes and a pump in a washroom so we had running water, but we had to pump it every time, and of course, it wasn't hot. We would fill the tub part way and then bring a pot of boiling water from the stove to get a warm bath. "

Emma shook her head once and clicked her tongue. "Electricity is wonderful. We had power strung out here as soon as it became available. Akecheta put in electric pumps so we could have running water and flush toilets in the houses. We don't have a telephone yet, but probably will soon."

The kitchen door opened, and Jake stuck in his head and said, "I'll be in as soon as I see to Charlie and Pete." He then withdrew his head and let the door close.

Emma asked, "How did the horses take the trip?"

"Pretty well. Jake said Charlie's an old hand at train rides so he keeps Pete calm, but I'm sure they were both glad to have their feet on solid ground again."

Emma stood and handed Tammy to Nancy. "You two sit here and rest for a minute. I have to say hello to Charlie. He's one of my babies, you know. I've never met Pete, and since horses are my business, I want to go get acquainted with him. I'll be right back. If you need it, the washroom is right down the hall."

She followed Jake. As soon as Emma was out of earshot, Linda said. "She's wonderful. I never thought I'd see the day that a woman could wear pants and no one would even act like it was a strange thing to do."

With her free hand, Nancy thoughtfully fingered an earlobe. "I don't think Jake's mother is like any woman we've ever known."

"You're right about that. Did you see the way Dan jumped to attention when she told him what to do? I never saw a man do that before, at least, not for any woman but his mother."

"No, never, not ever. I wonder if Jake's father lets her talk to him like that."

Without turning away from the stove, Brenda said, "He holds his own with her. They love one another something awful."

Tammy stirred and started to cry. Nancy unbuttoned her top and gave the baby her breast. She told Linda, "Dan took all of our things to the other house. I'll have to go find her diapers."

Linda stood and walked to the door. "I'll get one for you."

Nancy sat peacefully watching her daughter have dinner until Linda returned with an armful of baby supplies. She set them on the table. "I brought some other things you might need until we get ready to go over there for the night."

Her stomach full, Tammy drifted off to sleep and Nancy buttoned up her dress. She was pinning a dry diaper on Tammy when they heard the sound of an automobile driving up to the side of the house. A moment later, a tall, slender man with copper-colored hair and wearing a vested suit, came into the kitchen. He grinned at Nancy and Tammy. "Is this my grandchild?"

Nancy knew immediately this was Jake's father. The only difference between the two men was the lines at the corners of this man's eyes, their clothes, and Jake's beard. "It is," Nancy said. "Her name is Linda Taima Belk, and we call her Tammy. I'm Jake's wife. My name is Nancy, and this is my sister, Linda."

"I am much more than pleased to meet you. I would have been here earlier, but I got held up in court and couldn't get away. Around here they call me Ike or Akecheta. I'm Jake's dad."

Nancy laughed. "You didn't have to tell us that." She pointed to the red curls on Tammy's head. "She didn't get this from me."

He held out his hands. "Let's get a good look at her."

Nancy held up Tammy, and Akecheta took her in his arms. He sat in one of the chairs and gazed down at her. "She's about the most beautiful thing I ever saw."

Nancy grinned at him. "You sure you're not saying that just because she looks like you, are you?"

He chuckled. "Maybe so, maybe so." He looked up at Nancy. "Thank you. Thank you for bringing our boy back to us, and thank you for this precious little girl."

"We're happy to be here, sir."

"Sir? Please, like I told you, call me Ike or Akecheta."

"Okay. Emma calls you Akecheta, so I will, too. That's a name like Taima, from Indian language, only hers is Paiute. I named her after the friend who helped deliver her. In her language, it means Thunder."

Akecheta threw back his head and laughed. "Taima, thunder? That'll go fine with Akecheta. In Kansa, that means fighter. Between the two of us, you may not have a peaceful day. Maybe she'll grow up to be a lawyer like me and my daughter. I do most of my fighting in a courtroom these days. Shelby's name means 'a sheltered place,' so she brings peace. Taima can join my firm and be the loud voice in the partnership."

Amazed, Linda asked, "Your daughter Shelby's a lawyer? You mean a girl could go to school to be a lawyer?"

"She can here. Manhattan has been at the forefront of women's rights from its beginning. Susan B. Anthony campaigned here in 1867. She didn't get what she wanted back then, but women have had the vote in Kansas since 1912. The rest of the country didn't get it until 1920."

Nancy started crying. Akecheta got the same expression on his face that Jake did when she cried. "I'm sorry. Did I say something wrong?"

"No," she sobbed. "You said something I can't hardly believe. All my life, people have been telling me that I couldn't do anything but marry and have babies. That was all I could dream about, or even think about, because I was a girl. Now, I find out that Tammy's grandmother has a college degree in something that only men used to study, and you tell me that her aunt is a lawyer, and my baby could be a lawyer, too, if she wants. I always loved books and I used to read about women who went to school, but I knew I couldn't do that. It's like a whole other world has been shown to me, only it's too late for me."

"It's not too late for you."

Nancy sniffled and blew her nose on one of the diapers. "Yes, it is."

"No. It isn't."

"But I'm married now, and I have a baby."

"That didn't stop Emma," Akecheta replied.

"You mean she went to school after she got married?" Nancy gaped.

"She'd already finished her first year when we got married. She didn't have our daughter, Shelby, until a few days after the summer of her junior year was over."

"You mean they let her keep on going to classes when she was showing she was in a family way?"

"Emma was determined to graduate. She was ready for a fight, and everyone who knows her was in no way ready to take her on. In reality, I think the whole town was cheering for her to graduate, the women especially. For two years after we married, everyone at the school sort of ignored the subject. No one talked about it, and when she was pregnant, we all pretended that she was just putting on weight."

"But what about her senior year? How could she go to classes and take care of a little baby?"

"That was her grandmother's doing. Emma would feed Shelby before she went to school in the morning, Grandma Adele would give her bottles of cow's milk during the day, and Emma would take over again when she got home. When she finished her senior year she was exhausted, but she graduated with honors."

Akecheta was beaming with pride. "Grandma Adele brought Shelby to the ceremony and she slept through the whole thing until her mother's name was called to go up and get her degree. Then she woke up and started screaming. Everyone in the place started laughing, even the dean." He grinned at the memory.

"So if we had some money, there might be a chance for me to go to school?"

"More than a chance. Money isn't a problem. You can take some tests to see where you should start out, and then we'll arrange it, one way or the other. Believe me, if Emma thought that was what you wanted, she'd move heaven and earth to make it happen."

From the other side of the table, a small, soft voice said, "What about me? Nancy didn't marry, so she got to finish the twelfth grade, but I didn't even get to the ninth."

Nancy and Akecheta both turned to look at Linda. He grinned at her. "You, too, Linda. Emma would be rooting for you as well."

Both Nancy and Linda were crying when Emma and Jake came into the kitchen. Jake grabbed his father and they greeted one another with a bear hug. When they let go, Emma said, "What's going on here? Why are these women crying?"

Akecheta wrapped his arm around Emma's waist and kissed her cheek. Nancy caught the look of obvious affection that passed between them. "I was just telling them about you graduating from college, and I said that they could both go to school if they wanted. Linda here wants to know if she can finish high school."

Emma drew in a sharp breath. "Of course you can. I'll practically insist on it. What would you like to study?"

Nancy and Linda looked at one another and both shrugged at the same time. Nancy said, "I don't know."

"No matter. We'll look through the school catalog and you can see what sounds good to you." She looked at her husband. "Where's Shelby?"

"You know how she is." He looked at Nancy and explained, "She hates the car and only rides to the office with me when she's running late. She changed clothes there and is riding her horse

302

home. She left an hour before I did. Said she wanted to stop at the mercantile before they closed to get something or other. She ought to be right behind me."

He had barely finished talking before the screen door slammed, and a beautiful young woman with copper curls swirling around her head charged into the room. She was carrying a store bag and wore culottes, leather gloves, and a western hat dangling down her back. When she saw Jake, she dropped the bag on the table and grabbed him. He lifted her off the floor in a hug while she kissed his cheek. She shouted, "It's about time you showed up. Mom has been meeting every east-bound train for the last three days."

Nancy wondered if all the Belk women yelled when they talked. Then Shelby turned her attention to the baby. "Oh, oh, look at this. Give her to me," she demanded, in the same loud voice Emma had used at the station. Once again, Nancy turned over the child. Shelby sat down to gaze at her. "How old is she?"

"She's almost two weeks."

"Oh, she's so beautiful." She kissed the still sleeping baby's forehead and nuzzled her cheek. Looking up at Nancy, she almost cried when she said, "Most little ones like her are still sort of ugly. I can't get over how beautiful she is."

Jake guffawed. "You're only saying that 'cause she looks just like you."

Shelby stuck her chin in the air and grinned. "She does, doesn't she? Well, thank God for that! You're a right handsome man, but you wouldn't do very well if you were a woman."

Akecheta put an arm around Jake's shoulder and said, "True enough, but we do make handsome fellas, don't we?"

Emma looked at Nancy and jerked her head in her family's direction. "Look at the three of them, congratulating themselves on how good looking they are. I don't suppose there's any chance of Tammy being humble if she grows up around them."

Just about that time, Brenda slapped a plate of fried pork chops on the table. "That's enough bragging on yourselves. Sit down and eat before dinner gets cold."

She put down another place setting for Linda while Emma and Shelby placed the vegetables on the table. Jake went to the door and called for Dan to come eat. He popped into the kitchen immediately.

"You must have been waiting right outside," Emma said. "Is that because you're hungry or is it because we have another pretty girl in here?"

Both Dan and Linda blushed, and Nancy ducked her head to hide her smile. Dan took off his hat and hung it on a row of pegs by the door. "I got to wash up," he said and went down the hall to the washroom. He was back in a minute and sat down at the place next to Linda.

Shelby shifted Tammy to one side. Emma said, "You can't eat and hold on to a baby. I know just the thing for her." She got up and left the room, returning a moment later with a large wicker laundry basket, padded with a folded blanket. She set it in a corner. "Put her in here. She can sleep a little while we eat."

Shelby carefully laid the baby in the basket and watched her for a moment to see if she would wake up, but Tammy didn't move. "She's a good sleeper, isn't she?"

"Right from the start," Nancy said.

"Thank God for that," Emma said. "Jake was the same way, but Shelby here only slept a few hours a day when she was a baby. She didn't cry, but she wanted me or Grandma to be where she could see us every minute."

Shelby picked up the bag she'd been carrying. "I brought her a present. I had to guess what size, so she won't grow into them for a while. If you want, you can exchange them." She handed the bag to Nancy, who opened it to discover two fancy little dresses, one in a pale yellow and one in pink, both embroidered with flowers along the hems and sleeves. Nancy held them up for everyone to see. "Thank you so much. They're beautiful. How did you know we had a girl?"

Shelby shrugged. "I guess wishing made it so."

As they waited for Brenda to sit down, Nancy watched Dan. She tried to be discreet, peeking glances from the side. *I wonder if that's his regular seat, or did he choose that one because he wanted to sit next to Linda?*

Brenda placed the last dish of food on the table and sat down. Akecheta held out his hands to Emma and Shelby, who were on either side of him, and they all joined hands. When Jake took Nancy's hand in his, he held it up to his lips and kissed it. She was overcome by feelings of peace and happiness.

Akecheta said a brief blessing that concluded with, "And thank you, God, for the return of our son and for the extra blessings of his family that has come home with him. Bless them and protect them and help them thrive. And we especially thank you that our granddaughter didn't inherit her Grandma Emma's hair. Amen."

Emma smacked him lightly on the arm. "Smarty-pants."

He ducked away from her and chuckled. "Did you want her to have that hair of yours?"

"No. Thank God she doesn't, but you're a smarty-pants all the same."

For a few minutes, the kitchen was filled with the sound of dishes being passed and plates filled. After everyone had begun eating, Akecheta said, "Now, son, tell me what you've been up to the last three years, and how we came to get you back home with us."

Jake swallowed hard and said, "I'll leave out some things in the interest of having a pleasant meal, but what I want first is legal advice."

Akecheta put down his fork and assumed a serious manner. "Legal advice?"

"Nancy and I were married according to Nevada customs, but I want to make sure we're legal in Kansas. I don't know if Vanessa ever divorced me. If she didn't, I want to get that done, and then we can have another ceremony here to make sure we're man and wife anywhere we go."

Akecheta nodded. "That's easy enough to take care of. I'll send an associate to Kansas City to look her up."

Nancy took a deep breath and said, "What about Linda? I want her to be free to live her own life."

Akecheta frowned. "Linda? I'll see after whatever she wants." He looked down the table to where Linda sat. "What do you need?"

Linda looked panic stricken. She glanced around the table and then leaned closer to Nancy and stared down at the table. In a voice hardly any of them could hear, she said, "I was married in Nevada."

Akecheta asked, "So you want a divorce?"

Linda bit her lip. She nodded her head, but didn't answer aloud. Nancy poked Jake in the side with her elbow, and he spoke up. "There's more to the story. Nancy and Linda were brought up in a town built by renegade Mormons. When Linda was only fourteen, she was married against her will to a man who already had other wives. He was a beast, and I'll tell you more about him later, when we're alone, and it won't spoil everyone's appetite, but she needs to be free of him. What do you think?"

Akecheta crinkled up his nose. "Well, I'm no expert on marriage law. I do mostly business and a few criminal cases, but I doubt that her marriage would be legal anywhere for a number of reasons. She was underage. She was coerced. He was already married. The law is funny, though, so better safe than sorry. Say, if one of those Arabian sheiks comes here with a bunch of wives, we recognize it, because it's legal where he comes from. Of course, plural marriage isn't legal in Nevada anymore."

Shelby spoke up. "I'll handle it. Whatever her standing here, I think we should file for a divorce, just to cover all the bases." She was sitting two chairs down from Linda, but she leaned forward to look her in the eye. "Don't you worry about a thing. You're in my hands now. I'll take care of you."

Linda teared up. "Thank you," she whispered.

Nancy stole a glance at Dan to see his reaction, but his face revealed nothing about his thoughts. They'd only been there a short while, but he was clearly smitten with Linda right from the moment he saw her. *How will he feel about a girl who's already been married? I know men set a high value on virginity. Will he forget all about Linda as a possible sweetheart? Will any man be able to love her?*

Chapter 27

Nancy was holding Tammy in her arms when Emma, carrying an armload of bedding, led her and Linda across the street and up to their bedrooms in the Belk house. She flipped on the electric light in the first room. "We had this house wired the same time we did ours, but there isn't running water yet."

Nancy was shocked to find the space almost as large as her whole cabin had been. A four-poster bed, made up with a ruffled spread and a pile of fancy pillows, sat in the middle of one wall, and there were three pieces of furniture to store clothing.

A rocking cradle with bouquets of flowers painted on each end was in one corner. Emma pointed at it. "Tammy can sleep there. I didn't keep any baby beds, but I couldn't bear to part with that. It was Shelby's and Jake's when they were first born. Akecheta made it himself. It'll hold her until she's about three months old. When we go into town to get you whatever you need, we'll order a proper bed for Tammy, and she can have her own room set up."

"Her own room?"

Emma handed the linens to Linda and then unlocked and opened one of the windows. "There,

310

that'll bring some fresh air in here. I told you, this house has five bedrooms. You can get a better look at it in the morning. We'll buy anything you girls need."

"You don't have to spend a bunch of money on us," Nancy protested. "We can get by."

Emma waved a dismissive hand in the air. "Don't worry about money. You need more clothes, and so does Linda. We may not be rich, but money isn't a problem for us."

Emma hugged Nancy again and kissed both her and Tammy on the cheek. "I owe you so much, Nancy. If I spent every penny I had, I couldn't begin to pay you back for what you've done."

Emma stopped at the door and said, "Now, the washroom is off the kitchen downstairs. I already put in a night-light in the hall so you can see your way after dark. You get some rest. I know you must be exhausted. Come on, Linda, I'll help you make up your bed." Emma gave Nancy one last kiss on the cheek and then she and Linda left.

When Nancy heard the door close, she laid the baby in her cradle and pulled the soft blanket up to her chest.

She looked around the room again. It was amazing. She went to the light switch and flipped it down. Poof! The lights went off. She flipped it up again. The lights went on. Nancy giggled like a naughty child. It was magic to her.

She heard Jake trotting up the stairs. He came in and looked around the room. "This sure doesn't look like our cabin, does it?"

"Not hardly. It's wonderful."

"I'm going to run downstairs to the washroom."

"I already used your mom's, but I bet ours is wonderful, too."

Nancy undressed, and when she turned down the bed covers, she could tell that the sheets and blankets were store-bought. She ran her hand over the fabric. It was so soft, it was almost like silk. She slid between them, closed her eyes, and sighed at the feel of them on her skin. Jake came back upstairs and started undressing. Hearing her sigh, he looked over at her and asked, "What?"

"What, what?"

"You're sighing, like you do when something is bothering you. Is anything wrong?"

She gave him a blissful smile. "No, not a thing. I feel like a princess in this house and in this bed."

He smiled with one side of his mouth. "Well, if you don't look too close, you might believe me when I say, here comes your Prince Charming." He switched off the electric light and got in next to her. They wrapped their arms around one another, and for a while, lay there in silence.

Nancy was drifting off to sleep when Jake said, "I know my mom is different from the women you were raised around. She can be a little rough around the edges sometimes, and she only wears a dress for church. I hope you'll take to her once you get to know her."

Nancy opened her eyes. The room was filled with moonlight. Jake was leaning on one elbow and looking at her. She hooted, "Take to her? I *love* her. She's—she's the biggest woman I ever saw, and I don't mean her size, I mean her personality. Look at the things she's done--gone to college, bred horses without her husband telling her what to do. She even runs her own business, and so forth. I never knew a woman who did any of those things, and that made me think I could never do them. I love that she wears pants."

Nancy cupped her palm on Jake's cheek. "I love the way she was so happy to see us when we got here. I can see how much she loves you and how much she already loves Tammy. I love Shelby too, her being a lawyer and all and not the least bit stuck-up. I love the talk about me and Linda going to school, even though I don't see how that could happen for me."

"Why not?"

"You mean, you wouldn't mind?"

"No. Why would I mind?"

"You told me you didn't go to college. Most husbands would hate to have their wives step out ahead of them in the world like that."

"Well, now. That's something I'd have to think on. My mom and dad were awful disappointed when I wouldn't go to university after I graduated high school. I have a feelin' they sure would like to see me go now. Maybe I'll sign up for a few classes and take the same ones you're takin', since I get the feeling you're already a lot smarter than me. Runnin' the farm won't leave me a lot of time, but you can help me with my homework."

"You mean it isn't too late for you?" Excitement sparked in Nancy.

"No. While you were sittin' on the porch and feedin' Tammy after dinner, I talked to Dad about what kind of work I should do here. He thought I could take over the farmin' part of the load."

"Your family farms, too?"

"Well, when Mom and Dad were growing up, his family owned this property, and my mom's family owned the part across the road. At the time, they were both farms. Once my mom graduated, she and her grandpa turned that side into a horse ranch, making most of it for grazing, corrals, and such. They built a stable and the other buildings they needed, like a smithy shack and a foaling barn."

He hiked a thumb toward the window. "The acreage on this side is used for raising the grain and hay to feed the horses and the other livestock, and our food. Dad did have a foreman taking care of it because he spends his work days in town practicing law, but that man left a while back. Dad will hire helpers to come in and get the harvest a few weeks from now, but he hasn't found a new foreman. I'm it. You might say it was providence working on our behalf."

"He has other livestock?"

"We keep chickens and pigs, one boar and half a dozen sows, usually, and four or five dairy cows."

"Cows, but no bull?"

"We don't have a bull because they're harder to handle. When it comes time, they take the cows down the road to the Winslow place and breed them with his bull. Mr. Winslow gets one of the calves for pay."

"Winslow? Is that Dan's family?"

"That's his dad."

"Why is Dan working here instead of there?"

"I asked dad about that. I was surprised to see him here. Dad says Dan and his father had a falling out. Dan came home from Kansas State

University after studying agriculture all fired up with new ideas for the farm. His dad was happy to keep on doing things the way he'd been doing them, said he'd gone to college there, too, and liked things just fine the way they were. One thing led to another, and one day Dan showed up here and asked for work. Mom was an old flame of Mr. Winslow, and they're still friends, so she took Dan on so's he wouldn't run off somewhere like I did. I wouldn't be taking work away from him. He's strictly interested in the horse side of the street."

Nancy sat up in bed, drew up her knees, and hugged them. "Dan's dad was an old flame of your mom's? Tell me about that."

"I don't know a lot, only that Mr. Winslow was sweet on Mom from the first time he saw her in elementary school. He courted her all the time my dad was gone to New York to study law, but she never paid him much mind. When Dad came home after he graduated and still wouldn't talk about getting married, Mom told him if he didn't quit lollygagging about it, she'd marry Mr. Winslow. That got Dad's dander up. He told her she wasn't about to marry anyone but him, so they tied the knot a few months later, right before Mom started her sophomore year."

"I can't imagine a woman acting like that. Your mother is about the most amazing woman I ever heard of. I want to be just like her."

"Now, take it easy there," Jake asserted. "I love her something fierce and wouldn't mind a bit if you took on some of her spirit, but I don't know if the state of Kansas is big enough for two of you. Besides, I love you the way you are already. Don't lose yourself trying to be like someone else."

"I don't imagine I could get to be like her overnight," Nancy laughed, "but I'd like to do some changing. We'll have to see how much. The one thing that excites me the most is the idea of going to school and getting more education, not only for me, but for Linda, too. When she got married off, she had to stop going to school, and she cried over it something awful. At least I got to graduate, and it wasn't easy either."

"Wasn't easy? Why not?"

"All the other girls were already married. For the last two years, I was the only female in my grade. I took a lot of teasing from the boys. Some of them were downright nasty about it."

"I'd like to go back there and punch them all in the face."

"It's too late for that now. I'm glad I stuck it out, though. If I could go to college, I'd be setting an example for Tammy."

"What if we have more babies?"

"I don't know how I could handle that, but it's exciting to think about it."

Jake yawned. He closed his eyes and rolled over on his side. "Let's talk on it some more tomorrow. I'm 'bout to pass out here."

Nancy lay back down, turned on her side facing the window, and wriggled into a comfortable hollow on the feather mattress. She was drifting off to sleep when she heard a crunching sound outside, like someone walking on the fallen leaves. It snapped her awake. Her stomach churned and sweat broke out on her forehead.

She slipped out of bed and went to the open window, barely moving the lace curtains. She peeked out from the side of the frame so she wouldn't be visible to anyone who might be there.

In the bright moonlight, she saw two raccoons, one, the largest she'd ever seen and, another, a bit smaller, making their way across the yard. *Go to bed Mr. and Mrs. Raccoon. It's getting late.* She watched until they disappeared from her sight. When her heart stopped pounding, she closed and locked the window and then went back to bed. Jake mumbled, "Something wrong?"

"No, I was just thinking, I'd like for us to have a few dogs."

"Mom has a whole passel of 'em."

"I know. I'd like one or two of my own."

"Fine with me. I'll see about it first chance I get."

Chapter 28

A rooster crowing, followed closely by Tammy demanding breakfast, woke Nancy. Jake was already gone. She changed and fed the baby, dressed, and went into the hall. Linda was just opening her door.

Nancy said, "I wonder if I have anything here to make breakfast."

"Let's go see."

They went down the stairs to the kitchen and started looking around. An empty electric refrigerator stood with its plug lying on the counter and the door ajar. There was a cabinet with dishes, a pantry with pots, pans, empty Mason jars, and linens, but no food. The rectangular table in the center of the room was smaller than the one at Emma's house, and the six chairs around it were as much as it could comfortably hold.

Linda said, "I guess Emma expects us to eat breakfast at her place."

"I guess." They walked across the road and knocked on the screen door to the living room. Brenda appeared from the kitchen, wiping flour off her hands with a kitchen towel. She pushed the door open and stepped aside for them to enter. As they walked by her, she asked, "Why are you knocking?"

Nancy shrugged. "It didn't seem polite to just walk in."

"You're family now. You don't have to knock, but to tell the truth, most of the time, we all come in the kitchen door."

"All right. We'll do that from now on. There wasn't any food in my—our—the house. I thought maybe Emma wanted us to eat over here."

"She does. Emma, Jake, and Dan have already eaten and gone to work. Ike and Shelby will be down in a minute, so you'll have company at the table."

They went into the kitchen. Nancy sat at the table and nested Tammy, stomach down, across her knees. Linda asked Brenda, "How can we help you?"

"Sit down and relax. I don't need any help."

"I feel bad about you waiting on us. Can't I do something?"

Brenda waved a spatula in her direction. "To tell you the truth, as big as it is, this kitchen is only big enough for one woman to work in it. I'm happy to take care of it all on my own, and the rest of the house, too. When you get yourself together, I'll help you get the Belk House going. You'll need groceries and such. The whole place needs a good cleaning because this Kansas dust settles down overnight and the doors and windows probably need greasing. When we went over to get your room ready, I noticed that the door in the kitchen squeaks something awful. "

Nancy slowly rocked her knees back and forth, and patted Tammy gently on her back until she burped. "There we go," she said. She picked up the baby, and held her in her arm. "Brenda, would it be all right if I asked how you came to work for Emma? I don't want to be nosy, but everything here is new to me. I never knew anyone who had a housekeeper before."

"Well, we went to the First Baptist Church together and we've known one another since Emma first came to Manhattan."

"She wasn't born here?"

"No. She's originally from back east. Her parents died in an accident when she was nine, and she came here to be raised by her grandparents. My son, Tommy, had an awful crush on her, but of course, she never had eyes for anyone but Ike."

"Tommy? I thought Dan Winslow's dad had his eye on her."

"He did, and so did a half-dozen other boys, but she wouldn't give any of them the time of day. She was fixed on Ike from the get-go. Anyway, when my husband died, we found out that he was a fool when it came to money. I never knew what we had or didn't have, and it turned out he'd mortgaged the house for some reason or other that he didn't bother to talk over with me. I never worked outside my home a day in my life, and I couldn't buy groceries, much less make mortgage payments. The church gave me money at first, but they couldn't go on supporting me. The house went into foreclosure and, even though the bank didn't run me off because they didn't have a buyer who wanted to move in, it wasn't mine anymore."

She swallowed hard, cleared her throat, and went on, "I didn't know how I could get by. Then, one day Emma came to me and said, 'I need some help at the house.' She saved my life. My job here is the same work I've been doing all my life, cooking and cleaning. I have my own room, and she treats me like one of the family. How many people do you know who tell their hired help to sit down with them at the table?"

Nancy shrugged. "I never knew anyone who had hired help before. All I know is what I read about in books, and they sure didn't do that in there."

Akecheta, dressed in his business suit, came into the kitchen. Shelby was right behind him, wearing her riding outfit. Nancy asked her, "Aren't you working today?"

"Sure am. I ride a horse into town when I can and change at the office. I have more clothes there than I do here."

She sat down next to Linda. "I want to work on your case as soon as possible, so tell me everything about your marriage."

Brenda served the meal, and while they were eating, Linda told Shelby details of her marriage, how old she had been, and that it was against her will.

"Tell her the worst part," Nancy said. "She needs to know."

Linda gave a short nod and swallowed hard. She glanced at Akecheta and her face turned red. "I can't talk about things like that in front of a man."

Nancy cocked an eyebrow. "Tell it. She needs to know what he put you through."

Akecheta stood and said, "I'm going out to say good morning to my wife. I'll see you at the office, Shelby."

Linda kept her eyes on the table, and when Akecheta was gone, told Shelby, "He would have relations with me twice a day, sometimes more, especially the first year. He did it to me so much I was bleeding from it all the time. He wanted me to make sons for him, and when I didn't conceive, he would beat me. It got to where I was afraid of starting my monthlies, because I knew it would mean a beating, and every time, it would be worse than the last."

Shelby slapped her palm down on the table and everyone jumped. "That bastard! I wish I could get my hands on him. He raped you over and over and then beat you because you didn't get pregnant? I'd like to shoot him."

Brenda patted her hand. "Calm down, Shelby. If you want to kill this monster, you have to get in line behind your brother and your mother and maybe even me. I may be getting old, but I can still pull the trigger on a shotgun."

Shelby put one arm around Linda's shoulder and hugged her. "I'll start the paperwork today to make sure you're free of him and he can't ever hurt you again."

She was starting for the door when Nancy stood and said, "I want to go with you so I can see the rest of the place and meet some of the horses."

"Sure, come on. Linda, you want to come, too?"

"No," Linda whispered. "I'll stay here and help Brenda clean up."

Nancy laid the baby in her wicker laundry basket. "Will you call me if Tammy wakes up?"

Brenda waved a hand. "You go on. We'll see after her."

They went out the back door, and Shelby led Nancy through a stable with a dozen stalls on each side. The smell of hay, manure, and disinfectant mingled with the aroma of leather and saddle soap.

Two cats sleeping by the door squinted up at them and yawned as they walked by. Another cat skittered away. Nancy looked back and forth. The stalls were all empty.

"Where are all the horses?"

Shelby pointed to the back door of the stable with her chin. "Mom turns them out in the morning and lets them graze, all except the ones she's training."

At the end of the stalls, Dan was rubbing oil on a strip of leather. The room behind him was lined with rows of saddles, halters, bridles, and other horse wear. Shelby said, "This is the tack room. Mom keeps all of her horse outfits here. The horses have a better wardrobe than she does. Morning, Dan."

He looked up at them, nodded, and smiled. "Morning, Shelby, Nancy.

They walked out the back door to a clearing of about sixty feet. There was a corral on one side with a half-dozen horses milling around and another farm building on the other side. Just beyond that was a larger corral, three times the size of the first. A saddled horse stood outside with its reins trailing on the ground.

Jake was sitting on the top rail of the fence and the four dogs were sitting on the ground under him, peering through the rails at Emma. Shelby pointed to the dogs, which were lined up from the largest to the smallest, as if someone had placed them in order of their height. "That big yellow one there is Ditto. Mom had his daddy before she had him and he looks just like his father. That's how he got his name. The next one is Talley, then Squeak, and Elwood."

Emma was in the center of the ring wearing boots, a set of buckskin pants and shirt, and a western hat. She was holding a rope tied to a beautiful, chestnut-colored horse with white stockings on all four legs that went up to his knees. He had a wide white streak down his face. He was trotting in circles around the perimeter. Shelby nodded at the horse. "That's Jeremiah. He's two years old now, still a colt, really, but ready to be sold--if Mom can bring herself to part with him. I notice she hasn't gelded him yet. That means she's thinking he'll make a good stud. She has a hard time letting any of them go. It's her business, what she does for a living, but every time she sells one of these horses she delivered into this world and trained, she goes to her room and cries."

Emma clicked her tongue twice and the horse picked up his pace, cantering smoothly. After a few minutes, she said something to him in a language Nancy didn't understand, and he slowed to a walk and then stopped. Emma walked up to him, shortening the rope into loops over her palm as she went. She patted his neck and scratched under his forelock, murmuring, "Good boy. Good boy."

She led him out of the corral to the paddock gate. He stood quietly while she opened it and unsnapped the rope from his halter. He rubbed his muzzle against her shoulder and then wheeled around and raced off to join the cluster of horses at the other end of the field. Emma stood next to Nancy and they watched as Jeremiah ran around the others in a circle, whinnying loudly and tossing his head before he joined the herd and started eating the lush grass.

Shelby laughed and nudged her mother's side. "Look at him! That one's a show-off for sure. He acts like he knows he's your favorite."

"He is. He has even better lines than his daddy. The others that were born that spring are all spoken for, but I haven't taken an offer for him. He's really smart and shows the most promise. It's hard to let him go."

Shelby said, "I have to be getting to work or my boss will be chewing me up and spitting me out."

Emma hooted, "Like you have to worry about that. One of the advantages of working for your dad is coming into the office when you want."

Shelby kissed Emma's cheek. "See you tonight, Mom." She gave Jake a wave of her hand

and Nancy a quick hug. "Kiss that baby good-bye for me."

Shelby strode over to the horse standing outside the corral, tossed the reins over its neck, grasped the saddle horn, bent both knees, and with a jump, almost flew into the saddle. She turned the horse and trotted off toward the road to town.

From where he was sitting on the fence, Jake called to his mother, "Which one of them is next?"

Emma looked at the horses in the smaller corral and nodded toward one of them. "Bring me Ginger, that little sorrel filly."

He jumped down from the rail, took the looped lead rope from Emma's hands, and went through the bars of the corral. As he walked toward the horses, they scattered and trotted away from him. Talking to them, he walked slowly into the herd, moving this way and that, until somehow he had separated the sunset-colored filly from the rest. She stood against the rail and fidgeted, pawing the ground with one foot. Jake stood in the middle of the ring and faced her. He reached into his pocket, held an open palm in her direction, dropped his head, and looked at the ground. He didn't move for several minutes. The filly walked slowly up to him and stuck out her head to lip up something from his hand. He snapped the lead rope onto her bridle, led the filly out of the small corral, then handed the rope to Emma, who walked her into the training corral.

Nancy was mesmerized. She knew Jake had complete empathy with Charlie and Pete, but didn't realize he could work his charms on other animals as well. "You're wonderful! How did you get her to come to you?"

Jake shook his head a little. "I surely do like you thinking I'm wonderful, but you have to give Mom the credit. She pets and talks to her horses every day from the first day they're born, and as soon as they're old enough to eat it, they get an apple slice every time she touches 'em. That filly knew I had something she liked and she wanted it, so she came to me."

Nancy hugged him and whispered in his ear. "I understand her. I'm the same way."

His face turned red. He whispered back, "How much longer do we have to wait?"

"I don't know, and I'd be too embarrassed to ask your mother." She bit a lip. "Your mom said Brenda would help me with my house cleaning. She raised a family. The next time we're alone, I'll kind of work it into the conversation."

Nancy watched while Emma led the filly around the ring a few times. When they stopped, Emma patted her on the neck, scratched under her forelock, and talked to her for a few minutes, all the while, rubbing one hand over her neck and head, and up and down her front legs. When she was finished, she led her out of the corral and said, "This could be a good one for Tammy. They have the same color hair. Akecheta's first horse had hair like his."

Nancy was shocked. "Tammy? She's only two weeks old."

"Ginger here is a yearling. By the time Tammy's two, this young lady will be ready to go to work."

"Can you put a two year old on a horse?"

Emma cocked her eyebrow at Jake and chuckled. "Depends on the two-year old. Both Shelby and Jake rode in the saddle in front of me from the time they were old enough to sit up. The first time I put Shelby on a horse by herself she took off like she had somewhere to go. Jake here cried until I took him down. He loved the horses, but he wasn't ready to ride alone until he was four or five."

"Weren't you afraid they'd fall off?"

"I had an older mare that was very gentle and quite small. I knew she'd take good care of them."

The sound of Tammy crying wafted from the house. "I better go," Nancy said. "I need to wash the clothes and get to know the house."

Emma nodded. "Don't be afraid to ask Brenda for help. She knows where everything is. If you want, you can eat with us for a while. I'd like for it to be a permanent thing, especially for dinner, when we can all be together. That way you won't have to cook."

"I'd feel like I was putting an extra burden on Brenda."

"Once you're all recovered from birth, you would probably be a help to her. I don't know if it's good for you to be standing on your feet too much so soon after having a baby. Don't overdo it and get yourself all worn out. That train ride must have done you in."

"Linda will help me."

"Make a list of anything you need. If we don't have it on this side of the road, we'll buy it for you. When you feel up to it, we can go into town and do some shopping."

"Thank you. It may be a while. I am a little tired from the trip."

Chapter 29

Everything that happened that first full day in Manhattan was a revelation to both Nancy and Linda. Once Tammy was fed and back in her cradle, they started upstairs and explored the house. There were four large bedrooms on the top floor. When Nancy and Linda had looked them over, Nancy said, "We may as well take our dirty clothes down with us."

"After a week on the road and on the train, that's about everything we own," Linda answered. They went downstairs with their arms full. On the bottom level was a large living room, dining room, pantry, and kitchen. The washroom, with a sink, bathtub, and toilet, was next to a small bedroom down the hallway.

Hanging on the wall of the washroom was a copper laundry tub. Linda took it off the hook, set it on the floor, and dropped the laundry in it. She said, "Let's take this out to the back porch. I imagine that's where the water pump is for the laundry. We'll have to get some soap from Brenda—both laundry soap and bath soap."

Hearing Linda's tone of authority, Nancy thought about how her younger sister had already been responsible for a home of her own for almost two years and how much she suffered there.

Nancy went to the kitchen door first. When she opened it, it squealed loudly in protest, and the girls both laughed. "This must be what Brenda was talking about. We'll have to get it oiled." When she stepped onto the porch and turned to hold the door open for Linda, she shrieked, "A clothes washer, an electric clothes washer. I don't believe it!"

In her surprise, Linda dropped the laundry tub and it landed on the wood floor of the porch with a thunk. The two girls stood staring at the appliance. Linda said, "I've seen these in the Sears Roebuck catalogue." They examined the machine and then Linda said, "We have to ask Brenda to show us how it works."

Nancy started down the steps. "Let's finish looking around the rest of the property first. There's no telling what else we'll find."

They walked through the barn. Farm tools hung neatly on one wall. Stall doors were standing open. It was organized and swept, and eerily unoccupied. When they went out the back door, Nancy stopped so shortly, Linda ran into her. "Look!" She pointed to the building in front of her. "It's our cabin!' She started crying.

A replica of the cabin in the Sierra Nevada Mountains stood about ten yards from the back door of the barn. As she walked toward it, Nancy said, "Jake told me he had one like it at home, but I forgot. He said he used it as a sort of pattern when he built the other one."

Linda peered over her shoulder. "Let's look inside."

Nancy walked slowly up the steps and opened the familiar door. The fireplace and the building itself were almost a perfect copy of the home she had loved, but the contents were very different. A wrought iron bed with a large quilt covering it stood on one wall. The house was built before closets came into style, and a large wardrobe with drawers on the bottom stood on one wall. An electric lamp was on a small table next to the bed, and when Nancy looked at the wall next to the door, she saw a switch plate the same as those at the house. "It's been wired for electricity."

There was a large bureau, a wardrobe, and a table and two chairs made of finished wood with machine-turned spindles and legs. "All of this furniture was probably bought at a store. Jake made ours with his own two hands."

The windows had glass panes. Nancy was both thrilled and disappointed. It was similar to her cabin, but so different inside that seeing it only reminded her of her loss. "It's nice," she said sadly and shrugged. "Emma said I could use this for a workroom or something like that."

"What kind of work?"

"I don't know. I don't have any hobbies. The house is so big, we'll never use all of it. Jake said it's only a few weeks until harvest time. Maybe he'll have to hire help. They could live here." She looked slowly around the room, her eyes lingering on any similarities she could find to her old cabin. "But I don't think I want them to live here."

They went out and looked around, finding an empty smokehouse, a deserted outhouse, and a shed with more tools in it. There was an orchard with rows of various fruit trees, heavy with ripening apples, pears, and peaches. The garden, which had been planted, was filled with food ready for picking. Nancy said, "I'm glad so see this. Emma's pantry had canned food in it. We can use those empty Mason jars from our house and help Brenda with the canning."

"We've seen everything here. Let's go see her about that soap."

They found Brenda in the kitchen putting a pie in the oven. Nancy said, "I hate to bother you, Brenda, but all our clothes are dirty, and we don't know how to operate the electric washer. Could you help us?"

Brenda's face broke out in a huge grin. "If you've been washing clothes in a tub all your life, you're going to love it!"

"They don't have power in Smithville yet. It's so far up in the mountains it would cost too much to get it there."

Brenda asked, "You don't have any soap over there?"

Nancy shook her head. "No, nothing but the dishes, pans, and empty Mason jars. That's why we came over here. There isn't anything in the cupboard at all."

Brenda went to the pantry, took a cloth tote from the shelf, and began filling it. "I reckon when that last foreman's family moved out, they probably took everything they could carry with them." She stuffed the bag with things from the shelves, starting with soaps and toilet paper. "Whatever you need, we probably have it here. Come on and get it, anytime."

"Thank you so much," Nancy said. "We'll try to do as much as we can without bothering you. We don't want to put a bigger workload on you. I told Emma that we'd help you any way we could. I see the garden is full of vegetables, and the trees have tons of fruit on them. We both know how to can. Maybe we can help."

Nancy's voice trailed off. *I had to leave my beautiful garden just when it was ready to be harvested. I hope Taima gathered the crop.*

"I could sure use help with that," Brenda admitted. "Most of the time, I'm just fine, and you

336

have your hands full taking care of that pretty little girl of yours, but canning is one thing that uses up a lot of energy."

Linda spoke up, "We have to do something to make up for all the work we cause. I could peel potatoes for you, or help you with the laundry and cleaning, things like that. I need to be useful somehow."

Brenda nodded. "That would be good, long as you stay out of my way. We'll work it out." She looped the handles of the bag over her arm and said, "I've got about an hour before I have to take those pies out of the oven. Let's go see what we can get done at your place."

They followed her across the road and around to the back porch, where she showed them how to put water in the washer, how much soap to add, and how to put the clothes in, a few pieces at a time. "Now, we started with the light colors and we'll let them wash about ten minutes. While they're doing that, let's see what else you're going to need."

They sat at the table while Brenda suggested supplies, and Nancy wrote them down on a piece of paper. After they did that, she said, "I didn't see any rope on the clothesline posts. You'll have to add that to your list. Bring your things across the road and hang them on our line for now. The pins are in a bag at the first post. Linda, don't let her carry that wet laundry. She shouldn't be picking up anything heavier than little Tammy for a while."

"I won't," Linda said, as she went to the pantry.

Nancy thought it was the perfect opportunity to ask the question she and Jake had in mind. "How long does it take after you have a baby before you can go back to doing--everything you did before?" She could feel herself blushing.

Brenda smiled at her as if they were sharing a secret. She tapped her finger on her chin. "Hmmm, well, for some things, like light housework, it's only a few weeks, for other things, it's about month and a half, sometimes, two months, depending on when you feel completely back to normal. You'll know. Now, let's show you how to use that wringer so's you don't mash your fingers up in it."

Nancy borrowed kitchen supplies, cooking pans, and kitchen linens from Brenda and began making breakfast in her own house, but the whole family ate together at the West house in the evenings. It was a chance for everyone to see Tammy and discuss their day.

On Monday, Akecheta announced, "Linda, today was the first day of fall classes, so I went to see Miss Blair at the school. She said to bring you in tomorrow morning and they would find the right class for you."

Linda didn't speak, but pressed her lips together, blinked back tears that sprang to her eyes, and gave her head a sharp little nod.

Akecheta added, "Be ready around eight in the morning." He looked at Nancy. "What about you? Are you ready to start school?"

"I've been thinking about it," Nancy answered, "but I decided that I should wait a year. I have a lot to do at home right now, and with Tammy barely three weeks old, I'm not sure I'm strong enough yet to take on anything else. To tell the truth, I don't think I want to be away from Tammy all that time."

Shelby said, "I don't blame you. I'm tempted to take her to work with me just so I can look at her."

Jake poked his sister in the arm. "Why don't you just take a big mirror? That'll remind you what she looks like."

Brenda told Shelby, "You could always marry that Jim Blake fellow who's so fond of you and have one of your own."

Shelby shook her head. "I'm very fond of Jim, but I'm not ready to get married, and I don't know if I'll ever want to have babies. I have my work to keep me occupied. I like being an aunt. I get to hold her and love on her, but I haven't had to change a diaper yet or get up in the middle of the night. Aunthood—if that's a real word, may be the best of all worlds."

Nancy was startled. She had never heard a woman say she didn't want babies. She tried to remember Shelby's age. Jake had told her Shelby was about two years older than he. That would put her in at thirty or so. *What a strange world this Kansas is.*

The next morning, Linda put on her best dress and, carrying the baby, Nancy went across the road to see her off. The automobile was parked by the side of the house. They were walking up the front porch steps when Akecheta came out the door. "Morning, girls, you're right on time. You look very nice, Linda." He handed her a brown bag. "Brenda made you a lunch. I forgot to tell you to bring one with you."

"Thank you," Linda said softly, her head down. "I didn't know if I would need any paper and pencils or anything."

"Miss Blair will see to it that you have what you need for today. If there's anything else, we can pick it up at the store before we come home."

Linda took in a sharp breath. "How will I get home? The school must let out a lot earlier than you'll be ready to leave work."

"I hadn't thought about that. Tell you what, before I drop you off at the school, I'll show you where our offices are, and you can come on over there after school. It's right down the street, so you can't get lost. If you have homework, you can do it in one of the empty offices, or maybe Shelby can find some sort of work for you to do, filing or something, until we're ready to leave. If we put you to work, we'd give you some sort of pay. Then when you graduate from college and start looking for a job, you'll have experience."

"College? My head is crammed full just thinking about going to high school."

He nodded. "You're right. They would say I'm putting the cart ahead of the horse. Let's go."

Linda hugged Nancy quickly, kissed Tammy on the forehead, and trotted down the porch stairs. As she got in the car, Nancy heard her tell Akecheta, "I never rode in a car before. I'm a little excited about it and a little afraid."

He laughed. "I'll drive careful." He got behind the wheel, backed the car out of the drive and onto the road, put it in the forward gear, and drove off.

Part of Nancy wished she were in the car with them. She watched until they disappeared down the road. *I still haven't ridden in a car.*

She sighed. *Don't be jealous. Be happy for Linda. Maybe you'll be going to school next year.*

Linda came home that night excited to tell everyone the news that she had a wonderful day. At dinner, she bubbled over with her story of the day's events. "Miss Blake gave me some tests and put me in the eleventh grade class. Can you believe it?"

Emma nodded. "I believe it. You're obviously a very bright young lady."

"Thank you. I had to stop going to school in Smithville when I married. I was only in the ninth grade there, but I kept on reading and Nancy was good to teach me her lessons when I could get away from---him."

Emma asked, "What kind of school was it?"

Linda shrugged. "One room, one teacher. Muriel taught everything from first grade to twelfth grade."

"She must have been very good."

Linda and Nancy said in unison, "She was." They looked at one another and laughed.

Nancy added, "Muriel didn't have any children of her own, and she used to say that we were her family, and she wanted us to have the best education she could give us. She was always having my daddy send away for books, and she had a very nice collection of her own. We could read anything of hers we wanted. Of course, the boys weren't much interested in reading, but most of the girls were. When we finished one, she would ask us questions about the story and what we felt about the people in the books. She was a wonderful teacher."

Shelby put in, "I'm surprised to hear you call her by her first name."

Linda said, "She never married. I think no one asked for her because she had a twisted foot and couldn't get around very well. It would have been hard for her to take care of a house and children. Being a spinster, she didn't get the honor of being called by her last name."

Shelby narrowed her eyes. "Oh! I see, the *honor* of being called by your last name because you were married. As if a single woman didn't have the right to the same respect as a married woman. What a bunch of hogwash! Well, then, I suppose everyone will have to call you Linda, because I started work on your case today, and according to Kansas law *and* Nevada law, you never were married. You were underage, you did not give your consent, and I'm sure there was never any marriage certificate, because if he had asked for one, they would have put him in jail for bigamy."

Linda clapped her hands together. "So I was never married?"

"Nope, but I'm still filing for divorce papers, just to cover all our bases."

Nancy asked Akecheta, "What about me and Jake? Have you found his other wife?"

Akecheta shook his head. "That'll be a while yet. My associate left for Kansas City, on the

Missouri side, this morning. He'll go to the courthouse there first to see if he can find out if she got a divorce. If she didn't, he'll start trying to track her down."

"What happens then?"

"He took the divorce forms with him. If she didn't die from the flu or something else, he'll try to get her to sign them, and you two can have another wedding to make it all legal here in Kansas."

Nancy's heart sank. Her future could depend on some person she had never even met. "What if she won't sign them?"

"That's a little more complicated. I've authorized him to offer her money. He'll start at a hundred dollars. From what Jake has told me about her, she'll probably take it."

"What if she doesn't?"

"He can go as high as a thousand dollars."

Nancy gasped. "A thousand dollars? That's a fortune."

"It'll be worth it to get rid of her. Jake will work it off to pay us back. He's going to be taking care of five hundred acres. Farming isn't an easy job."

Jake's mouth dropped open. "Five hundred acres? It was only two hundred a few years ago."

"We bought the Kennedy place when the old man died. It was too good a deal to pass up. It was right next to our property, and had been lying fallow for the last five years because he wasn't able to take care of it. We didn't plant it this year either, but I've had Dan spreading our excess manure there, so the soil is very well rested and should be incredibly fertile. Come spring, you can hire some help to get it cleared and plowed. Corn would be a good crop for the first year."

Jake nodded. "Sounds good."

The dinner conversation went on without Nancy's participation. Her thoughts went to the cabin behind her house, and she had only that on her mind for the rest of the evening. She was taken aback by the strength of her emotions. It wasn't her Nevada cabin, her and Jake's cabin, the place where they had met and fallen in love and made love, but it was similar enough that in her mind, it belonged to her. She remembered she told Linda the first time she saw it that it would probably be used by hired help, and now she hated the thought of someone else living in it.

Akecheta told Jake he could hire someone to help with the farming in a few weeks when harvest starts. No one will want it before then. Emma said I could use the cabin for a workroom. If I make it mine now, the hired help can just sleep somewhere else. What can I do in there? What sort of work would be important enough to claim the cabin as my own?

Chapter 30

Nancy had a secret. Each morning, after Jake went to work in the fields and Linda left for school, she carried things to the cabin and started claiming it as hers. One of her sweaters hung on a peg. She put flowers from the rose bushes in the front yard in a vase on the table. An extra wicker laundry basket became a second cradle for Tammy, and Nancy left one of her baby blankets in it permanently. She brought her little sewing box over and left it open on the bedside table.

During dinner a few weeks later, when Jake said, "I think I'll talk to some of the boys in town and see if they're free to come help get in the crops," Nancy's heart started to pound.

If they live in town and don't have a car, they probably won't want to work all day and then go all the way back. They'll expect to sleep here. Oh, God. I know it's greedy of me, when I have that great big house all to myself, to want that little cabin, too. Please forgive me, but I can't let anyone else have it.

After the Sunday morning service at the little Baptist Church, she drew Linda aside and told her, "Just for tonight, I'm going to sleep in the cabin. If you miss me, don't worry."

"What are you going to tell Jake?"

"I'm expecting he'll be there with me."

Linda's face drew into a grimace. "Oh, that."

Nancy hugged her. "It isn't always like it was with Abner. When you're with a man you love and he loves you, it's wonderful. Someday it will happen for you, and then you'll know what I'm talking about."

That evening, as they were walking across the road after dinner, Nancy wrapped her arm around Jake's waist and whispered in his ear, "It's been two months since Tammy was born. I think I'm all healed up. I sure have been missing you."

He looked down at her and smiled in a way that was almost shy. "Really?"

"Really, but I have something different I want to do."

"You'll get no argument from me. What is it?"

"I want us to sleep in the cabin out back. I already cleaned it and got it ready."

He nodded slowly and smiled. "I think I'd like that."

When it grew close to bedtime, Nancy fed Tammy, carried her upstairs, and put her in the cradle. When she came back to the kitchen, Jake asked, "You going to leave her up there?"

"She's been sleeping through the night for a while now. Linda is right in the next room to look

347

after her if she wakes up and needs something. If you want, I'll leave the windows open here and in the cabin. If she starts crying, I'll hear her."

"No, leave it shut. It's getting to where the nights are a little chilly."

"Don't worry. She'll be fine."

In the cabin, she had put fresh linens on the bed and had several bouquets of roses sitting around. She closed the door and turned to face him. "Let's make it like the first time," she said, and began unbuttoning his shirt. They undressed one another and then he picked her up in his arms and laid her gently on the bed.

Their lovemaking was sweet and emotional and satisfying. Later, they lay together with his arm around her shoulders and her head on his chest. She said, "I can't tell you how much I love you. When I think of what Linda went through with Abner, this is all like a miracle to me, that I have a man I want to be with in this way so much, a man that I crave."

"It's a good thing to hear, that your woman wants you."

They fell asleep in one another's arms, in the cabin that wasn't quite identical to their cabin in the mountains, but where the passion and the caring were every bit as strong.

Chapter 31

Not hearing the roosters' crowing from across the road, they slept until the sun was up, something rare for a man who was now a farmer. As Jake dressed and Nancy made the bed, she said, "I think we should spend the night here every now and then. It can be like a little getaway for us."

He hugged her from behind and kissed her neck. "We can do that anytime you like."

He waited while she slipped on her clothes, and they walked hand-in-hand back to the house. The air was heavy with the scent of the ripening fruit and the rich garden soil. Not even a hint of wind ruffled the leaves of the trees. As they went up the back steps, Nancy shivered.

Jake wrapped his arm around her. "It doesn't seem that cold to me, but you girls are more delicate. You should have worn that sweater you have hanging on the wall in the cabin."

"I'm not cold, not really. I just got a funny feeling, is all."

He held the screen door open for her. "What kind of feeling?"

"I don't know how to explain it, but it's gone now."

In the kitchen, he filled the big metal coffee pot with water and set it on the stove while she started setting the table. She said, "I'm surprised Tammy isn't yelling for her breakfast. She usually wants to be fed as soon as the rooster starts crowing."

She shivered again and turned slowly to look at him, her eyes wide. "Jake?"

He frowned. "What?"

She ran past him, bolted down the hallway, and charged up the stairs with him a few steps behind. Outside the door to Tammy's room, one of the baby's blankets was lying on the floor. She flung open the door, ran in the room, and found the cradle empty.

She grabbed the front of his shirt and twisted it in her fists. "Oh, God! Oh, God! Where is she?"

"Calm down," Jake spoke sternly. "Linda probably has her."

The sound of a baby screaming split the air. "There she is!" They ran to the hallway, stopped, and listened.

Nancy cried out, "She's in Linda's room." She opened the door. The crying was louder, but there was no sign of the baby or her sister. "Linda!" she called at the top of her voice. "Linda?"

Jake cocked his head to one side and listened. Then he walked to the wardrobe, opened the door, and pushed aside the dresses hanging there. Linda was sitting with her knees drawn up in the corner of the space, holding Tammy against her chest and rocking back and forth. When she saw Jake, she cringed, as if he were going to hit her. Jake asked, "Linda, what's wrong?"

Nancy held out her hand. "It's all right now, Linda. You can come out. We're here."

Linda's eyes were wide with fear. She drew even further back against the wall and shook her head in short jerks. She rasped, "He's here. He's going to kill us."

"Abner? Abner was here?"

When Nancy turned to look at Jake, he was gone. She reached out to her sister. "Tammy's crying because she's hungry. I have to feed her, Linda. Give her to me."

Linda shook her head again. She crouched there, panting as if she had run a long distance, and clutching the baby tighter. Tammy let out a piercing wail. Nancy held out both hands and pleaded. "You're holding her too tight. You're hurting her. Let me have her."

Jake reappeared with his rifle in his hands. "He can't hurt you now, Linda. If he shows his face, I'll shoot him."

Reluctantly, Linda handed the baby to Nancy, but made no move to get out of the closet. Jake held out one hand. "You're safe. I'll protect you." Linda reached out her hand to him and stepped out as Jake pulled her to her feet.

351

Nancy sat on the side of the bed, unbuttoned her dress, and gave Tammy her breast. The baby latched on and began eating greedily. She asked, "What happened?"

"I was sound asleep and woke up like someone had shook me, only when I opened my eyes, there was no one there. I thought I must have been dreaming. I tried to go back to sleep, but couldn't. Something made me get out of bed and go to the window. When I looked out, I saw him. The sun wasn't up yet, but the moon was bright enough to make out his shape and size. He was walking around from the front of the house to the back. He had his rifle in his hand. I ran and got Tammy, and we hid in here."

"Did he come in the house?"

She shook her head. "I don't think so. I listened as hard as I could, but I never heard the door squeak. Tammy was still asleep. She never let out a peep until you came in. I guess she heard your voice and it made her hungry."

In a soothing voice, Jake said, "Maybe it was all a dream."

Linda shook her head violently and scowled. "It wasn't a dream. I saw him. He's here, and he's coming to get us."

Jake patted her reassuringly on her shoulder. "If he was really here, he'd have tried to get inside."

Linda's whole body was shaking. She clutched his arm. "I don't know why he didn't, but I saw him out there sneaking around the house. *He was here!* I'm not imagining it."

Nancy knew her sister wasn't dreaming. "She's right, Jake. That must be why I was shivering. I must have sensed that something was wrong. I don't know how. Maybe I smelled him in the air. He always had the odor of the smoke from his blacksmith fire on him, even in church on Sundays. Since Tammy was born, it seems like I can hear more and see better and smell things I couldn't before."

Jake nodded. "Then Linda must be right. He's here." Nancy could see that he had fear written on his face, too. He sucked in a long breath, hissed it out slowly, and asked Nancy, "Do you think you could fire a gun?"

She shook her head. "No, oh--I don't know," she rasped.

"Stay right here." He went out and came back a minute later with the holster and Colt strapped on his waist, the rifle still in his left hand, and the smaller Smith and Wesson in his right hand. He laid the rifle on the bed and held the smaller pistol in front of him, gripping it with one hand in front of the other. "Hold it like this, with two hands. That keeps it steady. If you have to pull the trigger, keep your thumb away from the hammer here so it's out of the way. If you have to use it, pull back the trigger fast, but without jerking it. I'll only be gone a few minutes. The dew is still on the grass, so I'm going out to the yard to look for tracks. When I come back in, I'll call out when I open the kitchen door so's you'll know it's me. If you hear the door squeak, and I don't call out, it may be him. Give Tammy back to Linda and get ready. If he shows his face in here, shoot him."

He pointed at his chest. "You'll want to close your eyes when you pull the trigger, but don't let yourself. You have to keep your eyes open. Aim right here, in the center of his chest, like you were trying to shoot the button off his shirt, and keep pulling the trigger until the gun is empty. You're not likely to hit his heart with one shot. Just aim for the same spot and keep firing. Keep the gun pointed down a little unless you aim to use it. Be sure you don't shoot anyone else. Do you think you can do that?"

Nancy's heart was pounding. Biting her lip, she nodded her head. He said, "All right then. I'll only be gone a few minutes." Before he left, he took the still shaking Linda by the elbow and guided her to the chair by her window. "Sit down, Linda. Everything's going to be all right."

He kissed Nancy's cheek and started to say something else, but swallowed hard and shut his mouth. Looking frightened, he left them there and went out to look for traces of Abner.

Chapter 32

Jake was back in only a few minutes. He hollered, "It's me," as he opened the back door. When he entered the bedroom, Nancy saw that, in spite of the chilly morning, his forehead was covered in sweat. His voice was hoarse when he said, "There are footprints in the grass that would fit Abner's size."

Linda let out a little scream. He held up a palm. "Now, that doesn't necessarily mean it was Abner. Lots of men have feet that big."

Nancy was beginning to shake. "How many of them would be sneaking around here in the middle of the night?"

He wiped his face with the back of his forearm. "You're right. It had to be him."

"What are we going to do?"

"We're going to tell Dad. He'll know how to handle it. Let's go over there."

Linda jumped up. "We can't go out in the open. What if he's out there, hiding in the bushes and just waiting to kill us?"

"If that was what he wanted to do, he could have picked me and Nancy off already. I'm sure he's gone—for now. I followed his tracks around the house. He had a horse tied to the front fence. I could tell he got on it and rode off toward town. I think he came here before daylight to scout out the house. Whatever he has in mind, he wasn't ready to act on it yet. Come on. We can't stay holed up here forever. I don't think we have anything to be afraid of for now, but it doesn't hurt to be careful. Linda, can you take the pistol?"

She shook her head rapidly. "I'm afraid of guns. I'd never be able to shoot one."

"All right, then." They all walked down the stairs, out of the house, and across the road without speaking a word. Jake went first, holding the rifle in both hands to be ready in case he needed to use it. Linda walked behind him, rocking the baby back and forth in her arms. Nancy brought up the rear, holding the gun out in front of her but pointed at the ground, her eyes darting around and straining to listen for any sound Abner might make if he were hiding. Nancy knew that a man as large and cumbersome as Abner would have a hard time being quiet if he moved. She heard nothing.

Instead of going around to the back door the way they always did, they went in the front. Emma was still in the kitchen, wearing jeans and a plaid shirt. She sat at the table with a plate of ham and eggs in front of her. Brenda was cooking at the stove. When they came in, Emma looked up with a smile. "I'm getting a late start myself this morning. Why are you coming in the front door?" When she saw their faces, her expression quickly changed. She stood and asked, "What's wrong?"

Jake said, "Abner was here last night. Linda saw him walking around the house."

Emma went to the hallway and bellowed "Akecheta!" so loudly it shook the dishes in the pantry. Nancy could hear him running down the stairs. He charged into the kitchen barefoot, wearing only his trousers. Shelby, still in her robe, came running after him. Dan came rushing in from the back yard.

Akecheta grabbed Emma's shoulders. "What?" he shouted.

"Jake says Abner was sneaking around their house last night."

Shelby said, "Oh, Lord!"

Jake began pacing the floor. "I really didn't think he could find us here. I was sure we'd be safe. How could he know where we were?"

Nancy took Tammy from Linda and laid her in her wicker basket. Still kneeling over the baby, she said softly, "It's my fault. I've been writing letters to my mother."

Jake whirled to look at her. "But she would never tell him. Besides, the sheriff said if he showed up in Smithville, he'd toss him in jail."

Like Nancy, Linda spoke with a flat, expressionless voice. "He wouldn't have to go all the way into town. He has family living on the south end of the main street. His brother works at the telegraph office where the mail goes. He probably knew from the first day how to track us down."

Nancy stared without hope at the floor. Desperation began seeping into her. "What can we do?"

Akecheta said, "I'll tell you what we can do. First, Dan, take the car and go get the sheriff." Dan gave a quick salute and ran out the back door. Akecheta said to Jake, "We'll take turns standing watch. I want one of us to be ready at all times, day or night. I'll—"

He was interrupted by Emma grasping his forearm with both hands. Her voice quavered when she said, "I wonder why the dogs didn't bark."

Shelby said, "Oh, no." The two women ran out the back door, and the rest of the family followed. Emma stopped in the yard and called, "Ditto, Talley, here boys!"

She was answered by a whining sound and ran toward it. All four of the dogs were lying at the far side of the house, a large, partially-eaten hunk of meat between them. Ditto, the large yellow dog, opened one eye and looked pleadingly at Emma without lifting his head. He wagged his tail once. Emma dropped to her knees and picked up Ditto's head. She opened his mouth with her fingers and stuck her nose between his teeth to smell his breath. She looked up. "Jake?"

Jake knelt beside her and smelled the dog's breath. "It smells like the gas the Germans used on us during the war."

Emma jumped up. "That's cyanide! Shelby, come help me!" With Shelby on her heels, she ran to the barn. They returned with a narrow hose, a funnel, and a bucket. Shelby stopped to fill the bucket at the water trough, and then held Ditto's mouth open while Emma carefully fed the end of the hose down the dog's throat.

Shelby put the funnel in the other end of the hose and held it in place while Emma took the bucket and poured a small stream in the funnel. When she was satisfied that enough water had gone in the dog's stomach, she pulled out the hose and began pumping his side. He coughed, and a spurt of water with chunks of partially-digested meat came shooting from his mouth. Emma kept pumping his side until the water stopped coming out, and then she moved to the next dog, Talley, and repeated the procedure.

It was too late for the two smaller dogs. Emma held one in her arms, got to her feet, and roared with anger, waving a clenched fist in the air. "I'm going to track him down and kill him right now. You, or the sheriff, or anyone else who wants a shot at him will have to stand behind me."

Akecheta brought a small piece of canvas from the barn and used it to pick up the hunk of meat. He held it out for Emma to see. It had rows sliced in it about a half-inch apart. When he used the tip of his finger to separate one row, it was lined with a pale colored powder. He held it near his nose and sniffed. "You're right. He used cyanide."

Nancy was shocked. "Where would he get that?"

Akecheta said, "Here and there. Sodium cyanide has some legitimate uses, especially in farming areas like this. It's a pesticide, and some people put it out to kill coyotes that are raiding the henhouse. Could be, he bought it at one of the farming supply stores."

He looked down the road toward town. "Last night probably wasn't the first time he was here. I think he must have come by sometime during the day and scouted out the place. The dogs don't pay much attention if someone comes around in the daylight. When he saw dogs, he'd have known there was no way he could sneak around at night without them telling us he was here. Poison was a very efficient way to get rid of them. Most everyone feeds their animals in the morning, so it wouldn't be hard to tempt them with a cut of meat later on in the day."

Emma asked Linda, "What time was it you saw him?"

Linda wiped away a tear. "I'm sorry, I just don't know. It was still pitch dark. That's all I can tell you. I ran and got the baby and hid in the wardrobe. I don't know how long I was in there."

"It couldn't have been too long ago or the dogs would all be dead."

Akecheta folded the canvas around the meat and said, "We best put this in the refrigerator until the sheriff gets here. I want him to see it. His dogs are two of Junior's brothers, and he takes them everywhere he goes. He won't take kindly to anyone who'd kill a dog."

Nancy said, "Dogs? Don't forget, he also killed your grandson."

Akecheta nodded. "I'll never forget that. It will get him a hangman's noose. Killing a dog will get the tie put around the back of his neck instead of the side, so he suffers a while before he dies."

"He murdered my baby in Nevada. If they caught him alive here, what would they do with him?"

"They'd likely send him back there for a trial."

Nancy shook her palms in front of her. "They'd try him in a place where half the jury would be on his side before they even heard the evidence. He might get off."

362

"He won't get off. He'll hang."

Calmly, Emma said, "I don't want him to hang."

Nancy looked at Emma's face. Her eyes were pinched half-shut, her mouth was a thin line, and Nancy understood, but Linda said, "Why not?"

"I want to be the one to kill him."

Akecheta gave her a long look. "Now, Emma, settle down. That isn't exactly the Christian way to feel."

She glared at him with fire in her eyes. "I know it isn't the New Testament way of thinking about forgiveness, but the Old Testament wouldn't find any fault in it. He murdered our grandson, and he tried to burn Jake and Nancy and little Tammy alive. He killed two of my dogs, and if he gets a chance, he'll kill the rest of us. I suppose someday I'll have to ask God to forgive me, but not yet. I can't stop hating him yet. A man like that has given up his right to live."

It was the same way Nancy had felt when Abner killed her baby boy, the Old Testament against the New.

Akecheta put an arm around Emma's shoulder and said, "I'm not disagreeing with you. We best be going in the house to wait for Sheriff Hanks."

She shook him off. "I have to get Ditto and Tally somewhere they can rest and recover, and then I have to bury Squeak and Elwood."

Akecheta handed the meat to Linda. "Would you take this in the house and put it in the refrigerator, please?"

She took the bundle and went to the house. Jake said, "Nancy, you might as well go with her."

"No. I'll help with the dogs."

Akecheta picked up Ditto, who raised his head and licked Akecheta on the chin. Jake picked up Talley, and Shelby and Emma lifted the two smaller dogs. They carried the animals to the stables, where Akecheta laid Ditto on a pile of straw in one of the stalls. Jake placed Talley next to him, and Shelby brought a pan of water.

Nancy leaned close to Jake and asked, "Do you think they'll make it?"

He shrugged. "It depends how much of that stuff got in their system. Mom flushed them out pretty good, but there's no telling if she got to them in time."

Akecheta said, "Let's get those graves dug, Jake."

They went to the barn, and the men picked two spades from where they hung on the wall. Nancy followed them a distance from the back of the barn, where a picket fence stood around a square of land. Emma took Elwood from Nancy's arms and stood by the fence. Akecheta pointed to a place at one side, and he and Jake began digging graves side by side. Nancy looked at the dome-shaped, wooden markers on small mounds that had names like *Foxtail*, and *Zipper* printed on them. She leaned close to Shelby and asked. "Are all of your pets buried here?"

"Only the cats and dogs. Mostly the dogs. Cats have a way of going off to die."

"What do you do with a horse if it dies?"

"We're lucky. Over the years, it's only happened a few times. You send for the knacker to come get it, and you never speak of it again."

"None of them are buried here?"

Shelby nodded to the largest mound in the far right corner of the fence. "Only one. Mom had them make a special grave for Takoda. He was her first horse. Dad gave him to her years ago, before they were married, and she couldn't bear to send him away."

When the graves were ready, Emma placed Elwood in his resting place first, then took Squeak from Shelby and laid him in his plot. She straightened their legs, adjusted the bodies, and then stepped back. Tears streamed down her cheeks as she raised her face to the sky and said in her loudest voice, "Lord, thank you for the time we had with Squeak and Elwood. They were good boys, and they did you proud."

She gasped loud sobs and fell into Akecheta's arms, her body convulsing with her grief. Over her shoulder, Akecheta tilted his head at the graves, giving a signal to Jake to finish the burial. He scooped Emma off the ground and carried her back to the house. A sobbing Shelby went behind her parents, but Nancy waited for Jake to finish his work.

When the graves were filled, Jake patted the mounds with the back of the spade to make them even. He picked up the other shovel, and he and Nancy walked to the house together, stopping in the barn to hang the tools back on the wall.

Chapter 33

With the sheriff's car following, Dan drove in the side yard. Sheriff Hanks, a country boy himself, came to the back door. Akecheta held it open for him, and Hanks took off his hat as he stepped inside. Almost as tall as Akecheta, he was in his 50's, with a ruddy complexion, brown hair, and the beginnings of a belly. "I'm sorry to hear about your troubles, Ike. We've been watching for him. He hasn't been seen in Manhattan, or I'd have taken him into custody. What happened here?"

Akecheta told Hanks about Abner sneaking around before sunup and poisoning the dogs. He took the hunk of meat from the refrigerator, showed it to Hanks, and said, "The two smaller dogs didn't make it, and we may still lose Ditto and Talley."

The sheriff's face turned a deeper shade of red. He ran his fingers around the brim of his hat and cleared his throat. Nancy thought she saw a glimmer of a tear in his eye. He said, "I feel like we let you down, Ike. To get here, this louse must have come through town at some time or other. I don't understand why no one saw him."

Jake spoke up. "Don't feel bad, Sheriff. Abner's the sneakiest man that ever lived. He may not even have come into town in the daylight. It would be more like him to stay in Ogden, rent a horse there, and pass through Manhattan after dark."

"That would explain it. If he's as big a man as you say, he'd stick out like a sore thumb anywhere he went. I'll call Ogden and Junction City and see if anyone there has seen him. We'll all keep an eye out."

Akecheta nodded. "Thank you, but I want to tell you in advance, if he shows up here again, he'll not get a chance to kill anything else."

Hanks looked at him for a long moment, and then nodded and said, "That would save us the trouble of extradition."

Chapter 34

Thinking that Abner had no grudge to settle with Shelby, Akecheta sent her in to work. He didn't go to the office with her, but refused to let her ride her horse. He insisted she take the car and made her keep a gun on the seat beside her.

Besides the usual routine of caring for the horses, Emma had the sick dogs to care for. They were only beginning to walk around the property in the last few days. She went about her chores, but even she had taken to wearing a sidearm, a snub-nose .38 Smith and Wesson, in a removable holster she clipped on her belt.

Akecheta, Dan, and Jake took turns standing guard over the Belk house where Linda, Nancy and Tammy spent all their time. The men wore pistols on their sides and carried a rifle in their hands. Except for the nightly dinners at Emma's, the women were afraid to step outside, and even when they walked across the road, they all went together. Nancy kept the window shades down, the draperies pulled together, and all the windows and doors locked.

By the middle of the week, with the sheriff still reporting no sightings of Abner, everyone's nerves were on edge. The slightest unexpected sound made Nancy jump. After a tense dinner one night, Emma said, "We can't keep on like this. We're more likely to shoot each other than Abner. Jake, you're always talking about how this man is so sneaky and would never come at anyone head-on. I've been thinking about that, and I realize we've been going about this the wrong way."

She looked around at the trees that circled the property. "He's probably watching us, and he can see you men taking turns standing guard on the porch with a rifle in your hands twenty-four hours a day. He isn't going to show his face. My guess is that no one has seen him in Manhattan because he hasn't been there. I think he's camping out in the woods around here and watching us. What we need to do, is get him to think we've relaxed our guard. That could draw him out."

Jake scratched his chin. "How do we do that?"

"Make it look like we're going about our business as usual. Akecheta can go to the office with Shelby. Jake, it would be normal for you to hire extra men to help bring in the corn. Choose one who's handy with a gun, and after you all go to the fields in the morning, he can double back and watch the house from far enough away that he won't be seen."

Jake said, "I'd rather be the one who doubles back."

Emma nodded. "Then you do it. For the amount of time you're away, Dan can watch the front and sides of the house from the upstairs window here. Once you get the men started working, you can come back, but Abner has to see you leave so he'll think he has a clear path."

Dan asked, "What can I do here?"

"Keep your weapons where you can reach them in a hurry, but don't wear them where they're visible. It's cool enough for a jacket. Wear one long enough to cover your Colt, and keep your rifle where you can reach it fast. Instead of wearing my gun clipped to my belt, I'll wear my loosest jeans and fasten it on the inside of my waistband. A vest or jacket for me will cover the grip so it can't be seen."

Nancy raised her hand as if she were in school. Emma smiled at her. "What is it?'

"So, Linda and Tammy and I will be in the house alone?"

"For a while, but someone will be watching all the time."

"I want a gun, too."

"Have you ever fired one?"

"No, but Jake told me how, and he showed me how to hold it. Maybe I won't be so scared if I have one."

Emma pursed her lips and looked at Nancy as if appraising her. "Shelby's Colt would be too much for you to handle." She asked her husband, "Is that little Derringer your Grandpa brought from New York with him in working condition?"

Akecheta nodded. "It hasn't been fired in thirty years, but it was cleaned before he put it away, so probably. I'll check it out and make sure it's usable."

"Do we have any ammunition for it?"

"None that I would trust in a crisis. That's thirty years old, too. I'd have to get some in town."

"Take it with you in the morning, get some bullets, and check it out to make sure it will fire."

He nodded and waited for his wife's next direction. Nancy listened to her mother-in-law, physically the smallest person in the room, making a plan for their defense, and watched the men going along without complaint. They were all accepting the idea that Emma knew the right things to do. She admired Emma more than ever.

Brenda, who had been clearing the table as they talked and hadn't said a word, put in, "Is there an extra gun for me? I wouldn't mind being the one to shoot him."

The tension in the room broke, and they all laughed. Brenda looked at them with her chin in the air. "I wasn't being funny. If he's watching us, he knows by now that we still have two dogs alive. Who's to say he won't come here first?"

Emma gasped, and said, "How stupid I am! I didn't consider that. I've been thinking about this as something that would ultimately happen across the road when he's already harmed us over here."

Akecheta nodded, and said, "What can we do differently?"

Emma shrugged. "I don't know. Stick to the plan, I guess. Dan and I will be armed on this side of the road. Jake will be on the other. We can't hire every man in town to come out here."

Nancy added, "Don't forget me. I'll have a gun."

Emma looked around the table. "Does anyone have another idea?" Her gaze went from one to another, and each shook his head in turn. She nodded. "So, we get on with our lives, keep our weapons close, watch our step, and wait for Abner to make his move. I don't think it will be a very long wait."

Chapter 35

Another week after the dinner conference in Emma's kitchen crawled by with everyone on edge. Nothing had happened. Except for Linda, they all wore firearms, Emma and Shelby's in holsters, and Nancy's in her pocket. Jake, Akecheta, and Dan also carried rifles everywhere they went. They watched and waited, with at least one of the men on guard at all times, but after seven days of tension and fraying nerves, there was no sign of Abner.

The men ate with their rifles propped against the table next to their chairs. At dinner one night, Dan said, "Maybe he's gone home."

Linda put her hand on his and said, "No. You don't know him. He'll never go home until he's killed us, maybe all of us, if he can. He's out there somewhere, watching and waiting for his chance."

The Derringer Nancy kept in her dress pocket all day and under her pillow at night had become so familiar it was almost an accessory, like the ribbons she used to tie back her hair. Each morning, Jake left with the hired help, got them going on the harvest, and then quietly worked his way back to the house, setting up watch just outside the perimeter of the property.

As Nancy and Jake got ready for bed Saturday night, Dan was at his post across the street, in a hiding place that allowed him to see the house, but not be seen. Jake would take the second watch.

Nancy put her head on Jake's shoulder. "Maybe Dan's right. Maybe he's gone. Maybe he got tired of waiting and went home."

"After what he did before, do you think he'd do that?"

"No," she sighed. "He's out there somewhere."

On Sunday, Dan and Akecheta stayed home to guard the two properties, and everyone else packed themselves in the car for the ride to church. Since he was the only man in the group, Nancy assumed Jake would drive, but Emma got behind the wheel, and Jake didn't make any attempt to replace her. It was another thing for Nancy to marvel at.

For the first time, the now familiar service in the little Baptist church building didn't comfort Nancy. The pastor preached about how God was always watching over us. Silently, Nancy disagreed. On the way home, Linda commented, "It was helpful to know that God is protecting us."

From the back seat, Nancy made no effort to keep the bitterness out of her voice when she blurted out, "I don't believe that sermon. Why wasn't God watching over my little boy to keep Abner from killing him?"

Emma looked over her shoulder. "I know how you feel. I don't understand a lot of things. The only answer for that is to remember where the Bible says that now we look through a glass darkly, and someday we'll be able to see everything."

"Right now, I don't understand anything at all." Nancy turned her head and stared out the car window. She didn't speak for the rest of the ride home.

At the house, Brenda and Emma put a cold Sunday dinner on the table. They ate with very little appetite and not much conversation. After the kitchen was cleaned, Jake and Dan, wearing their side arms under their jackets, escorted Nancy and Linda home. Linda was carrying a dish of leftover ham they would have for breakfast the next day.

As they approached their house, both Ditto and Talley, in the Belk yard, began barking wildly. Jake and Dan exchanged a look and Jake said, "I'll stay here with the girls and watch this way. You go see what that's about."

Dan headed back across the road. Jake, Nancy, and Linda walked around the house and stopped on the porch outside the kitchen.

Jake held his rifle in front of his chest and told Nancy, "You go on inside. I'll watch here until I hear from Dan."

In the kitchen, Nancy told her sister, "I think I'll put Tammy down for her nap and rest for a while. I'm so tired."

Linda opened the refrigerator door. "I could use a nap myself. I'll put this ham away and be up in a minute."

Nancy went to her bedroom and laid Tammy in the cradle. Yawning, and thinking of sinking down into her feather bed, she was still bending over the baby and arranging the blanket when the unpleasant odor of burning wood and man-sweat reached her. She knew what it was, and was jolted to attention.

When she turned, Abner was standing in the doorway holding a gasoline can in one hand and a pistol in the other. Too tall for the doorframe, his head was tilted to one side, and he leered at her from under bushy, black eyebrows. Dirt creased the folds of his hands, face, and neck, and his bib overalls were stained with grease and grime. "Nice to see you again, Nancy," he rasped. "Come on over here and give me a little hello kiss."

Nancy's heart pounded, and adrenalin surged through her. She backed away until she was pressed against the wall. "No! Get out of here before you get shot."

His mouth twisted in a macabre grin. The rancid smell of him filled the room, smoky from the blacksmith's fire, and musty--from hiding out in the woods for weeks.

From behind him, Nancy could hear Linda trotting up the stairs. She raised her voice. "Get out of here," she yelled. "Jake will shoot you if he sees you." Thankfully, the footsteps stopped.

Abner threw back his head and laughed wildly. His eyes were burning with hatred. "If he comes up those stairs, I'll see him before he sees me. It doesn't matter. We're all going to die today. This time, I'm going to finish the job I started. The only difference is, I'll go to be with the Lord and Joseph Smith, and you'll all burn in hell for your heresy."

Nancy reached into her pocket and found the Derringer. *I don't want him to see it or he might get to it before I can aim and pull the trigger.* Without taking it from the folds of her dress, she aimed it at his heart and pulled the trigger. The report of the weapon echoed in the room and the bullet slammed into the wall next to Abner.

His eyes flew open with surprise, and then he laughed again. He stuck his pistol into his belt and lunged at Nancy. He grabbed her hand, and ripped the skirt half-way off her dress as he wrenched the little gun away from her.

Abner twisted her wrist until she thought it would break, and then shoved her back against the wall so hard it knocked the wind out of her. He set the gas can down and tipped it over with his foot. The fuel bubbled out and seeped across the wood floor, running toward the far corner of the room. He pointed at the stream and laughed maniacally. "Looks like your floor is a little crooked. No matter. It'll all burn once it gets started. What can we use for kindling? Ah, I know just the thing."

He took a step toward the cradle and reached for it. Nancy screamed, "No!" and launched herself through the air, flying against his massive shoulder. He slashed out at her with one arm. She flew across the room, smashing the back of her head against the wall and falling in a heap on the floor. Dizzy from the impact, she shook her head, tried to focus, and attempted to get to her feet, only to collapse again, landing on her knees with a thump.

Abner drew a fistful of long, wooden matches from the lower pocket of his bib overalls and held them up for her to see. "Let's see if that fuel will burn."

Behind him, Nancy saw Jake appear in the doorway with his rifle raised. He pulled the trigger, and a blast echoed around the room. Abner dropped the matches and staggered back into the wall next to Nancy. He had blood gushing from a wound in his shoulder, but managed to push himself erect and stay on his feet. He bellowed a roar so loud the ceiling light shook. Jake was pumping another shell into the chamber as Abner charged like an angry bull, his head lowered.

Instead of stepping back, Jake took a step closer, and fired again. The second bullet hit Abner in his bulging stomach, but it wasn't enough to stop his momentum. He tackled Jake, and the rifle went flying across the room. The two men fell to the floor with their arms around one another in an odd dance hold, rolling over and over through the spreading pool of gasoline.

Nancy snatched Tammy from the cradle and ran for the door, passing Dan as he burst in. She stepped aside to get out of his way and turned to see what would happen. Dan raised his rifle, but Abner and Jake were joined like Siamese twins. Dan couldn't fire without taking the chance of hitting Jake.

Abner rolled over on top and stopped there, his fist raised high above his head, ready to smash it down into Jake's face.

Jake, flailing his arms and legs, struggled to free himself, but was crushed by the massive weight of his opponent. Dan fired, hitting Abner in the side. Like the other bullets, it seemed to do no significant harm. Abner got up on one knee, and wrapped his hands around Jake's throat.

With a clear target, Dan fired again into Abner's immense body. Abner fell on his side, lying next to Jake.

He rolled away and stretched his arm out in front of him. As he grasped one of the matches and struck it on the wood floor, a rifle blast came from behind Nancy. Abner's body jerked. Emma strode past Nancy holding up a rifle. She fired again.

Abner went limp and dropped the burning match on the floor. Flames shot up immediately and embraced Abner's overalls. They danced across the pool of amber liquid to the corner of the room. As the fire climbed the green trellises of the wallpaper, Dan grabbed Jake's arms, dragged him from the floor, and hefted him over his shoulder. He shrieked, "Let's get out of here!"

Nancy and Emma ran down the steps and out to the front porch as Dan followed. Akecheta, Shelby, and Brenda were all carrying weapons and running toward Nancy's house, but they stopped in the middle of the road when they saw Nancy and Emma burst through the door. Dan followed close behind them, carrying an unconscious Jake. They gathered in the road, and Nancy yelled, "Linda, where's Linda?"

From the back of the pack came a voice. "I'm right here. I'm all right"

They all stood frozen in the road, listening to Abner's animal-like screams coming from the upstairs of the house. Linda covered her mouth with her hand and sobbed.

Nancy gasped, "He must have been shot five or six times, and he just kept coming. How is that possible?"

Emma replied, "A man that big, sometimes it's hard to hit a vital organ. You'd almost have to get him right in the heart or in the head to stop him."

Akecheta handed his rifle to Shelby. He went to Dan and held out his arms for his son. Dan let Jake slide off his shoulder and into Akecheta's grasp.

Brenda gasped. When they looked at her, she was pointing to the bedroom window where the form of a man stood. He was covered in flames and desperately trying to beat them out. With a last scream of agony, he fell out of sight.

The blaze was crawling up the draperies and licking at the window frame. No one moved. "Should we try to put it out? Shelby asked.

Emma replied, "No, there's no wind, so it won't spread. I'm not going to have any of you risk your lives. The house is insured. Let it burn, and let him burn with it. Where he's going, he'll need to get used to the heat."

They all turned their backs on the inferno and walked away.

Akecheta carried his son across the road and into the house. Nancy followed close behind as he laid Jake on the sofa in the parlor. Jake coughed several times and began to waken. When he opened his eyes, Nancy was sitting on the edge of the cushion next to him.

He lifted his head and rasped anxiously, "Abner?"

Nancy held his hand. "It's over. He's dead."

Relief showed on Jake's face as he managed a nod and let his head fall back on the pillow. "Good."

Chapter 36

Nancy's family slept at Emma and Akecheta's home while their house smoldered. The fire didn't go completely out for two days. When the heat had drained away, the sheriff brought two deputies with him and they carried the charred remains of Abner to town. Not wanting to see it, all the women stayed in Emma's kitchen until the detail was gone.

Akecheta and Jake went to survey the damage and came back with the information that the yellow limestone had escaped the ravages of the fire, but the inside of the house was gutted. As they sat down to eat that night, Jake held Nancy's hand and said, "We'll rebuild. It will be good as new."

She looked at him with sad eyes. "It doesn't matter. We can live in the cabin."

He kissed the back of her hand. "I have to rebuild. Let me explain. It was my grandfather's home and my dad's home, and now it will be our home. Someday our children will raise their families there. I brought this trouble here with me from Nevada, and I need to wipe it away. I'm not going to let Abner's memory take my family home away from me."

384

Nancy objected, "Jake, I don't ever want to go into that bedroom again. I couldn't rest there."

"That room is gone. The whole floor is gone. The only things left of the house are the chimney and the outside walls. If you want, I'll switch things around so our room is on the other side of the house."

She saw the determination in his eyes. Nancy thought it over and then pleaded, "Would you do one thing for me?"

"I'd do anything for you. What do you want?"

"Is there any way you could you put in running water and a washroom on the second floor?"

Emma slapped her hand on the table and laughed. "A woman after my own heart."

Chapter 37

It took six months to rebuild the house. During that time, Linda took a bedroom at the Belk house and returned to school. Jake and Nancy still crossed the road to have dinner with his family each night, but while the reconstruction was going on, they lived in the cabin out back.

There, Nancy and Jake recaptured the happiness of those months in their other cabin, before Abner killed their son and tried to take their lives.

On the day they moved into the big house, brand new and sparkling fresh, Emma and Brenda gave a party for them. The house was decorated with furniture Nancy chose herself from the Wareham Mercantile in Manhattan, and there were gifts of new linens from Emma, dishes and glassware from Shelby, and cooking utensils from Brenda.

It was late in the evening before the kitchen was cleaned and everyone left. Jake wrapped his arm around Nancy's waist as she carried Tammy up the stairs and into the room that had been furnished as a nursery. It had rose-patterned wallpaper, a proper crib for the growing little girl, a chest for her clothes, and a table and chair made for a child's height.

Nancy tucked the sleeping child in and kissed her forehead. They stood and watched her for a moment before going to their own room. When they were in bed, Jake took Nancy in his arms. Before the lovemaking began, she murmured in his ear, "A person would think I have everything a woman could dream of, but there's something else I'd like."

In a husky voice, he said, "You know if you ask me now, I'll give you anything."

"From time to time, I'd still like for us to spend a night in my cabin."

"Your cabin? I thought it was our cabin."

"It is, but only when you're there. The rest of the time, it's my cabin."

He chuckled and slid his hand over her body. "Then I want it to be *our* cabin as many nights as you like."

The End

Other Books by Donna Mabry

The Manhattan Stories:

Jessica
Pillsbury Crossing
The Cabin
Tammy (in progress)

Stand Alones:

Conversations with Skip
Deadly Ambition
The Right Society
The Other Hand
Maude (in progress)

The Alexandra Merritt Mysteries:

The Last Two Aces in Manhattan
The Las Vegas Desert Flower
The Las Vegas Special
Rough Ride in Vegas
M.I.A. Las Vegas
Lost Luggage (in progress)
The Las Vegas Cats (in progress)

Get ready to make your move to Deerfield Springs! Please join us for lunch and learn helpful information to assist you in a stress-free move to the retirement life you deserve!

Basil's on Market

5650 Tylersville Rd
Mason, Ohio 45040

RSVP by November 11 to join in the FUN! **513-453-0017**

3664 West US 22 ◆ Loveland, OH 45140 ◆ DeerfieldSpringsRetirement.com